Guardians Of The Round Table 4
Frog Mage

Guardians Of The Round Table 4
Frog Mage

Avril Sabine, Storm Petersen
and Rhys Petersen

Cracked Acorn Productions
Australia

Guardians Of The Round Table 4: Frog Mage

Published by

Cracked Acorn Productions

PO Box 1365

Gympie, Queensland 4570

Australia

978-1-925617-86-3 (Kindle)

978-1-925617-87-0 (EPUB)

978-1-925617-88-7 (Print)

Genre: Young Adult Fantasy LitRPG

For Will. You didn't think we'd forget about you, did you?

**When all actions have repercussions,
it isn't really agame.**

Mallory had been so certain it was time for a challenge, that they could take on something of a higher level and survive. But maybe she was wrong. When an encounter with a frog mage doesn't go as well as expected, she begins to doubt their ability to take on greater challenges and complete some of the quests they'd planned to focus on.

*

This story was written by Australian authors using Australian spelling.

Name Pronunciation

Like many names there is more than one way to pronounce the following ones. These are the pronunciations used in this story.

Characters

Ahron (ah-ron)

Alamaree (el-ah-mah-ree)

Cila (sill-uh)

Danae (da-nay)

Deneg (den-eg)

Emica (em-e-cah)

Grotmur (grot-mer)

Hisoki (hiss-oh-key)

Jorgen (jaw-gen)

Kruth (kr-uth)

Sarisa (sa-risa)

Tivon (tiv-on)

Places

Buckneth (buck-neth)

Eridell (air-a-dell)

Inadon (in-ah-don)

Lilica (lil-e-cah)

Morlee (more-lee)

Sendale (sen-dale)

Shadhurst (shad-hurst)

Shadville (shad-vil)

Simria (sim-re-ah)

Surith (soo-rith)

Ursen (ur-sen)

Velkden (velk-den)

Wester (west-er)

Wildebay (wild-bay)

Foreword

Opening stats, Mallory's notebook entries recapping the previous adventures and other details can be found at:

www.avrilsabine.com/series/gotrt

The notebook entries will contain spoilers if you haven't read the book they refer to.

Chapter One

Sitting across the kitchen table from her brother, Mallory tried to focus on the bowl of cereal in front of her. Every time she looked up and caught her brother's gaze, she wanted to grin at the thought of how soon they'd be returning to Inadon. Since Norine sat at the table with them, that wasn't a good idea. It'd probably lead to more questions than they'd faced yesterday. Or at least yesterday in this world.

Neither of them had dressed in their school uniforms yet, trying desperately to keep things as normal as possible. Brodie's short, brown hair stuck up in all directions while her long brown hair, that was naturally streaked with copper highlights, fell in a tangled mess around her shoulders. It had taken a great deal of effort not to brush it before breakfast. Neither of them got ready for school any sooner than they had to. If they started changing the way they did things, it'd lead to questions they couldn't answer. And didn't want to answer since it'd lead to their mum taking the disc from them to prevent them from returning to Inadon.

Brodie added more cereal and milk to his bowl, both still sitting on the table from when he'd served himself before.

Norine frowned, her gaze focused on Brodie's bowl. "Haven't you already had enough? The amount you eat is ridiculous."

"I'm still hungry." Brodie shovelled more food in his mouth.

"At this rate, you'll have to get a job to help pay the food bill with the amount you've been eating lately," Norine warned.

Mallory tried not to laugh. A sound escaped, drawing her mum's attention. Picking up her empty bowl, she rose from the table. "Don't go looking at me. I'm not the one who eats almost constantly." She put the bowl in the sink, rinsing it out. "He's probably growing again. He always eats more before he grows."

"That's all I need." Norine sighed. "Between the amount of food you eat and how fast you grow out of your clothes I probably spend half my wages on you. I've a good mind to send you to your father's for the weekend so he can see for himself that I'm not exaggerating."

"It's not my fault," Brodie muttered. "And I don't want to go to Dad's. There's nothing to do there."

Norine started to speak, breaking off when her phone rang in the lounge room where she'd left it, the tune signalling it was her partner. "I wonder why Alicia is ringing at this hour of the morning." She stood up quickly, knocking over the milk bottle Brodie had left on the edge of the table. She reached for it as it headed towards the floor, not fast enough to catch it.

Brodie grabbed the bottle from mid air, barely glancing at it. Placing the bottle on the table, he returned to eating his breakfast.

Norine stared at him, the phone continuing to ring in the background. "How did you manage to catch that?"

Brodie shrugged, swallowing his mouthful. "Guess it was that point I put in dexterity."

Mallory barely managed not to laugh. It was close though. "Probably the fear it'd break if it hit the floor and he'd have no milk for breakfast tomorrow. You know what he's like about food."

Norine frowned at Brodie, glancing in the direction of the lounge room when her phone stopped ringing. "Can't we have a single conversation without one of you talking computer games?" She strode towards the lounge room, glancing over her shoulder. "Get ready for school. I need to ring Alicia back."

Mallory waited until Norine was out of hearing, returning to the table. "Do you think it was from the dexterity point?" Normally it'd be her brother knocking things over, not catching them.

Brodie shrugged, continuing to eat.

"I wonder how putting points in constitution will effect us in this world," Mallory said.

Finished his second bowl of cereal, Brodie took the bowl to the sink. "I wonder if the spells you've learned will have any kind of effect on you in this world."

"I doubt it," Mallory said. "There are probably no wands in this world to focus the magic."

"I forgot about that." Finished rinsing his bowl, Brodie turned off the tap.

Norine came back into the kitchen. "Alicia's car has broken down. I need to give her a lift to work. She'll never get a taxi at this hour." She gestured towards the sink. "Make sure you do the dishes before you head to school."

Mallory stared after her mum as she strode from the

kitchen, heading for her bedroom. They could leave early this morning?

Brodie nudged her arm. "Did you hear that? We'll be able to leave early."

"Shh." She glanced in the direction her mum had headed. "If she hears you, we won't. And we won't be able to leave too early. Mrs Torres will comment to Mum about it." Mallory glanced at the table. "You wipe that down and put everything away. I'll start the dishes." Before she began the dishes, she sent Ryan a text to let him know they'd be able to leave a little early.

The kitchen was cleaned and they were dressed and ready for school at the same time as Norine walked out the door, warning them not to be late for the bus. Mallory, who'd plaited her hair back out of the way, grabbed hold of Brodie when he headed for the door. "Give her a chance to leave. She hasn't even started the car yet." She kept her voice low.

"I'm not stupid. I just want to check out the front window so I can see when she leaves." Brodie pulled out of her grip.

"What do you think Mum would say if she saw you at the window?" Hearing the car start, and drive off, Mallory headed for the front door. "Now we can check."

Brodie reached the door first, pulling it open and looking outside. "All clear. We can go."

Mallory took out her mobile phone. "I'll send Ryan a text to let him know she's left."

Once again, they met him at the corner of their street, not wanting to risk Mrs Torres from across the road telling tales to their mum. That old woman loved getting them in trouble. Or at least that's the way Mallory saw it from past experience. Reaching the dull white van parked at the corner, she clambered in the front with Ryan while Brodie got in the back with Callum.

"I swear this van is looking worse today," Brodie muttered as he slid the back door shut. "We need somewhere better to leave from so you can return this piece of crap to your mate."

Mallory looked over to Ryan as she pulled the door shut. His long, dark hair was tied at the nape of his neck, his tall frame was filled out from hours at the gym and his shoulders were broad. "What's my surprise?"

Ryan chuckled, his dark eyes filled with humour. "No hello or anything?" He leaned towards her. "Such as a kiss."

Dropping her backpack on the floor at her feet, she pressed a hand against his chest, preventing him from coming closer. "I don't think you deserve one after making me wait this long to find out. It took me ages to fall asleep last night wondering what the surprise is." She wasn't about to admit to him that part of the trouble had been the excitement of returning to Inadon today.

Ryan chuckled again, settling back in his seat. "You need to wait a little longer." Ryan pulled out onto the road. "This is one of those kind of surprises where you have to see it."

Mallory took her purple notebook and a pen out of her backpack. "You have got to be kidding. How much longer do I have to wait? Does Callum know?" She glanced at the curtain blocking her view of the rear section of the van.

"He didn't tell me either." Callum drew the curtain open. He had the same dark eyes and hair colour as his brother, but his hair was kept short and his tall frame was wiry. "Although I really can't be annoyed since he bought me a coffee seedling yesterday."

"Close the curtain. I'm trying to get dressed," Brodie said.

"You haven't got your gear out of your schoolbag yet." Callum closed the curtain.

"There won't be time to get dressed, you'll have to

wait." Ryan glanced at Mallory. "And no, I'm still not going to tell you anything."

Chapter Two

Seeing it would be pointless trying to get any information out of Ryan, Mallory glanced at the curtain. "Have you named the seedling yet? And added it to the party."

"I'll wait until we're ready to go," Callum said.

"Need a hand?" Brodie asked.

"Not after last night's suggestions. I'm not calling it latte, or cappuccino," Callum said.

Grinning at Callum's words, Mallory opened her notebook. "What should I write down today?"

Ryan slowed. He pulled into a rutted driveway and stopped in a gravelled carpark opposite an old, red brick apartment building. "That will have to wait. It's time to get out. Bring everything with you."

Mallory shoved her notebook and pen into her backpack, swinging it onto her shoulder as she clambered out. "Why are we here?" She examined the peeling paint on the eaves of the building, the guttering rusted through in places. There were several doors across the front of the ground floor of the building, narrow windows beside them, and a centrally located door held open with a rock. Concrete steps were visible through the doorway.

"Because we're going inside one of the apartments."

Her gaze was drawn to a man who walked towards the carpark, glaring at them. She lowered her voice. "Is it safe?" She glanced at the man again. He continued to glare at them.

Chuckling, Ryan slipped an arm around her waist. He also carried a backpack. "This from the person who's faced hellions?"

"I had my wand when I faced them." Mallory glanced at Brodie and Callum who joined them, Callum carrying his coffee seedling. Like her, Brodie was still in his school uniform. Only Ryan and Callum wore jeans and a shirt. "Where is the surprise?"

"This way." Ryan headed towards the left, leading them along the side of the building to a door partway along. Like all the other doors, there was a narrow window beside it. This particular window had a lacy curtain hanging at it that had once been white and was now a greyish colour.

"Who lives here?" Callum asked.

Ryan unlocked the door and stepped inside, grinning. "No one."

Mallory followed him inside. "What do you mean by no one?" Her gaze swept the small living area, a kitchen to the right of the entrance with two rickety stools set at a bench that separated the kitchen from the rest of the room and an open space to the left for a lounge suite, a damaged television aerial jack in the wall. There were two doors on the far wall, both shut. The place was dimly lit with only light from the single window and door entering the room, but that wasn't what had Mallory stepping back.

"It's available for rent," Ryan said. "When they told me I could pick up the key and have another look by myself this morning I thought we could leave for Inadon from here."

Mallory stared at the cockroach that ran past her shoe. "Do they charge extra for the roaches? Or do they throw them in for free?"

"You're going to rent this?" Brodie did a slow turn. "We could bring Danni, Fang and Smudge back?"

Callum looked at the cockroaches that ran across

the kitchen bench. "You couldn't find anything better?"

Ryan shrugged. "Not in my budget and not within a five to ten minute drive from our homes. If it's too far away you'd be late to school, if we kept leaving in the morning like this."

Mallory took another step back when a cockroach ran directly towards her. "Do you think we'd be able to get rid of them?"

Callum opened one of the kitchen cupboards and rapidly closed it. "I don't like our chances. Considering the amount of dead bodies, there's still a lot of roaches here."

Mallory checked the time on her phone. "We've got half an hour left until we need to leave. Otherwise, we'll be late."

Ryan gestured towards two closed doors. "Bathroom and bedroom. You can get changed in one of them." He turned on the light before closing and locking the front door. The bare bulb hanging from the ceiling didn't help much.

Mallory eyed the two closed doors, looking at the stained ceiling when she heard the sound of footsteps running overhead. They were followed by a woman yelling at someone to stop making so much noise.

"The irony." Callum also looked upwards.

Ryan chuckled. "You should have seen some of the other places I looked at yesterday. This place is a palace in comparison."

"A cockroach palace." Mallory hurried out of the way of another cockroach that scurried towards her, opening the door on the left. It was a bedroom. The carpet was faded and the walls patched and painted in a slightly different shade over the patched sections. There were no windows or furnishings. But there were more cockroaches of varying sizes scurrying around. "I thought cockroaches hid during the day and only came out when it was dark and quiet." She opened the second door. The bathroom contained a shower, with no shower curtain, and a toilet with a black coloured lid and seat. The floor and shower were covered in tiny tiles that may have once been white but were now grey in the middle and a darker grey around the edges of each one.

Callum peered over her shoulder, still holding the coffee seedling. "Give me an outhouse on Inadon any day. They're a lot cleaner than this."

"It can be cleaned," Ryan said.

"I think you'd need an industrial pressure cleaner to get this place clean," Callum said. "And even then the cockroaches would probably still be here."

"Having a pool party?" Ryan asked.

Callum chuckled. "Wouldn't surprise me."

Mallory turned to face Ryan. "What if we all put money towards rent and utilities? We could find something better and possibly with two or three bedrooms." She glanced at the shower that had mould along all the edges and corners. "And with a bathroom we can use when we return from Inadon." They might even be able to get a washing machine and clothes dryer so they could bring their clothes back to clean rather than always needing to hand wash them.

"What about four bedrooms and then we can have one each," Brodie said.

"Four bedrooms is way out of our price range. Particularly around this area," Ryan said. "Even in the older suburbs bordering ours."

Mallory eyed the bathroom again. "We better get ready. We've got a lot planned for when we return to Inadon."

"Taking on more of the dark forces so we can be paid more when we return here," Brodie said. "Then we'll be able to afford any place we want."

Callum's gaze was focused on the seedling he continued to hold. "We'll have to talk to the wagoner about his friends who might be interested in growing coffee plants."

Mallory stepped inside the bathroom, turning on the light before she closed the door. The entire time it took her to change into her jeans and a t-shirt, she kept an eye on the cockroaches that scurried around the bathroom. Shoving her school uniform in her backpack, she took out the leather boots that were in a plastic bag inside it. After slipping them on, she shoved her sneakers in the plastic bag and put them in her backpack. She opened the door and stepped into the main part of the apartment. "I'm going to end up having nightmares about cockroaches."

Brodie came out of the bedroom at the same time as Mallory exited the bathroom, also dressed in jeans and a t-shirt. "Don't be so lame, Mal. They're cockroaches. Not like they're undines or something."

Mallory pointed at Brodie's head. "Is that a cockroach crawling across your hair?"

Brodie frantically brushed at his hair. "Where? Is it gone? Can you see it?"

Mallory laughed. "Don't be so lame. It's not like they're undines."

Brodie glared at everyone when they laughed. "Very funny."

"Yeah, it was." Mallory crossed the room to stand beside Ryan. "What options were there other than this place?"

He took out his phone. "The only decent one in this price range is a bit out of the way. You couldn't always be guaranteed to get to school on time." He pulled up an image of a townhouse and showed it to her.

The dwelling looked old and worn, but tidy. "That's much better than this." Mallory looked up at Ryan. "What about the ones you said were too expensive for you? We seriously need something better than this place. Anything we left here would get full of cockroaches." She glanced at Brodie. "They'd probably eat our food too."

"I can put money towards rent and stuff." Brodie came closer, his gaze drawn to the phone Ryan held. "What else is there?"

Mallory tried not to smile, but she wasn't successful.

Ryan tilted the phone so they could see the images as he scrolled through. "These are the ones in the next price bracket that are within a ten minutes drive of our places."

Chapter Three

Mallory stretched her hand out towards Ryan's phone. "Go back one. I recognise that place." Lowering her hand, she stared at the old cornershop that had been boarded up for as long as she could remember. It was about a five minute walk from their place.

"Cool. I'd live there," Brodie said. "Has it got any of the old shop stuff in it?"

"What's the layout like?" Callum asked.

"It has the shop at the front and a storage room behind that. At the back, that you reach through the storage room, is a kitchen, bathroom and two bedrooms." Ryan pulled up some of the photos for them to look at. The rooms were worn and faded. "There's also a small fenced yard out the back." He brought up an image of an overgrown yard surrounded by fence palings, the dark green paint peeling. A large fig tree with widespread branches was in the corner, the roots snaking across the ground.

"It'd be perfect," Brodie said. "I could bring Fang back with me. She'd love the place. Think we'd be able to put a pet flap in the back door?"

"It's got no lounge room, or living area," Ryan said.

"We could use the shop area for that," Callum said.

Ryan looked at each of them. "You like this one the best?"

Callum shrugged. "It's not far from home and it is on the way to school."

"I'll arrange a time for us to look at it when we return." Ryan locked the phone screen and slipped it into his backpack. "We need to get ready to go." He brushed cockroaches and their droppings off the kitchen bench and put his backpack on it. The critters scurried away when they hit the floor. After washing his hands, he took his laptop out of the backpack and set it up on the bench.

Mallory avoided the scurrying cockroaches, not wanting to stand on one, and placed her backpack beside Ryan's. She checked the time on her phone before she slipped it inside her backpack. "I didn't get a chance to write anything in my notebook."

"Better write down mum had to pick Alicia up this

morning." Brodie dropped his backpack beside the other two. He eyed the cockroaches on the floor. "Do you think the food in my backpack will be okay? How fast can they move? Are they quick enough to reach it in two seconds?"

"They can travel a metre in a second." Callum placed his backpack with the three already on the bench, keeping hold of the seedling. He turned to Mallory. "You should write down that Ryan needs to find better rentals for us to look at."

Ryan grinned. "Think I'd forget after all your complaints?"

Mallory scrawled the words in the notebook and returned it to her backpack, taking out the disc. She put it in the laptop drawer since it had finished turning on.

Callum sat the seedling, in its clay pot, on the bench beside the laptop. "How do I do this? Should I take it out of the soil? Or will the pot come with us?"

"Name it and add it," Ryan said. "I guess if the pot shouldn't come with us, it'll remain behind."

Callum ran a finger across a glossy, green leaf. "I still don't know what to call it."

"Bean," Brodie suggested.

"Not likely," Callum said.

"Better hurry up," Mallory said. "Or you'll have to leave your precious behind."

Ryan laughed. "That's pretty much how he's been treating it since I gave it to him yesterday. Even put it on his bedside cabinet when he went to bed last night."

"Name it and let's go," Brodie said. "If you don't hurry up and name it, I will. Those cockroaches look like they might be thinking about getting back on the bench."

Mallory looked at the time in the corner of the screen. "Three minutes left."

Callum rested his fingertips on one of the leaves. "Accept companion animal Precious."

"Bean would have been better," Brodie muttered.

Callum lowered his hand. "Do you think it'll work since it technically isn't an animal?"

"I don't know." Mallory looked at the gold words on the black screen that had replaced the bow, dagger, staff and sword inside a gold circle. As always, she couldn't resist reading them aloud, a shiver of excitement racing through her as she did. "Do you wish to return to Inadon?"

"Of course we do," Brodie said. "Stop messing around, Mal. Choose yes so we can go back."

Mallory chose yes as the time changed to eight.

Everything went black. Sounds, smells and sensations faded, slowly returning. They were in one of the bedrooms of Buckneth tavern, early morning light coming in the single window. Another shiver of excitement raced through her. She doubted she'd ever get bored with returning to Inadon. Even with this being their tenth day and the fourth time they'd returned, it still felt like a dream. An amazing dream.

Fang launched herself at Brodie with an excited bark and he scooped her up into his arms, laughing at her antics. "I missed you too, girl. We might be able to take you home with us one day."

"Can you see it? Did it come with us?" Callum bent to pat Smudge who wrapped an arm around his calf, chattering up at him.

Danae sat up in bed, a shadowy figure in the limited light. "Did you bring a coffee plant with you?"

Mallory finally found her wand and used it to light the candle on the chest that was between the two beds. She grinned when she saw the potted seedling behind Callum.

"Hell yeah. We don't have to worry about going through Hellfire for coffee." Brodie put Fang on the floor. "Kick it out of the party so we can get ready and go after the hellions."

Callum picked up the seedling, taking it away from both Fang and Smudge who were sniffing at it. He placed it on the chest near the flickering candle. As he spoke the words to remove the seedling from the party, someone knocked on the door.

Ryan opened it to find Welby and Roast. They were dressed for the day and Welby had his bow with him. "Are you going hunting already?"

"Soon," Welby said. "After we have something to eat. Did you want to join us?"

At a noise from Callum, Mallory turned in time to see the seedling drag itself out of the soil of the clay pot. Fine, hair like roots parted to become legs. It jumped off the chest and ran towards the door. A face had formed below the leaves at the top of the plant that hung down like thick strands of hair. The outstretched branches had appendages similar to fingers beneath the single leaf each ended in.

"Don't let him get away," Callum called out.

Fang pounced on the seedling, yelping and drawing back.

Mallory managed to capture Precious, dropping him when he bit her. "He drew blood." Checking her stats, she saw she was missing a health point.

Ryan tried to shut the door. He was too late. The seedling slipped out before he could. He dragged the door open, running after him, the two companion animals giving chase, Welby and Roast stumbling out of the way.

With a wistful look at the rest of her gear, Mallory followed the animals in their mad dash down the stairs. She waved Ahron's concerns aside as she caught up with Precious. She joined Ryan and the animals, surrounding Precious so he couldn't escape.

The seedling snarled, sharp teeth visible inside his wooden mouth. He shrank back against the door, swiping at Fang when her nose came near. The door swung open, sending the seedling tumbling across the floor.

"No!" Callum called out as he joined Mallory and Ryan, the rest of their party with him, along with Welby and Roast.

Precious picked himself up and raced through the open door, dashing between the wagoner's feet.

"That can't be good." Ryan pushed past the wagoner, running after Precious, throwing an apology over his shoulder.

Mallory followed, glancing over her shoulder at the wagoner who looked confused. "Sorry." Behind her, the rest of her party followed. Her attention remained on Precious who headed out of the village. She threw a fireball at him. It hit the ground beside him.

"Don't kill him," Callum called out.

"We can't let him escape," Ryan said. "We'd be responsible for whatever havoc he caused."

"But I need him." Callum caught up to Mallory.

"He's going to escape." She tried to run faster. It didn't help. She was soon overtaken by her brother, only Danae behind her. The half-elf was gaining on her though.

"Take him out, Mallory," Ryan ordered.

"No," Callum protested.

Chapter Four

Mallory launched another fireball at Precious. This time it hit. It barely slowed him. Taking a deep breath, and making sure there was nothing else flammable, she attacked with flame.

Precious instantly caught on fire, running around in circles, shrieking. Fang barked at him, staying back out of reach.

"We need water." Callum came to a stop near the seedling. "Or something to smother the flames." He started to remove his t-shirt.

Precious stopped shrieking, dropping on the ground to burn down to ashes.

Callum let go of the hem of his shirt, kneeling in front of the ashes, all that was left of Precious. "No." The word was low and drawn out. "He's dead."

Ryan stopped beside his brother. "I think this is

the moment where you're meant to say 'my precious' over and over."

Callum picked up the ashes. They trickled between his fingers, drifting to the ground. "He's dead."

Smudge leaned against Callum, making soft sounds and patting his arm.

Ryan rested his hand on Callum's shoulder for a moment. "We can go after hellion encampments so you don't run out of coffee. Then once we're finished on Ruby Isle, and after we set up base somewhere on the mainland, we'll go to Cape Barren."

"No we won't," Brodie said. "It'll be too dangerous. Are you trying to get us killed?"

Mallory glanced around the group, none of them ready for the day, other than Welby and Roast, and Danae was barefoot. There was no point arguing it out with Brodie when there were still so many other things to do. "We'll figure out what to do later. We need to get dressed and gather our weapons."

"Did you want to join us for the morning meal?" Welby asked.

Mallory shook her head. "Most of us have eaten." She turned to Danae. "Unless you wanted to."

"No, thank you," Danae said. "I'll have a couple of apples." She glanced at Brodie, smiling. "I'm sure we'll have more than enough to eat throughout the day. Even if it's only jerky or some berries we pick along the way."

Brodie's expression brightened. "We should pick berries before we go." He headed towards the tavern with Welby, Roast and Danae, talking about pies. Fang trotted at his side.

Mallory turned to Callum, who still sifted through the ashes, Ryan remaining beside him. "Callum? Are you okay?"

Callum rose to his feet, gathering up Smudge and holding him close. He rested his cheek against Smudge's face for a moment. "I thought it had worked. When he came back with us, I really thought it had worked.

Ryan slung an arm around Callum's shoulders. "You have coffee for now. We're gaining XP all the time and able to take on stronger creatures. It's simple. We level up and Hellfire will be a breeze. We've got this."

Mallory walked on the other side of Callum as they headed to the tavern. "We should ask Danni if there are some foods you can only get in Hellfire. That might change Brodie's mind about never going there."

Callum laughed softly. "Okay. We'll figure it out.

It's just bloody annoying this didn't work. I was so sure it had."

They reached the tavern bedroom to find Danae standing in front of the door. She gestured towards it. "Brodie is getting dressed. He's going to collect berries while the rest of us get ready."

Ryan turned to his brother. "You should go with him." He grinned. "Keep him out of trouble."

"What will you be doing?" Callum asked.

"Asking the wagoner where to collect our animals," Ryan said.

"Do you need a hand with that?" Mallory asked.

Ryan stepped close. "No. But I'm still waiting for that kiss you didn't give me because I wouldn't tell you what the surprise was. You do know surprises don't work that way."

Mallory slipped her arms around his waist, looking up at him to see the humour in his eyes. "Maybe I was planning to surprise you with a kiss."

Ryan chuckled, lowering his head. "I think I like your kind of surprise better."

Her lips met his, her arms tightening around him. Eventually, she drew back, smiling up at him. Behind her, she heard Brodie come out of the room and tell Callum to hurry up when he said he was joining him. "I'm sure your surprise will improve. When it doesn't come with cockroaches." She briefly kissed him again. "Are you sure you don't need help collecting the animals? If you don't, I'll stay here and pack the handful of things that are out."

"I should be all good." Ryan drew away from her when Callum came out of the room. He turned to Brodie. "Gather enough for two pies. We should be back well before dark. We can have one for afternoon tea and keep one for breakfast tomorrow." He entered the room, closing the door.

"Two pies. Even better." Brodie grabbed Callum's arm, tugging him towards the stairs. "Come on." He let go to hurry ahead, Fang walking alongside him.

Callum followed at a slower pace, once again carrying Smudge, smiling at the river otter who chatted softly to him.

Mallory watched them leave.

"Will Callum be fine?" Danae asked once they were out of sight.

Mallory nodded. "He'll be quiet for a bit and think it over. Once he settles on another plan, he'll be okay."

"That's good." Danae turned towards the door when it opened. She glanced at Mallory. "Did you want to get dressed next?"

Ryan came out, buckling on his weapons and

quiver, dressed in a black tunic and trousers, his hunting bow at his back, angled across the top of the backpack that was mostly empty. "I won't be long."

Mallory nodded, returning the kiss he gave her before he hurried down the stairs. She gestured towards the room as she faced Danae. "You can dress first." While Mallory waited, she looked over her stats, her mouth dropping open when she realised she'd earned experience points for killing Precious. She wasn't sure if she should mention that to Callum. It seemed kind of wrong, especially since Precious had once been a member of their party. Even if it had only been for a few minutes. That made her think of Ninette and she couldn't help wondering how she was doing now she was a warrior. Had her father found out yet?

Danae stepped out of the room, bringing two apples with her, a bite out of one. "I'll help you pack once you're dressed."

"Thanks." It didn't take her long to dress in her light brown shirt and black trousers, putting on her belt with the belt pouch, sheathed dagger and loop of canvas that she slipped the wand into. She picked up her satchel, slipping it over her head and one arm. Opening the door, she let Danae in and together they packed the handful of items that were out.

Danae gestured towards the waterskin of health tea. "Did you want some?"

Mallory shook her head. "I only lost a single point. That's not so bad since we levelled up. Fang should probably have some since she only has six health."

"I should buy more herbs for health tea next time we're in a town or large village," Danae said. "I've only got enough left for two more batches." She opened her belt pouch, taking out a small potion vial and searching once more through the belt pouch before looking at the vial. "And more postponed cycle tincture since I don't know how long we'll be down south."

"More what?" Mallory asked.

Danae slipped the vial back into her belt pouch. "A tincture to postpone your monthly cycle. I would have thought you'd be using it since you're an adventurer."

"How does it work? Can anyone have it? Are there negative side effects?"

"It stops your monthly cycle. Postpones it so you don't have to worry about it. You have to take a dose every twenty-nine days for it to continue to work. There are no negative side effects. Women also use it for birth control," Danae said.

"So I could have it?" Mallory asked. When Danae

nodded, she continued, "When could I start taking it?"

Danae took the vial out of her belt pouch and held it out to her. "Now."

Chapter Five

Mallory stared at the vial Danae held out. It would be a lot easier taking it than dealing with whatever medieval methods women had to cope with each month. She took the vial. "Do I need to have it with food or anything?"

"No. Just make sure you keep track of the days you spend in your world because they count too. You're better off having it early rather than late. Even up to ten days early."

Mallory downed the contents, handing the empty vial back. "I should have asked how much it costs."

Danae laughed softly. "It's not so expensive your brother will complain about it. A silver piece a dose. Less if you return the vial for refilling." Danae's expression became serious. "Doesn't your brother like me?"

"Of course he does." Mallory grinned. "You're

going to have to make all the moves though. He doesn't have the confidence for that. Not when it comes to girls. Anything else and he has heaps of confidence. When he talked about taking you out to dinner, that was his lame attempt at letting you know he's interested."

Danae grinned. "Thank you. I'd begun to think he wasn't. When I figured out how much he liked food, I thought that was the only reason he seemed interested to start with."

"He's interested." Mallory tried not to grin. It escaped anyway. "In you as well as your mother's cooking."

They were both laughing when Brodie and Callum entered the room, their companion animals following. Brodie looked from one to the other. "What's so funny?"

Mallory shared a look with Danae, both of them bursting out laughing again.

Before Brodie could finish asking again what they were laughing about, Ryan entered the room. He gestured back the way he'd come. "The horses and donkey are out the front." He turned to Brodie. "And Not For Bacon. It seems he got into a bit of mischief and isn't welcome back there."

"What sort of mischief?" Brodie asked.

Ryan grinned. "Apparently he's as interested in food as his owner."

Brodie glared at all of them when they laughed. "Are we going? Or are we sitting around here all day?"

Ryan gathered up some of the gear. "We're going."

Mallory helped, glancing at her brother. "We should give Fang some health tea before we leave. Get her health back up to normal."

"She needs her own revive." Brodie continued to speak about all the things he wanted for Fang as they saddled up and put the panniers and the rest of the gear on Bobbi. He gave Fang a dose of health tea while they talked to Welby, going over the directions to the hellion encampment again. It was about twenty minutes north east of where they'd found him on the road.

They headed in the opposite direction to Welby and Roast, leaving Buckneth behind. Mallory turned to Danae. "You were paid four gold, six silver and twelve copper pieces from the last lot of questing we did. So you've now got six gold, ten silver and twelve copper pieces in your bank account."

"She was also paid for the poppet and hellion, not just the quests," Brodie said. "What's the point of banks in this world anyway?"

"To protect your money so no one can steal it from you and so you don't need to carry large amounts around with you or carry it between towns. I'll be able to access the money from any demonic bank. It doesn't matter which one the money was deposited in," Danae said.

"Talking of hellions." Mallory glanced at Brodie before returning her attention to Danae. "How can we avoid Rass coming after us? I don't think we're a high enough level to cope with him continually tracking us down."

"Keep global rep low," Danae said.

"Is that to give us time to level up?" Brodie asked.

Danae shook her head. "No, it won't help with that. He'll level up too. It'll make it harder for him to find out where we are. If no one knows who we are, they can't tell him where we've been."

Mallory sighed. "I was looking forward to gaining global rep."

"We really need to go after a fire drake nest and work on getting better gear," Ryan said. "After we come back from Cutthroat Harbour."

"If it's not too late by then," Brodie muttered.

They continued to talk about fire drakes and all the items they needed, including a second horse. This led to Callum and Brodie taking a turn to ride, their companion animals going on Bobbi. The pig trotted alongside them, Brodie needing to tie another piece of rope to the one on the pig so he could hold onto it while the two of them were on Bug. Danae rode Augusta and Ryan led Bobbi. Mallory walked beside Ryan.

They were about fifteen minutes from the location where they'd rescued Welby when a mage came out from behind a cluster of trees. Mallory and Ryan were now riding Bug and she reached for her wand while Ryan dismounted from where he sat behind her. At least a dozen frogs, of various sizes and different shades of greenish-brown, followed the mage, jumping across the ground.

The mage held a wand in his right hand, wearing a tattered, brown robe. He appeared to be in his early twenties. "Hand over your coins and my frogs won't attack."

Brodie laughed, only able to draw a single throwing dagger since he held Not For Bacon's rope, which was back to its normal length. "You're going to have your frog army attack us?"

Mallory slipped off Bug's back. She didn't blame Brodie for being amused. Even to her the comment had sounded odd. Who sent an army of frogs after anyone?

Ryan held his swords ready. "We outnumber you. Last chance to rethink this."

Danae frowned. "Don't you live out from Wayholt?"

"I… no, of course I don't." The mage cleared his throat. "Uhm… your coins." He cleared his throat again. "Your coins or your lives."

Callum drew back an arrow. "Neither." He kept the arrow pointed at the mage.

"You asked for this." The mage threw a bolt of lightning at Ryan. "Attack now." The frogs jumped forward.

Mallory attacked the mage, rapidly throwing fireballs at him. She would be able to throw fifteen fireballs before her mana completely ran out and she'd have to wait for it to regen. Two of the frogs came towards her and she backed away, trying to focus on attacking the mage. It looked like she was going to need every one of those fireballs with how many frogs attacked.

The majority of the frogs went after Callum, making it impossible for him to use his bow. He tried to block them with it instead. "Stay on Bobbi, Smudge."

"They shoot darts." Brodie backed away from the two frogs that came for him, dropping Not For

Bacon's rope and throwing his knives at frogs. "What sort of frog shoots darts? That's just wrong." He nearly tripped over his pig. Fang jumped off Bobbi and barked at the frogs. Brodie glanced at her. "Stay back, Fang." He glanced at his pig. "You get back too."

Ryan attacked the mage, a cutlass in one hand and short sword in the other. "Danni, take the animals out of danger."

Mallory continued to throw fireballs at the mage as Danae led the horses and donkey away from the frogs, Not For Bacon unwilling to be caught. Mallory stumbled when one of her fireballs was reflected back at her. Pain arrowed through her, along with fear, and she breathed in sharply. It looked like they might be the ones outnumbered with how skilled the mage was and the amount of frogs he had. Not wanting to risk having her magic turned against her again, she drew her sword and ran towards the mage, sidestepping the frogs that came after her. The mage was the greater threat.

"I need help with these frogs." Callum continued to try and block them with his bow, his hunting knife now in his right hand. Several small darts were randomly sticking out of his body.

Chapter Six

Before Mallory could turn away from the mage she was attacking, Callum vanished. Smudge made his high-pitched warning sound and shock momentarily froze Mallory in place. Until the frogs turned their attention on her brother. She started to go towards Brodie.

"Forget the frogs," Ryan ordered. "Focus on the mage."

Having moved the animals back far enough, Danae joined the fight, Smudge remaining on Bobbi and continuing to make his warning sound. Danae shot an arrow at the mage. "I'm sure there's a mage who breeds frogs and lives out from Wayholt."

Mallory tried to focus on attacking the mage. She wanted to keep checking her brother was okay and the sound Smudge made grew more piercing.

"My pig took out one of these annoying little frogs," Brodie said. "How cool is that?"

Mallory smiled. Her brother was obviously okay with how satisfied he'd sounded. She threw another fireball at the mage.

"No!" The mage launched an attack at Brodie. "How would you feel to be little and overlooked?"

Not For Bacon ran in front of Brodie, chasing another frog and getting in the way of the attack. He shrank in size until he was small enough he could fit in someone's hand. The rope that had been tied around his neck fell to the ground.

"What? No." Brodie dived on the pig, scooping him up from in front of the frog Not For Bacon had been about to attack. "Leave him alone." He dropped the pig in his belt pouch before attacking the frog that had been going after his pig.

Mallory didn't know what to do. Darts punctured her body, taking away a health point at a time, frogs seemed to be everywhere and the mage randomly targeted each of them with his various spells. How were they meant to take on a hellion encampment if they were struggling to face a single mage and a dozen frogs? Admittedly, the frogs were about the size of a lap dog, but they still weren't doing too well against them. She threw another fireball at the mage, preparing to cast another one. He disappeared. She remained in place for a couple of seconds, stunned they'd taken him out. Turning to face the frogs, she lowered her weapons when they jumped towards the trees, retreating. "He's dead?" She much preferred it when there was a body to confirm the kill.

Ryan also lowered his weapons. "Let the frogs go."

Sheathing her sword, Mallory removed darts from her arm and legs. "What about Callum? How long until he returns?" She shied away from thoughts of what it felt like to use up a revive as she glanced at Smudge who continued to make his warning cry. She winced. "I hope it isn't too long." She started to move towards Smudge.

Ryan stepped past her, stopping in front of Danae who'd brought the horses and donkey forward.

Danae handed Bobbi's lead rope over to Ryan. "Any second now that the fight is over." She glanced at Smudge. "At least it should be any second."

Ryan patted Smudge who sat up on Bobbi, continuing to call out. "Callum will be back soon." He glanced around the area. "At least I'm guessing that's the problem and there isn't a tonne of enemies hiding nearby."

Brodie took Not For Bacon out of his belt pouch after he picked up the rope and put it in one of the panniers. "What am I going to do with my pig? I can't leave him like this. Look at him. He's so tiny and there are so many dangerous creatures. He wouldn't make a mouthful for most of them." Brodie frowned. "He's been eating my jerky." He glared at Mallory when she laughed. "He's had about a third of it. What am I going to eat?"

Mallory shrugged, her laughter fading as she opened her journal and checked everyone's health. Brodie had lost the least and was at twenty-two health points, Danae had seventeen, Ryan sixteen and she had the least health at eleven. So much for levelling up and having better stats. "I think we need armour." She glanced at Smudge who was still making his warning cry even though Ryan comforted him.

Danae patted Not For Bacon on the head. "Nobles buy farm sets for their children that are full of real animals that have been shrunk in size."

"So it won't hurt him?" Brodie asked.

Danae shook her head. "If you do want him a normal size, you can pay a mage to remove the spell, but it's costly."

Callum reappeared several metres away from them, running his hands over his arms. He shuddered. "That is the worst feeling."

Smudge stopped making his piercing noise, scrambling off Bobbi to bound over to Callum and launch himself at him.

Callum scooped him up. "I'm glad to be back too."

"You don't need to tell me how bad it feels," Brodie muttered.

Mallory glanced at all of them. "Should we be going after the hellions?"

"Not with how low our health is." Ryan took a health potion out of his belt pouch. "Mallory, have a potion too." He drank the contents, putting the empty vial in his backpack.

Mallory drank one of the potions she carried. "Now you don't have a potion in case you need one." She put the empty vial in Ryan's backpack.

Ryan shrugged. "Not much we can do about it." He turned to his brother. "You okay?"

Callum nodded, gesturing towards the pig Brodie continued to hold. "What happened? How did you end up with a teacup pig?"

Danae laughed. "He's certainly small enough to fit in a teacup."

Callum smiled. "I can't take credit for the name. It's a breed of pig back home." He glanced at Not For Bacon. "Not quite that small though."

"I hope you're not expecting to get him back to

normal size," Ryan said. "We've got other things we need to spend money on."

"As if. How cool is he now?" Brodie asked.

"Even though he ate some of your jerky?" Mallory gestured towards Brodie's belt pouch.

Brodie eyed Mallory's belt pouch. "You don't need yours, do you?"

She took a step back from her brother. "You're not having it."

"What am I meant to do with my jerky? If I leave it in my belt pouch with my pig, he'll eat it," Brodie said.

"Guess you'll have to eat the jerky first." Ryan strode towards Bobbi, gathering the lead rope. "Time to go. We'll see how many are at the hellion encampment before we decide if we can take them on. Callum and Brodie can have a turn to ride Bug."

Mallory walked beside Ryan, her hand remaining near her wand she'd tucked back in the canvas loop. "Do you think we've ended up with another enemy?"

"I hate when they have a revive," Brodie muttered. "We get nothing out of the fight."

"At least you got four XP." Callum cradled Smudge in his arms, the river otter clinging to him as he made soft sounds. "I didn't even get that since I wasn't here when you killed the frog mage."

Danae came alongside Mallory on Augusta. "I'm certain there's a mage who lives outside of Wayholt who breeds dart frogs. He's on the road to Wildebay."

"We should pay him a visit." Brodie chewed on the jerky he'd taken out of his belt pouch so he could put Not For Bacon back in it.

"We haven't decided which direction we're taking south yet. We might go along the coast instead of through Wayholt." Ryan glanced at Brodie's belt pouch, Not For Bacon poking his head out beneath the flap Brodie had buttoned shut. "Does that spell work on fire drakes?"

"No." Danae also glanced at the pig, smiling at him. "Only on domestic animals and some sentient races." She looked to Ryan. "Animals that have been shrunk magically don't sell for the same high prices that naturally small animals in certain breeds sell for. Someone with a high level barter can tell the difference. As can someone with certain magic spells."

"I wouldn't mind getting a spell that reflects spells back at mages. Having my own firespell thrown back at me hurt. I could take on higher level mages with a spell like that," Mallory said.

"The frog mage was a level two since we received four XP from him so the spell would probably only be a level two. Unless he's put all his points into intelligence to gain extra spell levels," Danae said. "I'm afraid I don't know all the spells and levels. There are too many of them. But you will gain a reflect skill at one of the higher levels of mage."

"What about the shrink spell?" Brodie asked. "What level is it? One or two? And the one to unshrink."

"Shrink reversal. I think it's level two, but they're some of the more expensive spells to buy," Danae said.

Brodie looked towards his sister. "You should learn them, Mal. Save us having to agist the horses and donkey. Shrink them down when we're not using them and make them normal size when we want to use them again."

"That's actually not a bad idea," Ryan said.

"You don't have to sound so surprised," Brodie muttered.

Chapter Seven

Mallory glanced at Ryan, most of her attention on their surroundings. They were getting close to the hellion encampment and she didn't want to accidentally stumble on any hellions. "Don't tell me you're going to start hassling me to level up mage too."

Ryan grinned. "Nah, keep alternating if that's what you want to do. We just might have to do some days of grinding."

"We keep saying that." Callum patted Smudge who continued to cling to him.

"I know." Ryan stopped, gesturing them all to do the same. "There always seems to be more interesting things to do, but we might have to make time for it."

Mallory peered ahead. "What did you see?"

Brodie breathed in deeply. "Not see. Smell. Someone is cooking meat."

Mallory caught the scent before the breeze shifted again. "That smells pretty good."

Brodie dismounted, reaching for throwing knives. "What are we waiting for? The hellions to eat all the food?" Fang, who jumped off Bobbi to stand at Brodie's side, whined. "See, even Fang agrees with me."

"We'll leave the horses and Bob here." Ryan tied the donkey's lead rope to a nearby tree branch.

Mallory went a little ahead, Brodie following her. The other three finished securing the animals before they followed. Mallory caught a glimpse of the encampment through the trees. She slowed her movements, being more careful where she stepped. She was hoping to get closer for a better look without anyone noticing them. When she was close enough, she hid behind a broad tree, peering around it.

Brodie stood behind her, looking over her shoulder. "Do you think that's all of them?"

There were three sitting around the fire, a hotplate propped up on some rocks, thick slices of meat cooking on it. At least two of them were hellions, skull tattoos high on their arms, clearly visible since both wore leather vests. The third one wore dark clothes and played with a throwing knife. "I don't know. There could be others inside the tents."

Two tents were set back to the left and right of the campfire. Well behind the hellions were two cages. In one was a russet coloured fox and in the other was a snowy white wolf that had a crystal blue tinge to its coat. They lay listlessly in the bottom of the cages as if injured.

Ryan joined them, shifting Brodie out of the way so he could peer over Mallory's shoulder. "Only three. We've got this."

Mallory kept her voice low, like Ryan and Brodie had done. "What if there are more in the tents?"

Ryan grinned. "Then we better take those three out before others can join the fight."

Callum and Danae joined them. After looking at the encampment, Danae turned to Ryan. "I'll focus on the hellion on the right if the rest of you want to take out the rogue playing with the throwing knife then help me with the hellion. We should be able to take out at least two before they can come close to us."

Ryan nodded at Danae's suggestion. "I'll take on the other hellion when he attacks while the rest can help you."

"With the armour those two hellions are wearing, I'd say they're also rogues," Danae said. "You can't become a hellion until you're at least level three so they'll be able to wield enchanted stilettos and throwing knives. It doesn't mean they will have them though."

"What can they do?" Brodie asked.

"Depends on the enchantment." Danae readied her bow.

Brodie pushed Not For Bacon's head back in the belt pouch. "Stay in there." He looked down at Fang. "And you stay back here. I don't want you to get hurt." He patted Fang on the head when she whined. "Give it time. When you're older and have better stats you can join the fight. Don't worry, you'll be close enough here that you'll gain XP."

Callum readied his bow, looking down at Smudge who leaned against his leg. "You too. Stay with Fang."

Smudge chattered up at Callum, sounding like he scolded him, continuing to cling to his leg.

"I mean it. Stay here where it's safe," Callum said.

Smudge tugged on Callum's leg, continuing to chatter at him.

Callum crouched in front of Smudge, running his hand across his head and over his back. "I'll be okay. I've got another revive. But you don't have any so I need you to stay where it's safe."

Smudge rubbed his head against Callum's hand before joining Fang and patting her on the head.

Mallory scanned the area. There were still only the three by the fire. If there were any others nearby, she couldn't see them. She took out her sword and wand. "I'm ready."

Ryan readied his hunting bow. "Spread out a bit and then attack."

Mallory shifted over behind the next tree, remaining out of sight. One of the hellions laughed at something the other said and she stared at them for a moment. Why did they have two animals in cages? Were they valuable? If they were, why hadn't they taken better care of them? She looked at Ryan, who nodded. Returning his nod, she again faced the encampment, throwing a fireball at the rogue.

The three of them leapt to their feet. The rogue ran towards them while the other two ran for cover behind the tents. Mallory began to stumble backwards, having thrown several fireballs at the rogue, worried he'd reach them. Thoughts of being killed by hellions flashed through her mind. The rogue was dead before he was halfway across the clearing. Not that it helped. There were still two hellions. She ducked behind a tree when a throwing knife grazed her arm.

"Set fire to the tents," Ryan ordered.

"There could be stuff in them," Brodie protested. "Good stuff we can sell."

"At least set fire to one," Ryan said. "It'll be safer than circling around."

Mallory used flame on one of the tents, the canvas catching light. When the hellion ran from behind it, headed for the other tent, she threw two fireballs at him. Three arrows struck him along with two throwing knives. The hellion didn't make it. But instead of his body remaining on the ground, he vanished.

"What's with all the enemies with revives today?" Brodie demanded.

"At least this one didn't see who we are," Mallory said.

Before anyone had the chance to comment further, a rogue ran out from inside the tent that was on fire. "Get out of the tent before yours is set alight too." He glanced at the second tent as he spoke, running directly towards where Mallory was hidden.

She threw several fireballs at him, the rest of her companions also attacking. He didn't make it to the edge of the clearing. A second rogue came out of the tent that wasn't alight, changing direction when he saw the other rogue taken out. It didn't help. He was dead before he could hide behind the tent, his body sprawled across the ground.

Callum pointed at the tent opening. "There's another one in there. He's lying on the ground. You can see him peeking out past the tent flap."

Ryan turned to Danae. "Follow me. We'll go around the clearing and take out the hellion behind the tent." He glanced at the rest of the group. "You lot focus on the one inside the tent." He hurried through the trees, Danae following him.

"The only thing I can think of is to cut the ropes like we did with the last one," Mallory said.

"That'd mean we'd have to get close," Brodie said.

Callum aimed at the tent. "Maybe I can shoot through the rope." He fired. The arrow missed. "It's a lot easier when you're aiming at a bigger target."

"I could try burning the ropes." Mallory looked along them. "If I burn them close to the ground, we might be able to put the fire out before it reaches the canvas."

Callum shot at the rope again. Once more he missed. "That was closer."

Brodie took out his stiletto. "We can't stand here all day. Burn the ropes. I'll get over there before the tent catches on fire."

Chapter Eight

Mallory used flame on the ropes of the tent, grinning when she was able to strike each one close to the ground. The tent collapsed in on itself and Brodie ran towards it. Mallory threw a fireball at the hellion hiding behind the tent. He ran towards the cover of the trees.

Before Brodie could reach the tent, an archer burst out of it, firing an arrow at him.

Brodie dropped to the ground, screaming. "My knee. He shot me in the knee."

Mallory focused on the archer, hoping Ryan and Danae took care of the hellion. "Brodie, move." She kept throwing fireballs at the archer, who again aimed at Brodie.

Brodie remained on the ground, clutching his leg. "I can't walk. My knee doesn't work."

Callum ran at the archer, hunting knife in hand. "Over here. You leave him alone."

The archer focused on Callum, who ran at him.

Mallory took a step forward, continuing to throw fireballs at the archer, wishing she could cast them quicker and worried at how fast her mana was going down. The archer staggered backwards as he let the arrow loose, missing Callum. She threw one more fireball and he collapsed on the ground. She took another step forward, leaving the shelter of the trees. Nothing attacked her. The journal icon appeared in the corner of her vision. Frowning, she checked, smiling in relief when she realised it was a notification that she'd discovered the hellion encampment. Closing her journal, she started towards her brother. She was halfway to him when another journal notification appeared. Before she could check it, movement had her stopping.

Ryan stepped out of the tree line on the opposite side of the clearing, Danae following him. He held both his swords. "We got the hellion. He tried to run." He frowned when he looked at Brodie lying on the ground. "What happened?"

Callum stomped out the fires that burned along the ropes. "He took-" He started to laugh.

Mallory grinned as she realised what Callum had

tried to say. "An arrow-" She too broke off as she tried not to laugh, the comment bringing to mind one of the video games she played. It was a comment she'd never expected to hear spoken by someone she knew other than in a joking fashion.

"It's not funny," Brodie said. "It bloody hurts. Where's the health tea?"

Ryan chuckled. "No more adventuring for you."

Mallory burst out laughing again, laughing harder when Callum joined her.

Danae looked at each of them, frowning. "I don't understand why this is so funny."

All Mallory could do was shake her head, while she ran the back of her hand across her eyes that watered from laughing so hard. Callum and Ryan weren't doing much better. Not that she knew how to explain video games to Danae.

Shaking her head, and looking thoroughly confused, Danae headed towards the animals, bringing them back. Fang ran ahead of her, stopping in front of Brodie to lick his face.

Brodie glared at them, patting Fang. "At least someone cares." He slung an arm around Fang, remaining on the ground.

Danae brought over the health tea, helping Brodie

sit up so he could drink it. "This is going to hurt." She reached for the arrow that pierced his knee.

He brushed her hands away. "What are you doing?"

"Removing the arrow." Danae again reached for it.

Brodie pushed her hands away again. "Hell no."

Mallory finally managed to stop laughing. "Won't the health tea help with the pain?"

"For the wound, but not all the pain from the broken bones." Danae grabbed the arrow, breaking the end off it and pushing it through the knee.

Brodie howled, Fang joining him.

The two caged animals stirred, also making noises.

Mallory dropped down beside her brother, picking up the waterskin of health tea he'd dropped, opening it again. "Have some more."

Brodie pushed it away. "I can't drink two cups. It's hard enough drinking one."

"I'll search the encampment," Callum said.

"I'll help," Ryan added.

Mallory checked Brodie's health. He was at seventeen health points after the health tea, which wasn't too bad considering what their health used to be like. She checked everyone's health. Callum and Danae hadn't lost any this fight, Ryan was down to sixteen so it was good he'd had a health potion earlier and she'd only lost three health points, putting her at eighteen. She frowned when Brodie remained on the ground. "How long will you need to lie there?"

"He needs an apothecary," Danae said.

Mallory frowned. "What for?"

"Because health tea and potions don't mend broken bones, only wounds. You'll need an apothecary that can use rapid mend or we'll have to buy boneset salve for him," Danae said.

Brodie stared at her, speechless for a moment. "A health potion won't fix this?"

Danae shook her head.

It took Mallory a moment before she could speak. "We can't take you home with a shattered knee. How would we explain that?"

Ryan joined them. "We can't. We're stuck in this world until he heals. We'll have to take him to an apothecary."

"How much will that cost?" Brodie asked.

Mallory laughed. "Should we be complaining about you wasting money?"

"It will depend on how quickly you want him healed and what treatments you go with," Danae said. "There's an apothecary in Wayholt that can do weak rapid mend. She also sells boneset salve."

Mallory rose to her feet. "We better finish

searching the camp so we can go to Wayholt this arve."

"I'd hoped to explore Bard's Hollow if there was enough time when we got back," Ryan said.

"How long will it take for my knee to be good again after being shot with an arrow?" Brodie asked.

Mallory couldn't resist smiling at his question. Glancing at Ryan, she quickly looked away as she fought the laughter that wanted to escape. Ryan had also found it equally humourous judging by his expression.

"I found a couple of books in that tent." Callum walked towards them, carrying the books. "Lucky it didn't burn down. Only the edges of the tent."

Before Mallory could ask what the books were, the fox made a high-pitched shrieking sound, more scream than howl. Mallory shuddered at the noise. "Do you think they'll attack if we set them free?"

Danae looked from the fox to the wolf. "That's a strange combination, almost like…" Her voice trailed off and she shook her head. "No, it couldn't be."

"Couldn't be what?" Ryan asked.

"Crystalline wolves are often used by weavers to prevent static in the material they're working with," Danae said. "They're usually shapeshifters because the wild creature can be aggressive."

"So we shouldn't let them out?" Callum asked.

"That's not all they're capable of." Danae took a step towards the cages, the fox once again shrieking. "They're used to prevent kitsune from using their abilities. It doesn't effect their shapeshifting ability though, only all their other abilities."

Callum glanced up from the body he was searching, Smudge remaining close to him. "As in a shapeshifting fox?"

Mallory looked from one cage to the other. Both creatures appeared half dead. "They're shapeshifters?"

Danae shrugged. "They might be."

Ryan strode towards the cages. "We can't leave them here." He bent to examine the padlock on the cage that contained the wolf. "Did anyone find a key?"

Callum held up a key. "I did." He tossed it towards Ryan when his brother held out a hand.

Chapter Nine

Mallory took out her wand she'd put away when she'd helped her brother. "Make sure you step to the side before you open the cage." Ryan was already low enough in health without her accidentally throwing a fireball at him if she needed to attack either of the creatures when he set them free.

Ryan unlocked the cage with the wolf, stepping to the side as he swung the door open. The wolf remained where it lay, raising its head slightly to whine. Fang, who remained at Brodie's side, echoed the sound.

"I think you might need to drag it out of there." Brodie patted Fang when she whined again.

"Open the other cage," Callum suggested.

Ryan shifted around to the other cage, standing back as he swung the door open. Mallory watched both creatures, keeping her wand ready.

The fox staggered to its feet, taking several steps before collapsing half out of the cage. It shrieked again.

The sound caused Mallory to shudder.

"I guess we now know what sound a fox makes," Ryan said.

Callum slowly shook his head. "Did you really have to go there?"

Ryan grinned. "Obviously."

Mallory lowered her wand. "I don't think they're capable of doing anything." Tucking her wand in the canvas loop, she cautiously walked forward. When neither creature moved, she knelt in front of the fox. "I just want to help you, okay?"

The fox opened its eyes, looking up at Mallory before closing them again.

Taking that as permission, Mallory carefully dragged the fox out of the cage. "Can you bring the health tea over, Danni?"

Danae crouched beside Mallory, bringing a wooden bowl with her. "I found this by the fire. It might make it easier for the fox to drink the tea." She tipped a cupful of health tea into the bowl, holding it in front of the fox.

The fox had barely finished drinking the health tea when it turned into a young woman, her clothes streaked with blood and dirt, bruises and cuts visible on her body. Her tangled hair was the same russet colour her pelt had been, her eyes a dark brown. She struggled to rise to her feet. "How can I thank you?"

Mallory helped the young woman stand up. "Is the wolf a shapeshifter too?"

Ryan finished dragging the wolf out of the cage then collected the wooden bowl and health tea from Danae.

"Yes." The young woman swayed on her feet, glancing at the wolf. "That's Jorgen. I'm Emica. Can you tell me where we are?"

Mallory helped her to a stool by the cooking fire. "Between Buckneth and Wayholt."

"We're back on Ruby Isle?" Emica asked.

Mallory nodded.

Emica momentarily closed her eyes. "I have to find my father before he goes after the king. What day is it?"

"The tenth day of the second month," Danae said. "Which king?"

"The one in Shadhurst." Emica glanced at each of them. "I was worried I'd lost track of the days. I still have time to find my father. We aren't due back in Shadhurst until the seventeenth."

"I thought the islands had dukes." Mallory joined

Ryan. She held the bowl of health tea while he held up the wolf's head. "Is it a visiting king?"

"The ancestral king," Emica said.

"When you say 'go after him', what exactly do you mean?" Danae asked cautiously.

"Take his crown." Emica leaned forward to peer inside a small pot hanging over the fire. "I'm so hungry, but this looks like that coffee the two hellions kept talking about. They were discussing investing in a coffee plantation when they returned home to the Cape Barren border."

"Coffee plantation?" Callum asked.

At the same time, Danae said, "Your father has to be stopped. Setting the ancestral king free could destroy the Green Isles."

Mallory began to wish she'd used the stool herself rather than give it to Emica. "All four islands?"

"Forget about that for now," Ryan said. "Are there any others who might return to the camp?"

Emica shook her head. "The other two hellions went with two hunters to take the preserved meat and dried herbs to their base. They never mentioned where it was. I need to find it. That's where my father should be." Picking up a fork from beside the fire, Emica prodded the meat on the hotplate. "They're a little overcooked, but I haven't eaten since yesterday around midday." She put them on one of the wooden plates that were in front of the fire. "You should have left one of the hellions alive so we could question him to find out where the base is. I need to find my father and stop him from trying to take the crown."

"What about f-" Brodie broke off when Callum nudged him. "What did you do that for?"

Assuming her brother had been about to ask for some of the food, Mallory spoke before he could try again. "We need to gather what we can and head back to Buckneth to see if Welby and Roast have returned and if everyone can leave for Wayholt today." The sooner they got her brother to an apothecary, the better. Nor was she sure if she should tell Emica where the base was. What if she got in the way of the rescue? Besides, how likely was it that her father would be able to get close to the ancestral king? Surely something that could endanger the islands would be extremely well protected.

"Aw, not more quests," Brodie muttered.

Mallory checked her journal. She read over the first quest. *The Sleeping King: Find a way to prevent the removal of the ancestral king's crown.* She had no idea how they could do that. She checked the second quest, hoping it was easier. *Dangerous Deeds: Help Emica find her father before he does something he'll regret.*

That didn't seem any easier. She had a look at the earlier notification, seeing it was the quest they'd completed. *Hellions In The North: You took matters into your own hands and took care of the hellion encampment. You earned fifteen experience points each.*

"How would your father get close enough to remove the crown?" Danae asked. "The tomb is heavily guarded."

"He's one of the Duke's personal bodyguards." Emica's words brought silence.

Mallory wanted to ask Emica to repeat herself, but she doubted that would change the words in the slightest. She had a bad feeling they'd have to take Emica with them. The stories from home often portrayed kitsune as tricksters. She hoped that wasn't the case on Inadon. That was the last thing they needed.

Ryan, who remained beside the wolf, stared down at him. "He hasn't shapeshifted. Should he have by now?"

Emica helped herself to the meat she'd removed from the fire. "He's probably hungry too." She put some of the meat on one of the other plates, holding it out to Mallory. "This might help. The sooner he's on his feet, the sooner we can get out of here and I can look for my father."

Chapter Ten

Mallory took the plate and walked over to Jorgen. He lifted his head as she placed it in front of him. He nearly ate it whole, but still remained in wolf form. She looked over her shoulder at Emica. "We might know where you can find your father, but we can't leave Jorgen behind and he looks too large for any of us to pick him up and put him on one of the horses." That was if they could convince one of them to carry the large wolf. Being around Fang didn't bother them, but Jorgen was a lot larger than Brodie's companion animal.

Emica set aside the now empty plate. "Ah, he might be deliberately staying in that form. I might have told him he could stop suppressing my abilities if he tried hard enough and that I'd strike him with lightning if I ever got the use of my abilities again if he didn't stop suppressing them."

Callum took the small pot off the fire, breathing in deep. "That smells good." He glanced at Emica. "Do you still plan to attack him?"

"No. I just wanted to escape and was frustrated. I know he can't help it." She smiled up at Callum. "Can I try some of that? It smells pretty good and I'm still hungry."

Callum had poured the contents into a cup and looked from it to Emica several times. "Okay, but it isn't going to fill you." He found another cup and shared the contents between the two, handing one over.

Emica sniffed the contents before taking a mouthful. She made a face. "It smells better than it tastes. I'm not sure if I like it. The drink is a little bitter."

"You can put milk and sugar in it," Callum said. "I don't mind it black."

Rising unsteadily to her feet, Emica made her way over to Jorgen, sitting on the ground next to him. "If you shapeshift, I'll share this with you." She held the cup under his nose before taking another mouthful.

Not knowing what else to do, and wanting to get back to Buckneth as soon as possible, Mallory joined Ryan in searching the camp while Callum drank his coffee, also continuing to search. She regularly glanced at Brodie who remained on the ground next to Fang and at Emica who tried to convince Jorgen she wouldn't attack him, that she just wanted to find her father. Eventually Jorgen shifted into his human form, his hair as pale a blond as Danae's, but not as white as his wolf coat. His hair hung around his shoulders, several thin plaits visible in the bottom layers of his hair, a scattering of glass beads in them. Like Emica, his body was covered in cuts and bruises, his clothes torn and bloodstained. Mallory paused in her search of the collapsed tent, wondering if she should offer him another cup of health tea.

"You're a traveller." Danae stared at Jorgen.

He handed the cup of coffee back to Emica, having taken a mouthful. "Is that going to be a problem?"

"Have you travelled to many places?" Danae asked. "I didn't think there were any travellers to be found on the Green Isles."

"I'm from Eridell." Jorgen took the cup from Emica, having another mouthful before handing it back. "I don't think I like it."

"You don't like coffee," Callum said.

Mallory laughed at Callum's tone. "You make it sound like it shouldn't be possible."

"It shouldn't," Callum said. "I bet if they had milk and sugar in it they'd like it."

"I don't see anyone offering me anything to drink. Or eat," Brodie muttered. "It's not like I can get up and get something myself."

Mallory picked up the bedroll she'd rolled up and took it over to Bobbi to put it on her back with the other one they owned and the tent. "Not everyone likes coffee." She didn't think her brother needed a reply. He was always complaining about being hungry so that was nothing new.

"I'm tempted to argue that comment, but the less people who like coffee around here, the more for me." Callum held up a small pottery jar. "I found some more. Five cups worth."

By the time they'd finished searching, besides the two books, coffee, bedroll and small hanging pot that had contained coffee, they'd also found a mixture of herbs in a tall, cane basket, a barrel of venison that had been preserved with salt, of which they only took ten kilograms, two charcoal coloured woollen blankets, a loaf of bread, a health potion, a flask of health oil, four cured deer hides, a pair of leather boots for Ryan, two steel throwing knives that Brodie added to his vambraces and a dozen venison and vegetable pasties which they shared since everyone was hungry. They left the wooden bowl and plates behind since they were dirty, along with the hotplate, which Ryan said was too heavy to take with them.

Since he didn't have one, Mallory gave the health potion to Ryan, who was sorting out the arrows they'd found and collected. The three of them now had twenty arrows each and there were four spare arrows tied to the outside of Callum's quiver.

Brodie argued about leaving the hotplate behind as Ryan helped him onto Bug, also complaining about the pain in his knee. Ryan shook his head. "We can't weigh the horses down with unnecessary items. They'll need to carry three people back to Buckneth. They don't need any extra weight and we've probably got enough on Bob without adding more to her panniers. Especially if the companion animals ride on her again."

"It's a hunter's hotplate," Danae said. "Suited for campfire cooking. Normally they're lighter than this one to make it easier to take on journeys. So it wouldn't help you, Brodie. The hotplate for cooking is different."

Brodie frowned. "When did you level up, Danni?"

"After we completed the quest," Danae said.

Brodie glanced at his knee. "I was hoping to level up today. I've only got three XP to go. How am I meant to do anything with a shattered knee? Why would anyone put an arrow through the knee? That's just wrong."

"So you can't run," Danae said.

"Maybe you can level up tomorrow," Mallory suggested.

"It will take longer than that for his knee to heal." Danae stepped in front of Emica when she headed for Bug and Brodie. "You can ride my horse."

"I can't share a horse with Jorgen. Even in human form he suppresses my abilities. Not as strongly, but being that close to him will make it worse." Emica glanced at Jorgen who stood near Augusta.

"Jorgen can ride behind Brodie." Danae glanced at the crystalline wolf shapeshifter. "He looks like he might need someone to help him stay upright."

Once both Jorgen and Emica were on the horses, they started towards Buckneth. Mallory walked beside Callum who held both the books, looking through one of them. She looked at the page, unable to make sense of the writings. "What is the book about?"

Callum kept his finger in place and closed the book to show her the cover. "Demonic Runes For English Speaking Scribes." He opened the book again to where he was up to. "There are sections written completely in demonic runes. I'll need to use the translation at the start of the book to figure out what it says. But I'll need pen and paper for that."

Mallory stared at one of the runes. "That looks like the mark on the back of copper pieces."

Danae glanced at the open book. "It is. Each coin has a demonic rune on the back. That is the letter 'c'. The demonic runes are put on them to prevent people from tampering with the coins."

Mallory stared at the book a moment longer. There was so much they didn't know. "And the other book?"

Callum held it out to her. "I haven't looked. It's locked and has what looks like demonic runes across the lock."

Danae hurried over to them. "Don't open it." She took the book from Callum, frowning as she checked the runes. "It says swarm. That wouldn't be pleasant."

"What does that mean?" Mallory asked.

"Demonic runes can be used for curses," Danae said. "If you open this book without breaking the curse or knowing the word for opening it, then you'll be attacked by a swarm."

"A swarm of what?" Brodie asked.

"The hellions were talking about it," Emica said. "They decided it was probably a swarm of biting insects and planned to take it to a mage to break the curse. Or a demon."

"We could do that," Brodie said.

"It wouldn't be cheap," Danae said.

Brodie groaned. "Why has everything got to be expensive?"

Chapter Eleven

Before Brodie could complain further, Mallory asked the question she'd wanted to ask earlier, when he'd been complaining about the hotplate. "What is health oil? Is it like a massage oil or something?"

Danae laughed softly. "No. It's for a lantern. You burn it and sit nearby and your health returns. Depending on the quality, it can be as many as a point each minute."

"How close do you need to be for it to work?" Ryan asked.

"Within a few metres," Danae said.

Mallory glanced at the pannier where the flask of oil had been stored. "We could light it now."

"I could do with regenerating some health points." Emica looked at Jorgen who was slumped against Brodie. "We both could."

They stopped long enough to take out a lantern

and the flask of oil. Mallory opened the lantern. "What about the oil in it? We've got nowhere to put it."

"Tip it out," Brodie said. "We all need health. It's not like I can help if we're attacked." He glared at his knee. "If that archer was still alive I'd put an arrow in his knee."

Mallory couldn't help smiling. She knew it probably hurt, although maybe it didn't since he'd had the health tea, but it was still amusing. Not something she'd ever expected to hear from someone. Other than in reference to one of her favourite games. Catching Ryan's eye, her smile became a grin and she looked away from his amused expression before she started laughing again.

Once the lantern was filled with the health oil, they continued towards Buckneth, only one hour worth of oil in the lamp. But they did have an empty oil flask now. Mallory kept watch on her stats, taking the pocket watch from Ryan. No one spoke as they waited to see how many health points the oil would regen. It was one health point every five minutes.

"That's rather good," Danae said.

Mallory checked all their health. Ryan was now only missing ten health points. If they waited until all of them had returned, there'd be five minutes worth of oil left. "We'll give it half an hour. That will give Danni and me full health and Brodie and Ryan will have four and five health missing."

"Six health points will help," Emica said. "The hellions kept our health low. Every time we healed after sleeping, they worked on getting our health low again, using a brass spyglass to regularly check it."

They remained silent as they continued towards Buckneth, Mallory keeping an eye on the time so she could put the lamp out once the half hour was up. She noticed some of the wounds on the two they'd rescued had healed, only the dried blood left behind.

Arriving in Buckneth before midday, they headed straight to the tavern. Ryan helped Jorgen off Bug then Callum helped Brodie. "Watch it." Brodie glared at Callum. "Are you trying to make my knee worse? An arrow to it wasn't bad enough?"

Mallory tried desperately not to laugh. It didn't help when she caught sight of the humour in Ryan's eyes. She hurried ahead of him and Jorgen, opening the tavern door and holding it while everyone traipsed inside. She brought more chairs over to the table in the corner. They'd barely sat around the table when the Buckneth hunter entered the tavern, heading straight for them.

Brodie broke off mid complaint, looking up at the hunter who stopped at their table.

Mallory was half tempted to thank the hunter for his interruption of Brodie's complaints, but they needed to work out what to do next. Wait for Welby and Roast to return or go looking for them and tell the wagoner they'd be leaving as soon as they found them.

The hunter inclined his head. "Had a talk with the wagoner this morning. He said you're interested in making a deal with me about some eggs. I'll give you the details for thirty percent of the profits."

"Thirty percent," Brodie exclaimed. "You've got to be kidding. We'd be the ones doing all the work."

"I'm the one with the information. I can wait until next time. You raid a nest and the mother isn't going to return to that location again," the hunter said. "She'll find somewhere safer."

"Fifteen percent," Brodie said.

The hunter shook his head. "Twenty-five. And not one bit lower. I've been laid up long enough and it'll take a good while longer before I'm fully on my feet. Not like there's an apothecary around here to take care of serious injuries."

"Sixteen percent," Brodie said.

The hunter gave him a look of disgust. "Don't insult me."

"When will the eggs be ready to take?" Ryan asked.

"She'll be laying them any day now. Be best to take them before the end of the month. Don't want to be cutting it too close," the hunter said.

"Twenty percent," Brodie said. "And that's our final offer." He glanced at his knee. "We'll be the ones risking ourselves and there's no guarantee we'll get anything out of it other than a few more injuries."

The hunter held out his hand to Brodie. "Done."

Brodie shook his hand. "So where's the nest?"

The hunter let go of Brodie's hand, taking a step back. "Come see me when you're ready to go after it. I'll tell you where you can find it then." With another nod, he strode for the door.

Jorgen looked from the hunter who stepped outside to those seated around the table. "You're going after drake eggs."

Even though it seemed more of a statement than a question, Mallory answered him anyway. "Yes."

"After he's well?" Jorgen nodded to Brodie.

Mallory took a deep breath. It was probably past time to share their plans. "After we've been to Cutthroat Harbour where the hellions took their captives."

"That's their base?" Emica asked.

"Until the nineteenth when they sail for the Hellfire and Cape Barren border," Ryan said.

Emica leaned forward. "I'm travelling with you."

"I am too," Jorgen said.

Emica glared at him. "No, you're not. How am I meant to regain my full power if you stay with us?"

"I wasn't the only one of my clan they captured. I need to see if anyone else survived." Jorgen met her gaze, determination in his. "No traveller would ignore the plight of another traveller. You don't turn your back on your family. Especially when they wouldn't turn their back on you."

"You're only saving a handful of people. Finding my father will save all those on the Green Isles," Emica said.

"Then you'll have to manage without your lightning," Jorgen said. "I am going after those of my clan."

Ryan rose to his feet. "This isn't getting us anywhere and it sounds like we need to get moving as soon as possible." He looked at Callum. "You see if the pies are ready and let the wagoner know there's been a change in plans. We need to leave today." He turned to Danae. "Can you stay with Brodie while Mallory and I find Welby and Roast?"

Danae nodded.

Ryan turned to Mallory. "You ready?"

With a glance at Brodie, who was muttering about being left behind and only having another three experience points left so he could level up, she nodded. "We should check with Ahron to see if they've been back."

Ryan slipped his arm around her waist as they headed for the bar. "Good plan."

Chapter Twelve

On learning Welby and Roast hadn't returned, Mallory and Ryan headed outside, going in the direction the two had taken that morning. "What if we can't find them?" Mallory scanned the area as they left Buckneth behind. All she saw was trees scattered around the place.

"Even if we have to leave here after dark, we will," Ryan said.

Before Mallory could argue about travelling at night, especially to Wayholt, she spotted Osbert senior striding towards them. "He doesn't look happy." She kept her voice low.

"That's an understatement," Ryan said softly.

Osbert hurried towards them, speaking before he'd come to a stop. "Find my daughter and bring her home. And take back that sword you gave her. I won't have it. Do you hear?"

Mallory nearly took a step back at the anger in his voice. "What happened to Ninette?"

"As if you don't know," Osbert said. "You happened to her."

Mallory frowned. "We didn't do anything to hurt her. We'd never hurt a friend."

"You gave her that sword." Osbert pointed a finger at them. "What did you think was going to happen if you let her become a warrior?"

Ryan took a step towards Osbert. "She was injured?"

"How do I know? Osbert demanded. "She took off when I told her to get rid of the sword or she wasn't welcome in my home."

"You threw her out?" Ryan asked.

Mallory heard the anger in Ryan's voice and stepped close to him in case she needed to prevent him from doing something crazy. Like attacking Osbert. Not that she'd blame him, but she was pretty sure the Guardians Of The Round Table would frown on that kind of behaviour.

"I won't have her be a warrior. You hear? I've been trying to discourage that nonsense for years. Then you come along and ruin everything," Osbert said.

"You threw her out," Ryan repeated

Osbert pointed a finger at Ryan again. "Find her

and bring her home. And take that sword off her." Turning, he strode towards his farm without another word.

Mallory stared after him, the journal icon in the corner of her vision. "This can't be good."

"Probably not." Ryan glanced around the area. "We need to find Ninette. As well as Welby and Roast. Then we can go back and listen to Brodie complain about a quest we can't complete. There's no way I'm returning Ninette to her father."

Mallory checked the quest. *Runaway: Osbert senior demands you return his daughter and take back the sword you gave her.* "There's no-" she broke off as a thought occurred to her, a smile forming. "You know, just because we take her back to him, doesn't mean we have to leave her with him. Same with the sword. Taking it from her doesn't mean we can't return it."

Ryan chuckled, starting to walk along the road. "I don't think that's going to help our reputation around here."

Mallory walked beside him. "Screw our reputation. I'm not about to make her return to that bully."

Ninette stepped out from amongst a cluster of trees. "Do you really mean that? You won't make me go back to him?"

Mallory hurried forward, looking Ninette up and down. "You're okay?"

Ninette nodded. "A bit hungry though. I walked out before I had the chance to have breakfast this morning. I came inside after taking care of my outdoor chores to find Pa had discovered where I'd hidden the sword under my bed. I don't know what he was looking for under there. I barely managed to say a word over all his yelling."

"Where do you plan to go?" Ryan asked. "I'm guessing you're not going to give up being a warrior and return home."

Ninette shrugged. "I have nowhere. Can I travel with you? Until I level up enough to travel alone."

"You want to join our party?" Mallory was pretty certain Brodie wouldn't appreciate having to split what they made even further when they returned home. Particularly since he didn't exactly get along with Ninette.

Ninette shook her head. "No, just travel with you so I can fight alongside you and gain some XP. Maybe until I gain a level. Or even half a level."

Mallory wanted to agree, but it wasn't exactly a decision she could make on her own. It was one the entire party had to decide on. Before she could come up with a reply, Ryan spoke.

"Help us find Welby and Roast and then we'll go back to the tavern and take a vote on if you can remain with us. We usually make these decisions as a group. We'll also get you something to eat."

Ninette pointed in the direction she'd come from. "I saw them headed that way about twenty minutes ago. They were tracking a deer."

Ryan gestured in the direction Ninette had indicated. "Lead the way."

They found Welby and Roast coming towards them, headed for Buckneth, a deer tied to a straight branch that rested on their shoulders. Walking beside them, Ryan and Mallory explained the situation, including telling them about Emica and Jorgen.

Welby nodded. "I have no objection to starting for Cutthroat Harbour sooner rather than later."

"Going today is a much better idea, but what are we going to do with the deer?" Roast asked.

"I'll sort it out when we reach Wayholt," Welby said. "I guess we'll be there for a couple of days depending on the level of the apothecary."

"What if it's only a low level apothecary?" Roast asked. "I can't wait around forever. I have to find Merry."

Ryan shrugged. "We'll figure something out. We

need to be in Cutthroat Harbour before Emica's father leaves."

"We've all heard about what might happen if the crown is removed from the ancestral king." Welby slowly shook his head. "I certainly don't want to find out if it's true."

Arriving back in Buckneth, they found the wagoner at the front of his cottage with his horses hitched to the wagon. Three chests were set sideways behind the seat, the rest of the wagon tray left empty. Mallory and Ryan left Welby and Roast to decide where to put the deer on the wagon while they went inside with Ninette.

Everyone was sitting around the table, two pies on it and Brodie complaining about wanting a piece. He looked over at them. "About time you got back. I'm starving."

Callum grinned. "Good thing you turned up. I don't know how much longer he would have waited to get started on the pies."

"I was only going to have my share," Brodie muttered. "And what's with the new quest that appeared in my journal?" He nodded to Ninette. "Is that why she's with you?"

Mallory sat at the table. She doubted her brother was going to appreciate what they had to tell him.

"We share out both the pies. There are too many of us for only one to be enough to go around." Using her dagger, she cut up the pies.

Brodie took his share. "Should have picked more berries."

Mallory waited until Brodie had a bite of his food before she explained what had happened.

Brodie glared at Ninette, who was cuddling Smudge, the river otter regularly reaching out his hand to pat Callum's arm. "Told you it was a bad idea. Now we're gonna be stuck babysitting her."

Ninette returned his glare. "I don't need a babysitter. I'd like to see you survive out there on your own."

Ryan glanced around the table. "We'll vote on it." His gaze rested on Danae. "You too."

Danae smiled at Ninette. "I don't mind. After all, who wouldn't want to be an adventurer."

Callum nodded to Ninette. "I vote yes too. We need someone to stay with the wagoner when we go to Cutthroat Harbour. No one else wants to wait behind and guard him so if Ninette would be willing to do that, she'd be doing us a favour. It's not like any of us are that much higher a level than her."

"I can do that," Ninette said.

"I guess that wouldn't be too bad then," Brodie muttered.

"Does that mean yes from you?" Ryan asked.

Mallory spoke before her brother could. "It doesn't matter if it is a yes. With my vote, that makes it majority rules."

Ryan rose to his feet. "That's settled then. Time to take Ninette to her father so we can finish off this quest and head to Wayholt."

Brodie struggled to rise from the table. "You're not completing a quest without me. I have three XP left to gain a CAS point."

Callum helped Brodie, wrapping an arm around his waist. "He can ride Bug."

They said their goodbyes to Ahron telling him they didn't know when they were returning in answer to his question. Leaving Bobbi and non-party members behind, except for Ninette, they headed towards Osbert senior's farm. They also left the sword they'd given to Ninette on the wagon, promising to return it to her once they started for Wayholt.

Osbert senior come out of the farmhouse before they'd stopped at his front door. He glared at each of them, his gaze finally coming to a rest on Ninette. "They take that sword back?"

Ninette nodded. "Won't make a difference though. I'm not coming home. I'm going to be a warrior."

"Stop being stupid," Osbert ordered. "Do you want to die young? That's what happens to warriors."

Ninette glared at her father. "Not all warriors."

"Too many of them die young. Is that what you want?" Osbert asked.

"I'm not about to spend my life taking care of sheep." Ninette gestured in the direction of the sheep pen. "You might like taking care of them, but I don't."

Osbert turned to Mallory. "This is your fault. She dies, then it's on your head." He pointed a finger at her.

Before Mallory could argue, Ninette stepped between her and Osbert. "This is my choice. If I die, it would be no one's fault but my own." She looked past her father to the farmhouse. "Are my brothers inside? I want to say goodbye to them."

Osbert crossed his arms over his chest. "You made your choice. You want to leave, then leave."

Ninette glared at her father a moment longer before turning and striding away.

"Keep walking and you might as well be dead to me," Osbert called after her.

Ninette kept walking towards the village, not looking over her shoulder.

"I thought our dad was a bit of a bastard at times," Brodie muttered. He turned Bug towards Buckneth. "No point sticking around here. We've got other things to do."

Chapter Thirteen

Mallory was the last one to start towards Buckneth. She stared at Osbert and he glared back at her. It didn't take long to decide there'd be no changing his mind. "One day, you will regret that."

"You don't know me."

She didn't answer immediately. "No, but I've met people like you before." Turning, she hurried after her companions, opening her journal since the icon for it had been in the corner of her vision once Ninette had walked away. *Runaway: You returned Ninette to her father who was displeased by the outcome. You earned two experience points each.*

"No! You've got to be joking. Two XP. I need one more for a CAS point," Brodie complained.

Mallory laughed, catching up with her companions. "No more adventuring for you." She couldn't resist paraphrasing the video game, even though only Ryan and Callum would get the reference.

Ryan grinned. "So it would seem."

Brodie glared at them. "None of you are funny. My knee is starting to hurt again. That health tea is wearing off."

"The waterskin of health tea is on Bobbi. Did you want me to hurry ahead and get it for you?" Danae asked.

"That would-" Brodie broke off. "We lost reputation in Buckneth. This is ridiculous. Why would they take rep from us? Two rep."

"I'm sorry," Ninette said.

Mallory glanced at Ninette. "It doesn't matter. We'll gain it back." She looked up at her brother, about to tell him to stop complaining when a voice called out from behind them, telling them to wait up. Stopping, she turned to see Osbert junior running towards them, a cane backpack on his back bouncing with his movements.

"Pa kept saying you'd come home." Osbert slipped the backpack off. The oblong opening at the top had a lid made from a thin piece of timber that was latched shut. "I knew you'd be back. Just as I knew you wouldn't stay. I packed all your clothes and things."

Ninette took the backpack from him, slipping it into place. "He wouldn't let me say goodbye."

"We heard." Osbert took fifteen copper pieces out of his belt pouch. "For you. From the three of us. All we had left."

"You didn't have to do that." Ninette didn't take the coins.

Osbert grabbed her hand and placed them on her palm. "Write to us. Send it to Ahron. I'll ask him to hold any letters so Pa doesn't keep them from us."

Ninette slipped the coins into her belt pouch and hugged her brother. She drew back from him. "I will. And I'll let you know where I settle in case any of you want to join me."

Osbert grinned. "Better be careful with that offer or you'll have all three of us living with you."

Ninette chuckled. "I wouldn't mind." She glanced towards Buckneth. "I better go. We need to get to Wayholt before dark."

"And before the apothecary shuts," Brodie muttered.

Mallory gave Brodie a look to warn him not to interrupt. There was a chance Ninette wouldn't return to Buckneth with them. She needed time to say goodbye to her brother.

Osbert took a step back. "I better get home before

Pa misses me." He grinned. "Or I'll be homeless and following you around the countryside before the day is over."

Ninette smiled, watching her brother go and raising her hand when he looked over his shoulder once he was several metres along the road. "Do you think they'll be fine?"

Callum clapped her on the shoulder. "Of course they will. And you'll level up before you know it and be able to make your own way in the world and find somewhere all of you can live."

Mallory started towards Buckneth, her companions going with her. "Look at all we've accomplished in ten days. I'm sure you'll be fine and your brothers will be too."

Danae smiled at Ninette. "Adventurers level up quicker than those focusing on crafting abilities. I'm sure you'll gain XP faster than you expect."

Reaching Buckneth, Mallory and Ryan spread out the bedrolls and blankets to make the tray of the wagon more comfortable and everyone visited the outhouse, Callum needing to help Brodie. He also had to help Brodie into the wagon. The companion animals were put in the wagon while Not For Bacon remained in Brodie's belt pouch, regularly poking his head out of the opening. Welby and Roast sat up the front with the wagoner while Jorgen and Emica lay in the back. As they started towards Wayholt, Brodie had another cupful of health tea.

Callum glanced at the waterskin. "Don't go drinking too much. I don't want to be helping you to the outhouse all night."

Brodie set the waterskin down beside him, frowning. "That's not fair." He looked at Callum. "You got to level up. And what are you going to do with all your CAS points? When are you putting them into something?"

"When I know what will be useful." Callum looked over his shoulder towards the wagoner. "Can we pull up for a minute?"

The wagoner drew to a stop.

"What's the problem now?" Brodie demanded. "Why are we stopping?"

Mallory had been about to ask the same question.

Callum turned to Ryan. "Give me a hand with Brodie. We'll set him down over there by those herbs and he can pick them and finally level up. It might stop his whinging."

Mallory laughed at her brother's expression. "I don't know if he deserves that after all his complaining."

Brodie sat up to make it easier for Callum and Ryan

to help him from the wagon. "How was I meant to know that's why we were stopping?"

Ryan helped Callum lay Brodie beside a cluster of herbs. "You do know you could have asked for help instead of complaining."

"I didn't think of it." Brodie breathed in sharply. "Glad I had some health tea. At this rate, I'm going to need another cupful."

Callum grinned at him. "I don't know how many more toilet trips our friendship can survive."

Brodie glared at everyone when they laughed. His glare faded when he picked three herbs. "Finally. I was beginning to think I'd never get that CAS point."

Once they were in the wagon and again headed towards Wayholt, Emica ran her fingers through her hair. "What I wouldn't give for a brush." She winced as her fingers caught in a knot. "And a bath."

Danae took a hairbrush out of her satchel and held it out to Emica. "I can lend you a brush, but you'll have to wait until we reach Wayholt for a bath."

"Thank you." Emica took the brush and tugged it through her hair.

Jorgen nodded towards the brush. "I wouldn't mind using it when you're finished."

Mallory glanced around her group, after resting her hand on her satchel. When they either nodded or shrugged, she took out the brush and handed it over to Jorgen.

He took it, separating his fair hair so that the eight thin plaits that were across the nape of his neck, in the bottom layer of his hair, were over one shoulder while the rest of his hair was draped over the other shoulder. There were a scattering of glass beads at various heights throughout the plaits. A couple of plaits had two beads in them.

"Did some of the beads get broken while you were captured or are they meant to be randomly spread throughout your plaits like that?" Callum asked.

Jorgen paused in brushing his hair. "You don't know about us?"

"Us?" Callum asked.

Jorgen inclined his head. "Travellers."

Danae smiled. "They aren't from here."

Jorgen lifted one of his plaits, holding it by a bead. It was dark blue with swirls of silver running through it. "We gain them for protecting the clan. When we fight to protect our family. Skirmishes don't count. Only battles or large fights." He let the plait fall from his fingers. "The beads can't break. They're enchanted." He lifted a plait with a blood red bead, swirls of gold through it. "We also gain them for helping other clans, for fighting at their side and protecting them."

"Can only travellers wear them?" Callum asked.

Jorgen continued to brush his hair. "Sometimes beads are given to those who aren't travellers, but have fought for us at great risk to themselves. They signify those who would protect travellers."

"Then travellers should take back the beads they gave the divine demon they follow. I heard you begging him to help you," Emica said.

"That's the problem with following a popular divine demon. They can't answer everyone, but when they do, they have a lot of power with which to help," Jorgen said.

"Follow a demon?" Mallory frowned. "A divine demon?"

"Is that like a divine being or a god?" Callum asked.

"The ancient gods haven't been heard of in centuries. No one believes they still exist," Emica said. "And demons aren't gods, but those who reach a hundred years and gain enough followers can become divine. They then regularly help those who choose to follow them because if they didn't, they'd lose followers and their power." Emica handed the brush to Danae. "Thanks for letting me borrow it."

The wagon jarred Brodie when they went over a

rock on the road, causing him to groan. "Why does Wayholt have to be so far from Buckneth?"

Mallory looked at the basket of herbs they'd taken from the hellion encampment. Danae had put the herbs Brodie had collected in it. "We should probably gather herbs to help pay for the apothecary."

Ryan grinned. "And so the rest of us can gain a level too."

Emica looked from them to the herbs set back from the side of the road. "You hardly get any money from herbs. You'd be better off hunting game."

Jorgen, who'd been laying down, sat up. "We should be out there collecting herbs. We've got no money, no food and no weapons."

Emica looked him up and down. "You expect me to gather herbs."

Jorgen shrugged. "You might have to if you want to eat. Or is collecting herbs too much like work to a noble?"

"Typical traveller," Emica said. "Always running down nobles."

Before Mallory could interrupt and prevent an argument, Danae spoke. "Wayholt isn't a very wealthy village. The apothecary will only be able to afford a certain amount of herbs. She will be willing to take some in trade though."

Jorgen turned to Mallory. "If you can give me the balance of what I need to buy a stiletto, I'd be willing to help you raid the drake nest without expecting any profit from the eggs. I can't save my clan without a weapon."

"I don't know," Mallory said.

"You can trust my word," Jorgen said.

"As annoying as travellers can be, they always keep their word," Emica said.

Mallory shook her head. "It wasn't that. I have no idea how much it's going to cost for the apothecary or how long we'll have to stay in Wayholt. Or even how much it'll cost to stay at the tavern there."

Danae glanced around the group. "Some of us could stay at my mother's place." She glanced around again. "Her home isn't very large."

The wagoner looked over his shoulder. "I always stay at the tavern. The rooms have two beds and for an extra copper piece a night they'll provide a mattress on the floor."

"I'd be willing to share," Roast said.

"I wouldn't mind sharing," Welby said. "But I was going to set up camp outside of Wayholt so I could sort out the deer."

"You could butcher the deer behind my mother's place," Danae said. "She won't mind. She's done the same herself when she needs a lot of venison for her cooking."

"Let's get this over and done with. Not that any sword that could be bought from money earned picking herbs could match the one my father gave me to celebrate gaining a journal." Emica jumped out of the wagon, striding towards the closest patch of herbs.

"We'll take the left-hand side of the road if you want the right." Jorgen followed Emica who glared at him as he drew near.

Mallory sighed. She wasn't sure how it was going to work out having the two of them staying with their party. Especially with how Jorgen interfered with Emica's abilities. Not that she could exactly blame the kitsune. You needed to be able to protect yourself in this world. And not being able to use your abilities would make that difficult.

Ninette gestured towards where Jorgen and Emica were picking herbs, several metres separating them. "Should I collect herbs on that side of the road too?"

"I suppose so." Mallory clambered off the wagon. "Time to level up."

Ryan joined her, the rest remaining with Brodie. It didn't take them long to gather enough herbs to level up and they returned to the wagon, putting them in with the herbs from the hellion encampment. Mallory also mended their clothes as she gathered, making sure not to let her mana get too low.

Danae spoke softly, Brodie having fallen asleep. "With the herbs you brought back along with some of the ones in the basket I'll be able to prepare more herbs for health tea. Possibly as many as another four batches, giving us six in total with what I still have."

"What herbs are we lacking to make more batches?" Mallory had the feeling that six batches weren't going to be enough.

"Calendula." Danae held up the herb.

Callum glanced at Brodie. "We should probably gather more herbs, not just calendula. I doubt the apothecary will be cheap. The more we can offer her in trade, the better."

Ryan grinned. "I bet you wouldn't have said that if he was awake."

Callum shrugged. "He can pick herbs when his knee is fixed."

"Okay. Let's get our XP up to ten each and see if we can find more calendula for health tea." Mallory jumped off the wagon, striding towards the closest cluster of herbs, the faint glimmer to harvestable resources making it easier for her to spot them as she drew near.

Chapter Fourteen

By the time they were finished gathering resources, they had plenty of herbs to trade and enough calendula that Danae could make twelve batches of health tea. Mallory didn't find it overly reassuring. What they needed was health potions. "Can potions be made while travelling?"

Danae shook her head. "Not easily. The apparatuses need to be set up and some potions can take anywhere between a few hours to a week."

"How much do the apparatuses cost?" Callum asked.

"Depends on which one and the quality," Danae said. "The cheaper quality ones have a greater chance for the potion making to fail."

Ryan grinned at his brother. "It's pretty much a given that everything is expensive."

Ninette returned to the wagon, putting the herbs

she'd gathered in her cane basket backpack. She glanced at Brodie. "How did he hurt his knee?"

Callum was halfway through the explanation when Brodie woke, complaining he was hungry. Emica and Jorgen returned to the wagon in time to hear him, clambering in. Both carried an armful of herbs. Emica set her herbs down at her side. "I'm starving too. How long until we reach Wayholt?"

"We still have a loaf of bread and honey," Brodie suggested.

"We haven't eaten properly in about a week," Emica said.

The wagoner looked over his shoulder. "You shouldn't eat too much today then. Might make yourself sick."

"I might make myself sick if I don't eat," Emica said.

The wagoner shrugged, remaining silent.

Narrowing her eyes, Emica looked at Jorgen. "Can't you sit further away from me? I was starting to regain my abilities."

"I'm at the opposite end of the wagon. What do you want me to do? Get out and walk?" Jorgen demanded.

"Don't be ridiculous," Emica said. "You could ride one of the horses."

"How about you ride one of the horses. Maybe you're doing all right after everything we've been through, but I'd probably fall off the horse," Jorgen said.

Mallory interrupted before Emica could do anything other than open her mouth. "Everyone want bread and honey?" When they all agreed, she sliced up the bread and spread it with honey, sharing it around, including giving some to the three sitting on the seat at the front of the wagon. They also gave some plain bread to Smudge, Fang and Not For Bacon.

"How did the hellions catch you and your father?" Danae asked Emica. "I wouldn't have thought one of the personal guards of the Duke would be easily captured."

Emica swallowed her mouthful of food. "It's the fault of that useless ship's captain. We were attacked on our way over to Eridell. We'd planned to visit family in the south. They invited us to a wedding, but my father said he didn't know if we could make it. He had to wait for permission to take extended leave. Then there wasn't enough time to let them know. Or at least it seemed pointless sending a letter when we'd arrive before it." Emica looked off into the distance. "We should have sent a letter."

"No one knows you're missing?" Ryan asked.

Emica shook her head. "I don't know how they knew about our plans. Someone must have told them. For all I know, there's a dark forces spy at the castle."

Brodie groaned. "Great."

Smiling, Mallory checked her journal since the icon was in the corner of her vision. Her smile vanished as she read the new quest. *Spy In The Capital: Discover who the spy is or notify the authorities in Shadhurst so they can look into the matter.*

"We're going to run out of room in our journals at this rate," Brodie muttered.

"That isn't possible," Danae said. "But it will make it hard to find a particular quest if you have a lot of them."

Mallory turned to Jorgen, hoping to avoid more complaints from her brother. "How did you end up being captured by hellions?"

"They tracked down my clan in Eridell and attacked, capturing several of us and bringing us here. I don't know where they took the others they brought back with me, but I was shoved in that cage to keep Emica from using her abilities against them." Jorgen glanced at Emica, two of the glass beads in his long hair clinking together as he moved. "I just want to find those who were captured with me and return home so I can find out what happened to the rest of my clan." He fell silent for a moment, his voice quiet when he spoke again. "I want to find out if any survived."

"Whereabouts in Eridell were you when they captured you?" Danae asked.

"Faryn."

"That's south of Merrow, isn't it?" Danae asked.

Jorgen nodded. "A few hours. We'd been in Merrow the week before. Do you know people there?"

"No," Danae said. "I'll be travelling there soon to attend the Alchemy Academy."

Jorgen inclined his head. "It has a good reputation. You've chosen well."

Danae smiled at him. "Thank you."

Brodie shifted slightly so he was closer to Danae. "It feels like it's taking forever to get to Wayholt."

Mallory managed to suppress a smile, glancing between Danae and Jorgen. She felt like telling her brother not to be so lame. To figure out what people did on dates around here and invite Danae out on one. Instead, she remained silent, as did everyone else. She alternated between mending Emica and Jorgen's clothes, shrugging when they thanked her. By the time Wayholt was in sight, all their clothes were mended and her mana had returned.

"Finally. It felt like we'd never arrive," Brodie muttered.

Ryan checked the pocket watch. "It's only half past four. It wasn't that long a trip considering we didn't leave until around one thirty."

"I'm surprised we didn't run into anything along the way," Callum said.

Ryan grinned. "Maybe we've cleaned up the road after the amount of times we've travelled along it." He returned the pocket watch to his belt pouch. "And got rid of the hellion encampment."

The wagoner took them directly to the apothecary and offered to wait out the front for them. Ryan turned to Callum. "Did you want to take those four cured deer hide to the trading post and see what you can get for them?"

"Shall I meet you back here?" Callum collected the hides.

Ryan turned to Danae. "How long will the apothecary take?"

Danae glanced at the herbs that had been collected and the ones from the hellion encampment. "It might take awhile to finish up."

"We'll head in and sell our herbs while you're

getting yourselves organised." Emica gathered her herbs and jumped off the wagon. "Hurry up, Jorgen. Don't let now be the exception to remaining close to me." She strode inside the apothecary shop.

Grinning, Jorgen gathered his herbs and hurried after them.

"I'll go with them." Ninette clambered off the wagon and followed.

Danae looked from the shop to the direction of her mother's home. "I should really let my mother know I'm here, but I need to buy more postponed cycle tincture."

"What's that?" Brodie asked.

Grinning, Mallory answered him. "To postpone a female's menstrual cycle. I'm going to get some too."

Brodie winced. "Do you think I want to hear about that? And what are you wasting money on it for?"

"Probably cheaper than the equivalent of medieval sanitary pads. And if you don't want to listen, go somewhere else," Mallory said.

"How? I'm the one who was shot in the knee with an arrow." Brodie gestured towards his knee, glaring at Mallory when she laughed. "Will you stop doing that?"

"I really can't understand how any of you can find it funny," Danae said.

"Don't worry, it's one of those things from our world. I'll show Brodie a Youtube vid when we return home and he'll understand." Callum grinned. "Probably won't find it funny though." He took a step away from the wagon, shaking his head at Smudge who wanted to be picked up. "I can't carry you and the hides." He sighed when Smudge continued to stretch his paws up to him.

Ryan held out one of the thin blankets. "You could make a sling to carry him."

Callum put down the hides, fashioning a sling to carry Smudge in front of him, needing to take off his bow to position it. Once Smudge was in the sling and the bow back in place, he gathered up the hides. He took a step away from the wagon. "I'll be back soon." He strode down the road in the direction of the trading post, Smudge peeking out of the sling.

Chapter Fifteen

Mallory glanced at the three seated on the front of the wagon, talking quietly amongst themselves, wondering if they'd been paying attention and if it was a problem who knew they weren't from this world. "We should probably get Brodie inside and see what the apothecary can do for his knee." She collected the tall, cane basket of herbs they planned to trade.

Ryan helped Brodie from the wagon, supporting him as they headed inside, Fang following and whining when Brodie complained of the pain.

Danae walked beside Mallory. "What is Youtube vid?"

She had no idea how to explain it to the half-elf. "Maybe one day we'll be able to take you home with us and can show you some of the things we talk about." Surely it would be okay to take her to their place when they finally sorted out one to rent. It wasn't like they'd invite anyone over. Well, maybe Ewen and Kern, but they knew about Inadon and the many races that lived here.

Danae smiled. "I'd like that." She stepped back to let Mallory enter first, Ryan and Brodie already inside.

Mallory entered in time to see the apothecary give Ninette three silver pieces, obviously having already paid Emica and Jorgen since they were headed for the door. She moved out of their way, waiting until the apothecary had finished with Ninette before she spoke. "Can you heal shattered knees? And we have herbs if you're interested in buying them."

The apothecary drew a chair out from the table, that was under the far side, for Brodie. "Do you have any canines for sale this time?"

Ryan helped Brodie to the seat. "Only herbs."

"Take them out of the basket and put them on the table and I'll see what you have. Then we'll discuss what treatment options I can offer." The apothecary gestured towards the table.

Mallory placed the basket on the floor beside the table and, along with Ryan's help, put the herbs where she'd been directed. "You can heal bones?"

The apothecary nodded, not speaking as she sorted

through the herbs, making notes on the parchment left on the table, using the nib pen beside it. Eventually she turned to them. "I can offer you eight silver pieces."

"Thanks." Mallory glanced at her brother, surprised he hadn't jumped in with a counter offer. She was taken aback by how drawn he looked. "Are you okay?"

"I've got a shattered knee, what do you think?" Brodie demanded.

The apothecary spoke before Mallory could apologise. "Everything in order. Now we've dealt with the herbs, you can figure out what you would like done."

"I want my knee fixed, of course," Brodie said.

"There are several options," the apothecary said. "I can set your knee for two gold pieces. It will take the normal length of time to heal, but will heal straight and strong."

"How long do broken bones usually take to heal?" Mallory asked.

"Anywhere between six to ten weeks depending on how bad the break," the apothecary said.

"There's no way I'm waiting that long for it to heal," Brodie said. "You'll all get miles ahead of me in XP."

"What other options are there?" Ryan asked.

Callum entered before the apothecary could speak, Smudge still in the makeshift sling. "Can it be fixed?" He handed Mallory six silver pieces.

Mallory slipped the coins into her belt pouch. "We were just about to hear the options." She dreaded to think what the costs would be since setting the bones was two gold pieces.

"I can use weak rapid mend on his knee every twelve hours which will reduce the length of time it will take to heal by five percent each time. You can also buy strong boneset salve, which can be used every twenty-four hours to reduce the length of time it will take to heal by fifteen percent. It costs forty gold pieces for a jar containing four applications. And no matter which option you choose, you need to keep off that leg so as not to disturb the healing process. You can hire crutches from me for five silver pieces a week and a deposit of two gold pieces," the apothecary said.

Mallory tried to calculate the cost, but all she could think of was forty gold pieces for the jar of strong boneset salve. They only had seventy-nine gold, fifty-four silver, and thirty-eight copper pieces. And one of those gold pieces belonged to Smudge. "We're going to be so broke."

"Guess you're not laughing about the arrow in my knee now," Brodie said.

Ryan chuckled. "It's always going to be funny. No matter how much it costs."

"Eighty," Callum said.

Mallory frowned. "What is eighty?"

"The treatment. Eighty gold pieces and we wouldn't be able to leave until after Brodie's final treatment on the morning of the fourteenth. And that doesn't include the hire of the crutches," Callum said.

Mallory stared at Callum. "Eighty. Are you sure?"

Callum nodded.

Mallory stared at Callum a moment longer before she turned to the apothecary. "How do you learn how to become an apothecary?"

"I still have the crafting ability book I used to unlock it if you're interested in purchasing it. Five gold pieces," the apothecary said.

"You should get that, Mal," Brodie said. "You've still got eight CAS points you haven't used."

"That wouldn't give you enough levels to be able to set bones let alone do weak rapid mend. You can set bones at level fifteen and do weak rapid mend at level thirty-five," the apothecary said.

"Can we afford everything for my knee?" Brodie asked.

She could see the worry in her brother's eyes. "Yeah." She didn't mention it wasn't going to leave them with much money.

"Get the crafting ability book," Ryan said. "That's if you're interested in levelling up apothecary." He glanced at Brodie. "Might be a useful skill to have."

"We can't afford it," Mallory said. "Not and pay for Brodie's treatments."

"We'll earn some coins over the next few days," Ryan said. "Get the book and that tincture you and Danni said you need."

Mallory nodded, hoping he was right. She tried to ignore the worries that crowded in. How were they going to be able to afford everything?

"Will everyone wait around long enough for Brodie's knee to heal?" Danae asked.

Mallory shrugged. "All we can do is ask." She turned to the apothecary. "I'll take the book, the salve, two doses of postponed cycle tincture, get you to set Brodie's knee, do weak rapid mend and hire the crutches. There's no way I'm helping him to the bathroom and we can't expect Callum to be stuck helping him. He can find his own way there."

"I'll need a couple of doses of the postponed cycle tincture too," Danae said.

Mallory shook her head. "One of those is for you.

We'll get more before we run out. After we earn some money." She tried not to think about how broke they were about to become. It felt like they were starting over again. She glanced at her companions and the gear they wore and carried. Almost.

"Thank you," Danae said.

The apothecary scribbled on the parchment before she faced them. "That will be fifty-two gold and seven silver pieces."

Mallory handed over the coins, using up all of the silver and most of the copper pieces. Her belt pouch felt a lot lighter and her heart sank as she calculated what they had left. Thirty-two gold and eight copper pieces. And they still needed another thirty-five gold pieces for the rest of Brodie's treatments. She hoped Ryan was right and they did earn money while they were stuck in Wayholt.

The apothecary tended to Brodie, setting his knee before she did weak rapid mend on it. She handed over the rest of the items and showed Mallory how much of the salve to use at a time as she applied the first lot to Brodie's knee before splinting it so he wouldn't be able to bend his knee and ruin the work she'd done.

Chapter Sixteen

Mallory slipped the salve and tincture into her belt pouch, giving the second tincture to Danae. The book she kept hold of, watching as Brodie struggled to use the crutches. Collecting the basket, she slowly followed him, thanking the apothecary.

"I'll be open at six. If you want me to do two weak rapid mends each day, make sure you're here when I open as I close at six in the evening. It'll only take me a couple of minutes to heal him in the evening before I close up for the day," the apothecary said.

"We'll be here." Mallory followed the rest of her companions outside, still trying not to think of how much money they'd spent. She put the basket in the wagon.

The wagoner turned in the seat to watch Callum help Brodie into the wagon. He nodded to Brodie's knee. "Everything sorted?"

"For now." Ryan climbed into the wagon. "We'll be staying here for a few days so the apothecary can completely heal Brodie's knee."

"How many is a few days?" Emica demanded.

"I need to rescue Merry," Roast said.

"We'll be able to leave on the morning of the fourteenth," Ryan said.

"I can't wait that long to go after my father," Emica said. "What if something else goes wrong and we're held up even longer? We should be leaving here on the twelfth at the latest."

"If I could gain twenty-seven levels, I could do weak rapid mend." Mallory glanced at the book she held. "But I can't see myself gaining that amount any time soon."

"Might be time for grinding," Ryan said.

"You need to pick six thousand six hundred and forty-two herbs," Callum said.

"You could gather vegetables and berries too," Danae suggested. "My mother is always in need of them for her cooking. And I don't think you'd be able to sell all the herbs if you gathered that many."

"How did you figure that out so quickly?" Mallory asked.

Callum chuckled. "It isn't exact. I didn't take into account the ten XP you've already gained for this level. Basically, I calculated that you'd need one hundred and thirty-six XP in twenty-seven levels time and we currently only need a hundred and ten XP for this level. Minus them and you get twenty-six which when halved and added to a hundred and ten will give you a hundred and twenty-three which is the average XP needed to gain another twenty-seven levels."

"I've already put up with enough pain today without having to listen to you explain maths to us," Brodie muttered.

The wagoner gestured to the road ahead. "Where am I taking everyone?"

"My place." Danae walked to the front of the wagon and sat on one of the chests. "I'll direct you."

Mallory returned her attention to Callum. "How would I be able to pick that many herbs in only a couple of days?"

"Danni and I could start some quests and you could join us before we finish them off," Callum suggested.

"Ninette and I could guard you while you gather herbs and if anything attacks you could throw a single fireball at each creature then return to gathering herbs," Ryan said.

"I couldn't ask that of Ninette," Mallory said. "It hardly seems fair."

"I don't mind helping," Ninette said. "I wouldn't have been able to become a warrior without your help."

"You're going to be so far ahead of us," Brodie muttered. "Even ahead of Danni."

"How would I manage to earn over fifteen hundred XP a day for two days?" Mallory asked.

"One thousand six hundred and sixty-five if you take away the ten XP you currently have for this level," Callum said.

"When I said we should leave on the twelfth, I meant during the day so we can reach the next village before dark," Emica said. "I bet none of you would want to wait around if it was your father being held captive."

Callum gestured towards Welby and Roast. "They do have people held captive. So does Jorgen. But going in alone won't save them. It'd probably only get you captured again."

"My father is due in Shadhurst on the morning of the seventeenth. He'll need time to reach there," Emica said.

"How long does it take to get from Cutthroat Harbour to Shadhurst?" Mallory asked.

"I'd need to look at the map," Callum said.

The wagoner pulled up in front of Sarisa's house, a

timber cottage with a hitching post out the front. He turned in the seat to face them, interrupting Emica who'd started to speak. "I'll be at the tavern if you need me."

Welby hopped off the seat. "Did you want to check with your mother to see if it's fine to dress and smoke the venison behind your house?"

Danae nodded. "I'll be back shortly to let you know." She glanced at Mallory, Ryan, Callum and Brodie. "We'll get Brodie settled inside first." She looked at Ninette, Emica and Jorgen. "Did you want to come in and see if we can make room for you too?"

They followed Danae to the door. It opened while she was still reaching for the door handle. Sarisa stared at first Danae and then those gathered behind her daughter. She wore a dark blue dress and carried a cloth covered basket by the handle. Her long blond hair was braided into a crown that went around her head making her pointed ears more noticeable. Her pale green eyes again focused on Danae. "You are meant to be in Simria."

Danae laughed. "I sent you a letter yesterday."

Sarisa looked from Danae to those gathered around her then back again. "You haven't changed your mind about the Alchemy Academy, have you?"

"No." Danae glanced at Brodie. "Let me get Brodie

settled and then I'll tell you everything. He was shot in the knee."

"I have to deliver food to the tavern." Sarisa nodded towards the basket. "They're extremely busy as there's a bard in the village that everyone wants to hear play of an evening. He arrived two days ago and people have been trickling into Wayholt ever since. His name is Deneg and he's spent time in the capital. Even played for the Duke."

Ninette tried to move forward, but it was a little impossible with how they were crowded around the door. "I can deliver the basket for you."

Sarisa smiled. "I'd appreciate it." She handed over the basket when a path was cleared for her. "Give it to whoever is behind the bar and tell them I have to decline their offer to work in the kitchen while Deneg is visiting. I will ask around to see if anyone else can help out though. Bring the basket back once they've emptied it and tell them I'll bring another basketful of food in the morning. More than the usual amount."

"I don't know what name to tell them," Ninette said.

"Sarisa."

Nodding, Ninette hurried away, the basket handle over her arm.

Danae led Brodie to the other end of the large room, that had a stone paved floor, to where two chairs faced a fireplace. A kitchen table and four chairs were across the room from them. Fang lay down at Brodie's feet once he was seated. "Did you need any more health tea?" Danae glanced past the cooking fire and brick oven, in the middle of the room, towards the open door. "I can get it if you need some."

Brodie shook his head. "It's not so bad after that salve and the healing." He looked at Sarisa. "Do you need to be a certain level to work in the tavern kitchen? Can the food be made while sitting down? How much are they paying?"

"At least level five, but the higher the better. They're looking for someone to do a four hour shift during the evening. For a fairly unskilled cook, they'll pay three copper pieces each evening worked. I daresay you could do most of the job sitting down," Sarisa said. "They're busy enough they'd accept any help even if it was limited. Although they might only pay two copper pieces instead of three."

"It's not like I can do much else at the moment." Brodie indicated his knee with a wave of his hand. "And I have enough CAS points I could take my cooking level up to seven."

Sarisa inclined her head. "I'll speak to them." She glanced at Danae. "After I find out what is going on."

Danae laughed. "Before I tell you everything I need to introduce you to some people." Danae ran through the names of those Sarisa hadn't met, including mentioning Ninette's name and leading her mother outside to meet the three who waited out there.

Chapter Seventeen

Mallory followed Danae and Sarisa to the door, along with Ryan, Callum, Emica and Jorgen. Smudge was still in the sling. "If people have been coming to hear the bard, will there be room at the tavern?"

Sarisa shrugged. "Probably not, but I couldn't say for certain."

Danae gestured towards the tent rolled up on Bobbi. "We could set that up behind the house for two to sleep in."

"I've often slept on my wagon," the wagoner said. "Or I can lay out the canvas on the ground under the wagon that I brought along to cover the tray when it rains."

"I could cut a couple of saplings and use them to create low arches above the wagon that we can drape the canvas over," Jorgen suggested. "We often do that when a traveller is old enough for their own home, but not yet able to afford a fully set up caravan."

"Like a wagon in the old west," Callum said.

"So everyone can stay here?" Danae turned to her mother.

Sarisa looked at each of them before facing Danae. "They can set up between the tree and the house. Make sure it's not past the tree. The cobbler won't want you too close to his place."

Danae threw her arms around her mother. "Thank you."

Sarisa wrapped her arms around her daughter. "It is nice to see you again."

Ryan took the map out of his belt pouch and gave it to Callum. "You, Mallory and Emica can figure out how long it will take to get to Cutthroat Harbour and how long her father will take to reach Shadhurst."

"His name is Hisoki," Emica said. "Captain Hisoki."

Sarisa stared at Emica, opening her mouth several times before speaking. "You are the daughter of the captain of the Duke's personal guards?"

"This keeps getting better all the time." Ryan slowly shook his head. "You couldn't have mentioned that earlier?"

Emica raised her chin. "I didn't know if I should completely trust you earlier."

"What made you decide you could?" Callum asked.

"It wasn't any one thing." Emica shrugged. "You could have left Brodie behind. Instead you're trying to figure out a way to heal him and take him with you. When you heard there might not be room at the tavern, you offered us somewhere else to stay. You also fed us, partially healed us, mended our clothes and brought us here. You haven't demanded anything in return, even when you were trying to figure out how to level up quickly." She nodded towards the map Callum held. "And you're willing to let me be part of the planning to rescue my father."

"Everyone gets a say," Mallory said.

Ryan took the axe out of a pannier. "We better get set up before it's dark." He glanced skywards. "It can't be too much longer."

Sarisa also looked skywards. "Half an hour at the most."

Jorgen gestured towards the axe. "I have ten levels in woodcutter if you need help."

Ryan handed over the axe. "That's good because I have none and would rather not put any of my spare points in woodcutter."

When everyone headed towards their various tasks,

Mallory followed Danae inside to the table, Callum and Emica behind her. Sitting at the table, she looked at the map Callum spread out after glancing at her brother who was talking softly to Fang and patting her. She was now curled up in his lap. Just like Smudge was curled up in Callum's lap, having clambered out of the sling once Callum had sat down.

Callum gestured towards the map of Ruby Isle. "Which roads would Hisoki take to Shadhurst?"

"You should probably call him Captain Hisoki." Danae turned to Emica. "Did you want us to call you Lady Emica?"

Brodie looked up from talking to Fang. "You're royalty?"

"No, a noble. And Emica is fine. Start using my title and bandits might think I'm worth robbing," Emica said.

"Like we need any more bandits attacking us," Brodie said.

Callum gestured to the map again. "Which road?"

Before Emica could answer, Sarisa spoke. "Help me prepare something for dinner, Danae. You can tell me what has happened while you were gone." She led the way to a bench beside a timber cupboard. Next to them was a closed door leading to the bedroom.

Once Danae had left the table, Callum again gestured towards the map. "Road?"

"He wouldn't take the roads. He'd travel in fox form and avoid most of the towns." Emica ran her finger across the map. "Probably take this path."

Callum used his hunting knife to measure the distance. "Lucky it's straight lines. Otherwise I'd need string or thread to figure out how far he'd have to travel." He compared his knife to the scale in the corner of the map. "At a guess, about fifty to fifty-five kilometres. Using a hunting knife isn't exactly accurate."

Mallory looked towards the other end of the room when she heard Sarisa speak a little louder.

Danae's mother looked at Brodie. "Him?"

Danae grabbed her mother's arm, tugging her so she faced the bench, whispering furiously.

Mallory grinned when she glanced at Brodie, who'd missed the exchange as he'd been busy talking to Fang and patting her. She returned her attention to the map. "How fast can a fox travel?"

"We are a little different to foxes," Emica said. "My father can also travel faster than me. Which isn't surprising since he's over four hundred-years-old."

Mallory frowned. "Four hundred years?"

"Four hundred and thirty-nine if you want to be exact."

"How many tails does he have?" Callum asked.

"Three." Emica nodded towards the map. "With my father's ability of swiftness that doubles his speed for twenty-three minutes, with only an hour cooldown, and being able to run long hours at twelve kilometres an hour, it'd take him a bit over three hours to arrive."

"I thought foxes could travel faster than twelve kilometres an hour," Callum said. "I'm sure I saw a documentary that said they could reach a top speed of fifty kilometres."

"He can, but he also wouldn't wear himself out like that and only keep it for times of danger." Emica again nodded towards the map. "How long will it take to get to Cutthroat Harbour?"

Sarisa turned away from the bench, holding a kitchen knife. "You're all going to Cutthroat Harbour?" She faced Danae. "You are going too? Why didn't you tell me?"

"I was getting to it," Danae said.

"You're not going," Sarisa stated.

"Haven't you been listening to anything I've said?" Danae asked. "I have faced bandits, a pirate, hellions, smugglers, chameleon vipers and even helped destroy two goblin settlements. I have a revive and there are only four more levels before I gain a second revive. It isn't like I'll be alone. There's a large group of us going."

"Chameleon vipers? Did you deliberately seek them out or stumble across them?" Sarisa demanded.

"Uhm… it was a quest." Danae looked down at the potato and paring knife she held, the potato half peeled.

Sarisa placed the knife on the bench, holding onto the edge of the timber. "I should never have let your father take you from here. You seem to think you can wander all across the island and face creatures far too high a level for you."

Brodie placed Fang on the ground, using his crutches to stand up so he could face Sarisa. "We'd never let anything happen to Danni."

Sarisa looked him up and down. "I don't think you're in any shape to protect anyone."

Callum rose to his feet. "But I am."

Mallory also stood up. "So am I."

Sarisa looked at each of them, still holding onto the edge of the bench. "One revive isn't much when facing an entire village of the dark forces."

"I'll have another one in four levels," Danae repeated.

"That doesn't mean you'll have those levels before you reach Cutthroat Harbour," Sarisa said. "If you go by way of Velkden it's less than eight hours away. Not far enough that you'll level up."

"What if we power level Danni too?" Callum asked.

Sarisa frowned. "Power level? Too?"

Callum nodded. "We're going to help Mallory gain twenty-seven CAS points in two days so she can do weak rapid mend to finish healing Brodie's knee."

"You think you can manage that in two days?" Sarisa asked.

Callum nodded again. "I've been thinking about it. All she has to do is pick the herbs and vegetables. She doesn't have to put them in anything or find them herself. A couple of us can locate the herbs and vegetables and one of us can put them in the panniers if Mallory leaves them on the ground. She should be able to get it done in less than two days. But just to be sure, after dinner we should take the lanterns and time you." He glanced at Mallory as he spoke the last handful of words.

"You are willing to do this for Danae," Sarisa said.

Everyone except Emica nodded. Brodie was the only one who spoke. "Of course we can. Once Mal has levelled up. She'll also have a healing spell she can use to help keep us alive."

Chapter Eighteen

Mallory guessed that now was not the time to argue about being support. She could remind her brother later. "We're not planning to march into Cutthroat Harbour and tell them we've arrived."

"I have sneak unlocked," Brodie said.

Again Sarisa glanced at his knee.

"And Mallory will fix my shattered knee before we arrive," Brodie added.

Sarisa turned to Danae, taking the potato and paring knife from her and setting them on the bench. "I had hoped you'd grow out of your interest in adventures and ending up in situations beyond your level." She took hold of Danae's hands. "Promise me you won't enter a fight if you have no revives left."

"I won't face any of the people of Cutthroat Harbour if I run out of revives," Danae said.

"Not exactly the promise I was hoping for," Sarisa said dryly.

Danae grinned. "At least you can stop worrying for now."

Sarisa crushed Danae to her. Stepping back, she slowly shook her head. "I never stop worrying. Not with how you rush into danger."

"I don't rush," Danae protested.

"Do you run away from it?" Sarisa asked.

Danae grinned, not answering.

Sarisa faced the rest of the room, about to speak when there was a knock on the door. Crossing the room, she opened it to let Ninette, Ryan and Jorgen inside. She took the basket Ninette gave her. "Thank you."

Ninette smiled. "Sorry I took so long. I checked the noticeboard to see what quests are available. Someone told me the mercenaries take all the good ones. From what I could see on the board it looks that way."

Sarisa set the basket on the floor by the door. She faced the rest of the room again. "Dinner will be ready in about an hour and a half. Plenty of time for you to test your theory." She turned to Danae. "You can take the lantern from the bedroom and the one from the bathroom. If you need a third one, you could probably take the one from the outhouse." She gestured to the two lit lanterns hanging from the ceiling. "I could also manage with a single lantern."

Danae threw her arms around her mother. "Thank you. We have two of our own. The ones from the bathroom and bedroom will be enough."

Ryan looked around the room. "What is going on?"

Callum folded up the map and strode towards the door. "We'll explain on the way."

Brodie looked towards the door. "What about me?'

Sarisa gestured towards the table. "You can help prepare dinner. Add those points in cooking first."

"Cool." Brodie grinned. "Level four lets me use an oven and level six lets me use enchanted tools and utensils. Level five is the best. 'You now have the ability to make poor quality food up to your level in cooking.' That's got to mean a major improvement in my cooking."

"Sit at the table and we'll see." Sarisa brought a bowl of unpeeled vegetables and a paring knife over to Brodie along with a bowl for the scraps.

Seeing her brother was happily settling in at the table and using the paring knife to peel the vegetables, Mallory followed everyone else outside, Danae having collected the lantern from the bedroom and lit it. At the corner of the house, she stopped and looked over the camp that had formed in the backyard. The wagon now had a piece of canvas stretched over arches of roughly trimmed saplings that were lashed to the wagon with rope. The tent was set up across from it, a campfire burning between them. The deer was hanging in the tree and Welby was skinning it. Off to the left of the tree were two buildings. An outhouse and a small, timber hut. Mallory smiled. The wagon made her think of old movies about the Wild West.

Danae glanced over her shoulder, having reached the hut. "You can have a bath this evening if you want, Mallory."

Mallory hurried forward, very little light left in the day. "You have a real bathroom?"

Danae opened the door. "Not like what you'd find in a city or large town, but it's more than some people have in Wayholt, or even Simria."

Mallory followed her into the building, looking over the area. There was a fireplace on the left wall with a pot hanging over kindling that had been laid for a fire. To the side of it was a timber bench, a jug and washbasin sitting on it and some firewood stacked beside it. In the other corner were two timber barrels and a wooden bucket on the floor in front of them. The floor was paved with stone and gently sloped towards the middle where there was a hole in the floor, a large tin tub beside it. There were another four barrels lined up along the wall to her right.

Danae collected the lantern. She nodded towards the closest barrels. "It looks like the water carrier has been recently because they're full."

"Water carrier?"

Danae nodded. "He carts barrels of water on his wagon that he fills at the well and people pay him two copper pieces for each barrel he fills."

"How do you get hot water?" Mallory eyed the tub. There were no taps and no drain hole.

"You heat it in the pot hanging over the fire. After you finish, you can wash your clothes in the tub and there's a wooden rack that folds up and is stored behind the barrels that you can hang your wet clothes over. We leave our clothes by the fire to dry and they're usually ready by morning. Once you finish with the water, you tip it out of the tub and into the drain in the floor. A pipe takes it out to the tree."

Mallory looked from the tub, to the fire and then to the barrels. A smile slowly formed. "I can't wait to have a bath." It would be more work than it usually took to have one, but how often did the chance to have a bath by a fireplace come along?

Danae laughed. "I thought you might feel that

way." She headed outside and towards the wagon where the panniers were being emptied into two of the chests the wagoner had brought with him. The other contained some of his things.

Mallory followed, closing the door behind her, still thinking of baths and fireplaces, half paying attention to Callum's explanation to Ryan, Ninette and Jorgen. She helped Danae pour the health oil into the empty flask and fill the lantern with normal oil, thinking about all the things she'd like to have in a base when they finally set one up. Instead of barrels, maybe they could have water tanks and gravity feed water into a bathroom so they could have showers as well as baths. They'd have to make sure the area had regular rain to fill the water tanks. And they'd probably need more than a single tree for the water they used. Maybe they could look at how septic systems worked when they were back home and figure out if they could do something similar. Or find some other system to deal with their used water. Guardians from their world should have come up with other methods. Maybe they'd learn more in a large town. An image of a well set up base slowly formed in her mind. Surely they'd soon get past this setback and start to gain money again.

Ryan placed the barnacle encrusted sword, given to

them by the merfolk, in front of the chests as it was too long to fit in them. "A pity Brodie's treatments will cost so much."

"We could see the blacksmith and ask how much it would cost to clean it up," Callum said. "It might not be as expensive as you think."

"We can visit him before we collect herbs." Danae handed one of the lanterns to Ninette who'd agreed to pick up what Mallory gathered. "He tends to work late."

"I don't suppose he'd sell stilettos for four silver pieces," Jorgen said.

"That's probably as likely as him selling swords for the same amount," Emica said. "We should have collected more herbs. We can't do anything without a weapon." She looked pointedly at Jorgen. "Or at least I can't if you plan to stick around me."

"Shapeshift into a fox," Jorgen said. "It isn't like you have no weapon when you can shapeshift."

"Same goes for you," Emica said.

Chapter Nineteen

Mallory interrupted before Emica and Jorgen could argue further. "We should get started. Sarisa only gave us an hour and a half before we need to return for dinner."

Ryan held out a short sword to Emica. "We don't have a scabbard, but you can borrow this spare sword we have. Maybe the blacksmith will have a secondhand scabbard you can buy." He turned to Jorgen. "I'm afraid we don't have any spare weapons suited to your class."

Emica stared at Ryan for a moment. "You'll lend me a weapon."

"Yes."

"How will I ever be able to repay you for that?" Emica asked. "And what if one of yours breaks and you need it back?"

Ryan shrugged. "We'll worry about that if it happens."

"We might get lucky and find another sword," Callum said.

Emica took the sword, looking it over. "Thank you. It feels better to have a weapon I can use."

Ryan picked up one of the lanterns and gathered the lead rope for Bobbi. "We'll see what the blacksmith has to sell."

Leaving the two horses behind, they headed through the village and past the tavern to the blacksmith shop where they left Bobbi at the hitching post outside. The blacksmith was working on making a sword, nodding to them in greeting as he continued with his task, his hammer ringing out against the metal of the sword. "Can I help you?"

"What would it cost to clean up a sword? It's encrusted with barnacles," Ryan said.

"About four gold pieces. Possibly more," the blacksmith said. "It depends on how much time it takes to clean and the type of sword it is. Such as short sword, longsword or greatsword."

"Thanks. We'll have to think about it." Ryan started to turn away. He stopped when Jorgen spoke.

"What is the cost of a stiletto? The cheapest you have available."

"And the cost of a scabbard." Emica sighed heavily. "The cheapest one you have."

"An iron stiletto is one gold piece and I have a secondhand scabbard I can also offer you for a gold piece." The blacksmith returned the sword to the forge, heating the metal.

"Thank you for your time." Jorgen started for the exit.

"Wait a minute," Ryan said. "We'll take you up on your earlier offer."

Jorgen faced him. "Of going after the eggs?"

Ryan nodded. "Two of you with stealth should mean we'll be able to take more eggs without being noticed."

"What about me?" Emica asked. "I can't afford that much money for a scabbard. Am I to carry the sword around all the time? If there was a bank around here I would be able to afford it."

Ryan stared at her for a moment before turning to Mallory.

She wanted to protest, but she remembered how awkward it had been when she'd had no sheath for her dagger. Hopefully they earned enough money to afford what they spent here. "We'll lend you the money for the scabbard."

Emica inclined her head. "I will repay you."

Mallory didn't doubt it. Not with the serious look Emica had. "I know." She took out two gold pieces, trying not to think about their dwindling supply. It was the right thing to do. They couldn't leave them to enter Cutthroat Harbour unarmed. Handing over the coins, she waited for the blacksmith to finish hammering the sword and return it to the forge.

He fetched a sheathed stiletto and scabbard, returning to his task the moment Jorgen had taken the weapon and Emica the scabbard. "You can have the stiletto sheath for free. It's always nice to have customers return. It won't last long, but it should do the job until you can afford something better."

"Thank you." Callum's gaze roamed over the blacksmith. "I for one don't mind returning."

Laughing, Ryan slung an arm around his brother's shoulders. "Time to go." He said goodbye to the blacksmith before heading outside, letting go of his brother to gather Bobbi's lead rope.

Callum waited until they were heading south east out of the village before he spoke. "We need to work on earning more money. We should go north again. That was good. We earned plenty and got some gear and all those books."

Ryan paused to light a lantern. "We just need to

go after the eggs when we return. That will fix our financial problems."

Callum lit the lantern he carried. "As long as we don't run into any other problems."

Danae turned to Emica. "Did you want to pair up with me to search for herbs and vegetables? None of us should wander off alone."

Emica glanced at Jorgen. "At least then my lightning ability might have a chance to work if I need to use it."

Callum turned to Jorgen. "Looks like you're stuck with me." He grinned. "Sounds okay to me."

Ryan chuckled. "Keep an eye out for trouble. You're not meant to be admiring the view."

"And for herbs," Mallory added.

Callum continued to grin, striding away without comment.

"I've spotted some," Danae called out.

Ryan handed Bobbi's lead rope to Ninette then took out the pocket watch. "I'll time you so we can see how you go."

Mallory hurried over to Danae and Emica, picking the two herbs and letting them fall on the ground before hurrying to Callum and Jorgen who'd called out. She went from one group to the next, going at a fast walk, occasionally breaking into a jog. Each time she picked the herbs or vegetables, she glanced at Ryan, wondering if he was going to share any of the details with her. When he continued to remain silent, she finally asked, "What rate do I pick them at?"

"It's only been five minutes. Not long enough to come to any conclusion."

"Is that all?" Mallory straightened, rubbing her lower back. "This is going to become very tedious very quickly." She hurried over to Callum and Jorgen, leaving Ninette to gather the carrots she'd pulled.

By the time twenty minutes were up, Mallory wanted to groan at the results. "Are you sure you counted that correctly?"

"Yep. It averages out at twenty-two resources a minute. Sometimes you get more, sometimes less." Ryan faced Danae as they reached her and Emica. "We need to be back in forty minutes. Can you start circling around towards Wayholt?"

Danae nodded, turning to Mallory with a smile. "You've managed to go up two levels. You have ten CAS points now."

Mallory picked the two herbs, letting them drop onto the ground. She straightened, pressing a hand against her lower back. "No wonder we don't pick herbs for long. This has got to be the worst way to power level." She dreaded to think how she'd feel after gaining another twenty-five levels. "Surely there's a better way than this."

"Not that I can think of." Danae hurried away, Emica at her side.

Mallory strode towards Callum and Jorgen, her pace a little slower than it had been before. "I keep reminding myself I can have a bath once I'm done."

"What bath?" Callum stepped back from the onions at his feet.

"There's a large tin tub in the small hut behind Sarisa's house." Mallory tried not to groan as she bent to pick the onions. "Although after another forty minutes of this I might just collapse on the bedroll."

Ryan chuckled. "Need someone to keep watch so you don't fall asleep in the tub and drown?"

She glanced at him with a slight smile, her tone dry. "Yeah, right."

Ryan grinned unrepentantly, giving her a half shrug.

Chapter Twenty

After another few minutes, Mallory's steps slowed even further. "Maybe Danni should pick a few resources so I can take a bit of a break. There's no point in wearing myself out and slowing down further."

"Another fifty-nine XP and you'll go up a level," Ryan said.

"It'll have to wait. I really need a break." Mallory rubbed at her lower back. "No wonder I was never interested in gardening." She stopped in front of Danae and Emica, groaning as she bent to pick the three herbs. Straightening, she looked at Danae. "You can have a turn for five minutes or so to give me a break. I'm starting to slow down."

"That will make my mother happy." Danae handed the lantern over to Emica then hurried to where Callum and Jorgen stood, Ryan at her side.

Emica looked from Danae to Mallory. "You're helping me now?"

Mallory glanced around the area, trying to spot some resources. "Yeah."

"This way." Emica led the way to a cluster of herbs. "We look for the next lot while we're waiting." She glanced at Danae who strode towards them. "You won't get the levels you need if you take too many breaks."

When Danae reached them, Mallory walked towards a sweet potato vine she spotted. "I won't get the levels I need if I push myself to the point of collapse."

"Will we still leave on the twelfth if you don't get your levels?" Emica asked.

Mallory examined the kitsune, clearly seeing the worry in her eyes. "We'll help you find your father."

Emica didn't answer immediately. "I don't want to lose him too." Her words were soft.

Before Mallory could say anything, Danae and Ryan reached them and they moved away to look for the next lot of resources. After she had a five minute break, Mallory returned to gathering resources. She noticed that Danae had a slightly better gather rate than she did and was now at seventy-eight experience points.

Mallory only lasted another ten minutes, not managing to gather as many as they drew nearer to the village. But at least she was able to gain a level and was now halfway to her next character level. A smile formed as she thought of how pleased her brother would be at her being able to do the healing spell when she reached the next character level and chose mage to put her point into. At least he would be until he began to focus on how far ahead she was. She stopped in front of Danae. "Your turn." She gestured towards the potato plant at her feet.

Before Danae could move, Callum called out. "Bear. Behind you."

Mallory spun, automatically drawing her wand. She managed to throw a fireball at it, three arrows striking it a moment before Jorgen attacked with his stiletto. He darted in and out, staying out of reach of the bear. Mallory stared at him for a moment before remembering she was meant to be attacking the bear, not marvelling over Jorgen's fighting technique. Brodie was the one who needed to see Jorgen in action. The way he darted in and out, always staying out of reach, was what her brother needed to learn. Ninette joined him attacking the bear. Before Mallory could throw a second fireball at the creature, lightning struck and it collapsed on the ground. Ryan hurried forward to skin the bear.

Mallory turned to Emica. "You don't need a wand to use lightning?"

Emica shook her head. "It's an ability, not a spell."

While Ryan skinned the bear, Danae gathered resources nearby. They continued towards the village once he was finished, having only managed to gain a pelt and five kilograms of meat. He also got two bones for Fang.

They gathered resources until Danae had gained another level and had one experience point out of the hundred and fifteen she needed for her next level. They strolled towards Sarisa's house, Mallory dreading the thought of continuing to level by gathering herbs and vegetables the next day.

Arriving back with a few minutes to spare, they sorted some of the vegetables out and put the herbs in cloth bags and sacks in the hope they'd be able to sell them in the morning. Some of the vegetables went in the chests with the rest of their gear while the majority of it was kept aside for Sarisa since she was letting them stay with her. They kept six carrots, fourteen potatoes, four onions, twelve sweet potatoes, two pumpkins and ten mushrooms.

Before they went inside, Mallory checked Brodie's

stats, noticing he'd gained one experience point. Once his knee was healed, he was going to be unbearable until he'd caught up with them. The scent of food cooking greeted Mallory as she stepped inside. She paused by the door, breathing in deeply, her mouth watering.

"About time you got back," Brodie muttered. "I'm starving."

Mallory put the vegetables she carried on the bench like Danae did, the rest of her companions doing the same. "When aren't you?"

Brodie shrugged. "I thought you'd have gained more levels by now."

"We ran into a bear." Mallory quickly spoke again when she noticed Sarisa's expression. "And Danni levelled up too. She only has another three CAS points until her next character level."

Sarisa served up the savoury pies she'd made with Brodie's help. "I'm glad you've started working on levelling up. Having a second revive won't completely stop me from worrying, but it will help."

Mallory watched Sarisa for a bit, wondering what her mum would have said. She was pretty certain she wouldn't have been so calm.

Since there wasn't enough room at the table, they took the food outside to eat at the campfire, sharing the pies amongst them, including the companion animals and Not For Bacon. Once the meal was over, Emica and Jorgen retired for the night, both exhausted. Ninette sat by the fire sharpening her sword with the whetstone she'd borrowed from Ryan. After learning Sarisa had spoken to the cook at the tavern while they'd been levelling up, and Brodie could work from eight till midnight, they offered to walk Brodie to the tavern since it was almost eight. Ryan carried a lantern and Smudge was once again in Callum's makeshift sling while Fang walked at Brodie's side.

They were nearly at the tavern when Brodie spoke. "Do you think you'll be able to level up enough, Mal?"

She would need to gain around fifteen hundred experience points a day for the next two days. A little under that, but she didn't want to spend the time figuring out the exact amount. She hadn't even managed to gain four hundred experience points tonight and dreaded to think about the aches she'd have after gathering herbs each day.

"Mal?"

A glance at her brother had her forcing a smile to her lips when she saw how worried he was. "Of course I will." Somehow she'd make certain of it.

"Cool. That way we can get going as soon as you level up. You can heal me on the way to Cutthroat Harbour."

Mallory nodded, not bothering to point out how short a trip it was as they entered the tavern when Ryan held open the door. She stopped not far inside the door, staring at the crowd. She'd never seen so many people in Wayholt before. The tavern was packed and not a single table was empty. There wasn't even standing room at the bar. The place was filled with a variety of races, some she wasn't sure what they were.

Ryan slipped his arm around Mallory's waist, nodding towards Brodie. "We'll leave you to it and be back around midnight to collect you."

Brodie glanced at Fang who remained at his side. "Do you think they'll let me keep her with me?" He patted the belt pouch. "And my pig."

Danae smiled. "They probably wouldn't notice the pig and as long as Fang doesn't chase the cat that belongs to the cook they won't mind her staying. But I doubt she'd do that. Not if you told her to stay away from the cat."

Brodie looked down at Fang. "You hear that, girl?"

Fang wagged her tail, looking up at him.

Brodie glanced around the group. "I'll see you

later." He headed towards the bar, swinging through the crowd on his crutches.

Chapter Twenty-One

Mallory watched her brother weave his way through the crowd, a little unsteady at times. "What are we going to do?"

"It's probably pointless gathering herbs without the extra help," Ryan said.

"I agree," Mallory hurriedly said. She would have agreed to any excuse that gave her a break from gathering herbs and vegetables. The morning would be soon enough to return to that task.

"We could pay a visit to the frog mage that lives north east of Wayholt," Danae suggested. "See if he's the same one that attacked us."

"How far is he out of the village?" Ryan asked.

"About ten minutes. He's on the road I take when I travel to Simria," Danae said.

Callum opened the door, holding it as everyone stepped outside. "I wouldn't mind paying him a visit."

Before he could close the door, music started. He faced the crowded interior. "That sounds pretty good."

Ryan chuckled. "Better than the noise we made."

Callum let the door close, patting Smudge who remained in the makeshift sling. "Which direction?"

"Should we collect the horses?" Mallory asked.

Danae shook her head. "It'd take us longer to get them saddled than it'll take us to walk."

The road was quiet, more so after the noise of the tavern. Mallory searched the trees as they headed out past the woodcutter's house. Nothing seemed to move. Or at least nothing that she could see. From the occasional soft noises, she had to guess something was out there. If they were lucky, it'd only be a few tiny rodents. A larger rustle in nearby shrubs had her slowing her pace. "Maybe we should do this during the day."

"We've got this," Ryan said. "Tomorrow we need to focus on levelling you up." He glanced at Danae. "Levelling up both of you."

She wasn't so sure about either of his statements, but she kept that thought to herself. "Can we break tomorrow's XP gaining up into three or four sessions? I don't think I can do it all at once. I feel like an old lady after all that bending and running around."

"Have some health tea when we return to my mother's home," Danae said.

"Have some…" Mallory's voice trailed off. "Really? That will help?"

Danae nodded. Before she had the chance to reply, several frogs jumped out of the shadows to land on the road in front of them.

"Those frogs look extremely familiar." Callum took out an arrow.

Ryan held up a hand, the lantern in the other. "Wait up. They haven't attacked yet. We'll see what they do if we keep walking."

Danae pointed to a location past the frogs. "His house is several metres from the road in that direction."

"Then I guess we go around them." Ryan tried to step past the frogs. They shifted to block his way.

Mallory readied her wand. "We might need to attack." She wasn't about to let them take out another one of her companions.

Ryan started forward again, drawing his sword. He'd barely taken a couple of steps when the frog mage hurried towards them, a ball of white light trailing behind him a fraction above head height.

"You leave them alone. Bad enough you killed one. You don't need to take out another."

Callum kept his bow trained on the frog mage. "You were the one who attacked us."

The frog mage stepped in front of the frogs, chasing them back when they tried to go around him. "I had no choice."

Ryan lowered his sword. "There's always a choice."

Callum returned his arrow to his quiver, keeping the bow in his hand. "Doesn't mean it'll be an easy option."

"You don't understand," the frog mage said. "They have Cila."

Mallory kept glancing around the area, glad of the extra light the mage provided. If he was stalling until help arrived, she'd be ready. "Who is Cila?"

The frog mage vaguely gestured behind him to where more frogs had joined the other ones. "She's mother of all these young ones. Every one of them."

Mallory stared at him for a moment. "Someone took your frog?"

Ryan chuckled. "Now there's a comment you don't hear every day."

"A bit like the arrow comment," Callum said.

Ryan chuckled. "Pretty much."

The frog mage glared at him. "It is not at all

amusing. They threatened to kill her. It's not often dart frogs live to be over fifty years. She's been with me since I was a child and I found her injured and near death, her children slaughtered."

"Why would someone steal a frog? Is there something special about dart frogs?" Callum asked.

"They want me to make them an invisibility potion. I have a recipe for an extended one," the frog mage said.

Ryan chuckled. "Brodie's going to be unimpressed when we meet up with him tonight."

Smiling, Mallory opened her journal since the icon had appeared in the corner of her vision. *Kidnapped Frog: The dart frog Cila has been captured and is in need of being rescued.* She didn't doubt her brother would complain. Especially with the number of quests they now had. He probably wouldn't believe any of them if they tried to tell him nine wasn't that bad.

"How dare you laugh at Cila's misfortune." The frog mage aimed his wand at them.

Ryan held up a hand. "Wait a minute. We weren't laughing at you or your frogs. We were laughing at a companion of ours who isn't with us."

"Where are they then?" The frog mage kept his wand ready.

Mallory eyed the frogs that had come close to him.

She didn't want to be attacked by them again. "He's working at the tavern tonight. Cooking."

The frog mage slowly lowered his wand. "It doesn't matter anyway. There's no way I can come up with the ingredients and make the potion before two o'clock tomorrow afternoon." His shoulders slumped. "I went to the mercenaries, but I couldn't afford to pay them. I offered every potion I have and the couple of spells I have no need of and still it wasn't enough."

Danae turned to Mallory. "Do we need to vote on it?"

Ryan sheathed his sword and picked the lantern up off the ground. "No. We'll find his Cila."

The frog mage stared at them, mouth open. "You will? I can't afford to pay any more than I had to offer the mercenaries. A variety of potions and two spells. And not high level spells at that."

Mallory smiled when she checked the quest update. *Kidnapped Frog: You have been offered a variety of potions and two spells for the safe return of Cila.* "Low level spells. Perfect." Especially since she was going to add a character point in mage very soon.

Again the mage stared at them for a moment before he spoke. "You are going to rescue my Cila?"

Smudge lifted his head up above the edge of the sling. He chattered excitedly at the frog mage.

Ryan chuckled. "Sounds like it's unanimous."

Smiling, Callum patted Smudge's head. "We'll need some details. Do you know where they're holding her?"

The frog mage shook his head, half turning away and gesturing in the direction behind him. "The night is getting a bit cool. My place isn't far from here and I can tell you everything I know."

Chapter Twenty-Two

Mallory glanced around the group, agreeing when everyone nodded. They followed the frog mage back to his cottage. There was a pond at the front door with barrels of water lined up along the side of the building, frogs peeking over the rims. Part of a large pond could be seen behind the house with several trees growing at the edge of it and a small jetty jutting out towards the middle. The cottage itself was made of timber, a window on either side of the door with the flickering light of the fireplace visible through them.

When the frog mage opened the front door, he had to shoo the frogs away that would have entered. He remained near the doorway, gesturing for them to enter. "Hurry. Before any of them try to sneak in. They make a mess of the potions if I let them in."

They trooped inside, sitting at the small timber

table, the mage clearing off a bench seat and bringing it over so they could all sit down. "I can't tell you much. I don't know what you'd find useful."

Callum absently patted Smudge. "Start at the beginning. Who took her."

The frog mage shrugged. "I came home from Wayholt several days ago to find her missing and all her children agitated. Someone had left a note telling me they'd be in touch with instructions of what I needed to do if I ever wanted to see her again."

"Did you look for her?" Danae asked.

He nodded. "They hid their tracks well. Even her children couldn't find her. I don't know how they managed to take her." He paused a moment. "When I realised there was no way I could find Cila. I went to the mercenaries. You all know how well that went."

"Is there some kind of law you could approach?" Callum asked.

"Wayholt isn't big enough to afford their own law," Danae said.

The frog mage glanced at Danae before he continued. "Exactly. It'd take too long to send for the soldiers. Even if they had the time to come. The Duke doesn't have a very large army."

His words made Mallory think of Hisoki. But she supposed the soldiers wouldn't necessarily be able to help. They could just as easily end up in trouble on their way here.

"The next day I found a note pinned to my front door. It demanded the potion in exchange for Cila. I can't afford the ingredients and I certainly don't keep any of them on hand. Who can afford the few hundred gold pieces the ingredients cost?"

"A few hundred gold pieces for ingredients?" Mallory was certain she couldn't have heard him correctly.

The frog mage slowly nodded. "You can see why I don't have the money to make one. And who is to say they'll return Cila if I did make it."

"I'd love a recipe for such a potion," Danae said softly.

"How are you meant to get the potion to them?" Ryan asked.

The frog mage glanced at Danae before returning his attention to Ryan. "I'm to meet them tomorrow afternoon. They told me to come alone. After they test the potion to see if it works, they'll return her."

"How do they test if a potion works?" Callum asked.

Mallory had been about to ask the same. The only thing she could think of, was using it.

"They said they'd return her two days after the job

is complete, but they never said when that would be." The frog mage gestured in the direction of the pond behind his cottage. "What am I meant to tell her children if I can't bring her home?"

Mallory was relieved Brodie wasn't with them. She doubted he'd be sympathetic about a kidnapped frog. Although she could see why her brother wouldn't be considering they had people that needed rescuing.

Ryan leaned his arms on the table in front of him. "Have you got a potion you can give them that looks like the one they want?"

"It'd be even better if it was a type of invisibility potion," Danae said.

The frog mage looked at each of them before he got to his feet and crossed the room to a wooden workbench that was covered with various apparatuses and two mortar and pestles. Beneath the bench were shallow cane baskets that he rummaged around in, muttering under his breath. Straightening, he faced them. "I can make an invisibility potion I and add food colouring to make it the correct colour. But that might render it useless." He returned to the table. "How will that help find Cila?"

Mallory met Ryan's gaze, pretty certain she knew what his plan was. "We'll follow the kidnappers back to their hideout. They won't have the chance to use the potion."

Ryan nodded. "Once we know where Cila is, we'll take them out and rescue her."

"You've done something like this before?"

Mallory wished she could tell him otherwise. "No, but I'm sure we can find her."

"Do you have another plan? One we could help you with?" Callum asked.

The frog mage rested his elbows on the table and lowered his head into his hands. "I have no choice." He raised his head to look at them. "Why do you think I demanded your coins?" He slowly shook his head. "You don't look that well outfitted. I was sure we could take you on and win. I brought plenty of Cila's children with me. Our overwhelming numbers should have meant we'd win."

Ryan checked the pocket watch before rising to his feet. "We'll be back at midday tomorrow. Get that potion sorted and you can show us where you need to meet the kidnappers." He met the frog mage's gaze. "We will rescue Cila."

The frog mage stared at him for a moment. "I really think you believe that."

Ryan grinned. "I do." He led the way to the door,

saying goodbye to the frog mage before they stepped outside.

Mallory tried to give the frog mage a reassuring smile before she left. With the worry she could see in his eyes, it obviously hadn't helped. "Why are we leaving all of a sudden?"

"If we're going to do this quest tomorrow, you and Danni need to do some levelling up tonight." Ryan led the way back towards Wayholt.

Mallory tried not to groan. She was unsuccessful. "Can we go back and get health tea first?"

Ryan glanced at the lantern he held. "We need to get more lanterns if we're to do this properly."

Callum walked beside Mallory. "Just remember the downside of drinking too much health tea."

Thinking of the outhouse, made Mallory think of the camp out the back of the cottage. "Where are we sleeping tonight? Emica and Ninette can share the tent while the wagoner, Welby, Roast and Jorgen can sleep on or under the wagon. But what about the rest of us. There isn't enough room. And where will we all sleep when we're travelling to Cutthroat Harbour? We just don't have enough gear."

"We'll gain more," Callum assured her.

Mallory didn't bother pointing out how much they were spending on Brodie's injury. "What do we do in the meantime? Are we sleeping by the fire or trying to find space in the wagon?"

"I can sleep in the bed I normally use when staying with my mother," Danae said. "The rest of you can either lay the blankets out in front of the fire inside or sleep out at the campfire."

"Inside sounds better," Ryan said.

They fell silent as they approached Sarisa's house. She was standing at the bench, preparing food when they entered. "What took you so long?"

"Ahhh…" Danae's gaze darted towards the exit. "We went for a walk?"

"You no longer think to let me know where you're going so I don't have to worry?" Sarisa asked.

Danae winced. "Sorry. I guess I've grown accustomed to not needing to do that."

"You haven't been gone that long," Sarisa said.

Mallory spoke before Danae had the chance to comment. "We're going to level up a bit while we wait for Brodie to finish at the tavern. It'll give us more of a head start on tomorrow's plans."

Sarisa looked from Mallory to Danae. "You plan to level up as well?"

Danae nodded.

"I've been trying to convince myself that levelling

up will keep you safe. I dare say it'll allow you to think you can face greater challenges," Sarisa said.

Smiling, Danae went forward and hugged her mother. "You might be right." She stepped away. "We'll be back a little after midnight. But don't worry if we're late. It won't mean we're in trouble or at least not in any more trouble than we can handle."

Sarisa sighed heavily. "I'm guessing the reason you returned wasn't to let me know what you plan to do."

Again Danae glanced towards the exit. "Not exactly."

"We came to get the lanterns," Callum said.

Sarisa inclined her head. She turned back to her daughter. "I sent Ninette out earlier to swap those vegetables you gave me for horse feed. She was able to get enough to last a couple of days. They should be fine staying behind the cottage for a few days. If you're going to be here longer, you might want to agist them elsewhere."

"I was going to buy feed tomorrow." Danae smiled. "That's a better option. Thank you."

Sarisa stared at Danae for a moment. "Be careful out there."

"I will." Danae grabbed the lantern she'd returned to the bedroom and they headed outside.

Chapter Twenty-Three

Only Ninette and Welby were awake and they sat by the fire, chatting. Mallory smiled as she listened to all the questions Ninette asked about the places Welby had visited. She waited until he finished describing one of the towns at the northern end of Ruby Isle before she spoke. "We're collecting herbs again."

Ninette scrambled to her feet, returning the whetstone to Ryan. "Do you need help?"

Ryan put the whetstone away. "That'd be good."

Mallory had a drink of health tea while Danae and Callum topped up the four lanterns, emptying one of the flasks. Callum lit one of the lanterns. "We're going to need to buy more oil tomorrow."

Mallory wanted to protest his comment. There always seemed to be something they needed to buy.

"Good thing we've got plenty of herbs to sell."

Ryan led the way out of the village, heading off in a different direction this time.

Gathering herbs and vegetables was a slower process with two less people. Mallory was able to gather for half an hour before she swapped with Danae. They continued to swap. Each time it was Mallory's turn, the length of time she gathered for slowly reduced. Excitement rose in her as she continued to level up, Danae also gaining levels. By the time they finished gathering herbs and vegetables and ended up back at the tavern, it was a quarter to twelve and Danae was now at character level two with one experience point of the hundred and eighteen needed for her next CAS point. Mallory had also reached character level two and had two experience points of the next hundred and eighteen she needed for a CAS point. She also had sixteen CAS points saved up and ready to use once she read Understanding The Crafting Ability Apothecary.

They tied Bobbi to a hitching post out the front, the panniers filled with herbs and vegetables. Putting out the lanterns, they left them hanging from the sides of the panniers.

Callum glanced over his shoulder as they walked inside. "I don't even know if we'll be able to sell everything tomorrow. That's a lot of herbs and veggies."

Mallory scanned the tables. Most of them were now empty. Or at least empty of patrons. Mugs, plates and spills from drinks littered most of the tables. Her gaze was drawn to a bard sitting on a tall stool, strumming what looked like a medieval guitar, the music soothing. He had shoulder length black hair swept back from his pale face. He smiled at her and his long, upper canine teeth became visible. When she continued to meet his gaze, he gave her a nod before glancing around the tavern at the scattering of patrons that had remained to listen to him play.

Ryan led the way to a table. "This one looks like it's been wiped down."

Mallory dropped onto a chair. "I don't know whether or not to have another health tea. I don't want to be up and down half the night using the outhouse." She thought longingly of the bath she'd planned to have. There probably wasn't going to be time to soak in the tin tub now. They had to be up before six in the morning. That wouldn't leave much time for sleeping.

"We should sort out our new character levels," Danae said. "I'm going to put my class point in archer and put two attribute points in constitution, two in dexterity and one in luck. Hopefully those extra points in constitution will keep my mother happy. I also have enough CAS points I can take my glassblowing to level five and put the rest in alchemy. I was worried about not having enough for alchemy if I added points in glassblowing so I could make basic quality vials. And other small glass items."

"Will nine levels in alchemy be enough?" Callum asked. "Do they have a required amount before you can attend the academy?"

Danae shook her head. "The higher your stats though the sooner you can learn more about potions. Level five alchemy gave me a ten percent chance of recognising herbs when gathering them and level six means I can now make double strength herbal tea. Level eight means I can use enchanted pruning shears and level nine allows me to use alchemy apparatuses. It's best if you don't level up past ten before going to the academy. Each time you gain a level they let you choose a recipe. Only a maximum of ten at a time though. Which is why it's best to collect the recipes regularly since they count levels from each time you've collected them. They count levels you learn outside of the academy as some students do extra work outside of classes in an effort to master the ability quicker."

"It's still a lot to drink to gain two health points," Callum said.

"I'll be able to make tinctures at level twenty-three. Once I visit the academy." Danae paused a moment. "You have reached level two archer. You can now use enchanted hunting knives, short bows and arrows."

"That sounds good," Callum said. "I can't wait until I can use enchanted gear. I wish I had a list of available enchantments."

Ryan grinned. "Maybe they have a book for that."

"I'm putting my character point in mage." Mallory glanced in the direction Brodie had headed in earlier. "Looks like I'll be able to use that healing spell sooner than we thought." Assigning the point to mage, Mallory read over the notification. *You have reached level one mage. You can now use level one spells. Each class level gained allows you to wield spells of that level if you have sufficient mana.* She thought of the spell in her satchel. She'd worry about learning it later. There were five attribute points to assign. "I'm putting two points in constitution and one each in strength, intelligence and wisdom."

Mallory checked the new stats. She now had twenty-seven health, as did Danae. Callum was the only one who didn't have that much health. His was at twenty-one. She smiled at the amount of mana she now had. Forty-five would allow her to cast a lot more spells before running out of mana and needing to wait for it to regen.

Callum checked Smudge, who was curled up asleep in the sling. "At this rate, we'll be able to leave for Velkden on the twelfth like Emica wants. Maybe we can sell some of the herbs and veggies there if no one wants them here."

Finished sorting her stats, for now, Mallory half listened to Danae and Callum discuss the possibilities as she took her notebook out of her satchel. She smiled when Smudge made soft noises in his sleep. Opening the notebook, she stared at the page, trying to decide what to write. A lot had happened. A grin formed. Including Brodie being shot in the knee with an arrow. She wrote in the date. Day Ten, Second Month, 514. It was hard to believe this was only their tenth day on Inadon.

Brodie joined them as Mallory was writing the last couple of lines, Fang at his side. He sat down on an empty seat, nearly dropping his crutches. Fang whined as she lay beside him. Brodie patted her on the head, looking around the table. "I'll be glad when my knee's fixed. There's no way I can work at the tavern tomorrow night. It's too hard on crutches." His gaze rested on his sister who was putting her notebook away. "Why haven't you put your points into apothecary? And what's with the new quest?"

Danae giggled. "It sounds like the type of quest where you will be able to join us at the end, to gain XP too."

Brodie slumped in his seat. "Three hours working in that kitchen and all I gained was three XP and two copper pieces. I thought I'd get more XP than that." He turned to Mallory. "I suppose you want the coins."

Mallory shook her head. They weren't going to make much of a difference. "You keep them."

Brodie's expression brightened. "I can?"

Mallory nodded.

Brodie victory punched the air. "Hell yeah."

Before Mallory could say anything, an orc strode towards them, grinning. He looked at each of them, his grin remaining in place. "What are you doing here? I thought you were heading to Eridell."

Chapter Twenty-Four

"Kruth." Mallory stared up at the orc who, at six and a half feet, towered over her. He had greenish grey skin, protruding lower canines and bulging arm muscles that were clearly visible since he wore a hide vest with his heavy cotton trousers. At each wrist was a wide copper bracelet, he had on leather boots and a longsword at his side. "What are you doing in Wayholt? Why aren't you at South Peak Mine?"

Ryan gestured to a chair at a nearby, empty table. "Bring it over and join us."

Danae glanced at the exit. "We can't stay too long."

"Why not?" Brodie asked.

"Danni's mum wasn't impressed at not knowing where she was earlier." Ryan turned to Kruth. "Are you visiting your brother?"

"If only." Kruth brought over the chair. "It's all terribly unfair. That goblin bait that was stuck in the dungeon with me started telling everyone I was the reason we were trapped and he was the one who got us out of there. The overseer objected when I got into a fight with him." Kruth paused a moment. "Twice."

"You lost your job?" Mallory asked.

Kruth nodded. "I'm staying with my brother until I can find another one. He had to go and write to our sister in Shadhurst. Paid extra to have it delivered quickly. And she sent a reply by drake. Threatened to visit and sort me out. Her and her girlfriend. Don't know what she's doing with some human. No offence, but you humans are rather squishy." He looked at Brodie's knee. "And easily broken."

"Letter by drake?" Mallory leaned forward. "How does that work?"

"They keep them in the capital. And a few private places in other towns. And also the military town of Shadville. They've been trained to find locations and return home after the letter has been delivered, and the reply picked up in some cases." Kruth slowly shook his head. "I don't know what Alamaree was thinking. Must have cost a fortune. It even waited for a return letter. You can only send a single page. They carry it on their back in a little tube strapped to their armour." Again he slowly shook his head. "Our parents should never have given her such a fancy name. Should have stuck with a good, strong orc name for her."

"Can any drake be taught to deliver letters?" Brodie asked.

Kruth shrugged, glancing around the table. "You never said what you're doing here." His gaze rested on Ninette. "And with an extra person in your party."

It didn't take long to explain about the trip they planned to make to Cutthroat Harbour and how Ninette had joined them to guard the wagoner. During their explanation, the music ended and the bard strode towards the bar for a drink, most of the patrons leaving since he was finished for the night.

Kruth leaned forward. "Are you looking for another guard? Grotmur tried to tell me I should take the job of helping one of the local farmers keep the birds out of his crops. What does he think I am? A scarecrow?"

"We can't afford it." Mallory glanced at Brodie's knee. "And we might not be coming back this way. One of our quests might mean we'll have to travel to Shadhurst." If they didn't find Emica's father they couldn't leave her in some random town. They'd also need to warn the Duke about the hellion's plans.

"I've been thinking of going to Shadville and seeing if I can get work there. Might even join the army. Or travel on to Shadhurst and work for one of the nobles. I'll help guard the wagon if you provide food and help me get as close as possible to Shadville," Kruth said.

The bard wandered over to them, smiling. His two sharp canines were visible again. He held out a pale hand, the other holding his instrument. "Allow me to introduce myself. I'm Deneg." His voice was deep and melodious.

Ryan shook his hand, introducing those at the table. "We enjoyed your music."

Deneg drew a chair over to the table and sat beside Callum without an invitation. "I overheard you talking about travelling to Velkden. I'm having trouble getting an escort there." He smiled, his canines again prominently visible.

Mallory looked from their table to where Deneg had been playing while they spoke about Velkden. "You've got good hearing."

Again Deneg smiled. "Something to make up for my inability to go out in the sun." He turned his smile on Callum. "Most of the time only having the night to enjoy doesn't bother me. There is usually plenty to keep me entertained." He faced Mallory. "I can pay five gold pieces if you can take me in my travel coffin to Velkden."

"Why do you need to go there?" Brodie asked.

Deneg smiled at Brodie. "There's someone I wish to visit. Someone who was once a travelling bard and who I'd like to learn some of their music from."

Mallory desperately wanted to say yes. Five gold pieces would help after all they'd spent. "We'll have to discuss it." She checked the journal since the icon had appeared in the corner of her vision. Like she'd assumed, it was a quest. *Visit To Velkden: The vampire Deneg offered to pay you five gold if you escort him to Velkden.*

"You'll discuss my offer too, won't you?" Kruth asked. "To work for you."

Mallory nodded. Before she could say anything, Callum spoke.

He gestured to Deneg's instrument. "Can I have a look at your gittern? I've never seen one up close before."

Deneg drew his instrument closer. "No one touches it but me." He smiled, softening his words. "It's my livelihood. I'm sure you can understand."

Callum nodded. "I understand, although I am disappointed."

Deneg briefly rested his hand on Callum's arm, smiling at him again. "If I have the chance to travel with you, maybe I'll be able to play a song just for you. Not everyone is as understanding as you've been."

Callum looked from Deneg to his gittern and back again. "I'd like that."

"Does that mean I can travel with you?" Deneg asked.

"We need to discuss it." Mallory rose to her feet, catching sight of Ninette trying to hide a yawn. "We should return to where we're staying. We've got an early morning ahead of us." And they weren't going to get enough sleep. She dreaded to think how hard that was going to make grinding for levels. The rest of her companions rose from the table, Smudge making sounds of protest at being disturbed.

"We'll let you know tomorrow." Ryan looked from Kruth to Deneg. "Both of you."

"I'll be here," Kruth said. "I try to spend as little time as I can with Grotmur. Better than listening to him complain all day and make stupid suggestions about what kind of work I can do."

"I'll be playing here between sunset and midnight." Deneg turned to Callum. "They've arranged an area for me in the basement. If you wanted to visit me an hour before sunset I could show you some of the other musical instruments I brought with me."

Rising to his feet, Callum nodded. "Thank you."

Deneg rose from his seat, again smiling at Callum. "I look forward to seeing you."

Callum watched Deneg stride away.

Brodie struggled to his feet. "I don't even want to think about tomorrow. Having a shattered knee makes everything so difficult. Even getting off a seat."

Kruth started to help Brodie.

"I can do this." Brodie's words were sharp and he looked down at Fang when she whined. "I'm okay." He sighed, turning back to Kruth. "Sorry."

Ryan chuckled. "You're lucky. He's usually crankier than this when he's sick. We all take cover when he's got a cold or anything."

"I'm not that bad," Brodie muttered, starting towards the door.

Kruth took a step towards Mallory. "You'll let me know tomorrow?"

Chapter Twenty-Five

Mallory nodded. "Don't worry. We'll talk it over and let you know what we decide." At Kruth's relieved smile, she headed for the tavern door with the rest of her companions.

Outside, they lit one of the lanterns and made their way to Sarisa's place. Ninette and Callum offered to sort the resources, including organising more vegetables for Sarisa, and tie Bobbi up with the rest of the livestock out by the tree while Mallory, Danae, Ryan and Brodie headed inside.

Sarisa was sitting by the fire writing on a piece of thick, cream coloured paper that had small, neat handwriting across half of it in alternating styles. She looked up as they entered. "I let your father know you're back here." Sarisa gestured towards the paper.

"What did he say?" Danae closed the door behind them.

"That he was expecting you home by now," Sarisa said. "I can arrange for someone else to escort you."

Danae moved closer to Brodie. "I don't need an escort."

Brodie swung himself forward on his crutches. "We'll make sure Danni catches a ship in time."

Callum crossed the room to examine the paper. "There are words forming on it."

Sarisa nodded. "It's a reply."

"How does that work?" Callum asked. "Can anyone use them?"

"Two pieces of paper are spelled to duplicate themselves. What is put on one, appears on the other," Danae said. "It's demonic magic. Some of the more powerful ones can do three and even four pages that duplicate each other."

"That's cool." Brodie dropped onto the second seat by the fire. "We need some of them."

"What would we use them for?" Mallory asked.

"To write to Danni when she's at the academy and we're off questing," Brodie said.

Sarisa looked at her daughter. "I hope you do attend. You've been wanting to go for years."

Danae smiled. "I levelled up. And I now have enough CAS points in glassblowing I'll be able to make my own basic quality vials and my alchemy is level nine."

Sarisa rose to her feet, leaving the paper and nib pen behind so she could envelop Danae in her arms. "What did you put your attribute points in?" She nodded when Danae told her. Letting go, Sarisa glanced at each of them. "I lit the fire in the bathroom and set water to boil. You might want to wash while it's warm in there."

While she waited to use the bathroom, Mallory helped Danae top up Sarisa's lanterns, using the last of their oil. There wasn't enough left to fill their own. Yet one more thing they needed to spend their money on in the morning. Mallory tried not to let the worries crowd in on her, reminding herself they'd gained money before. Yet it didn't help. If she didn't level up her apothecary soon, they'd be spending a lot more money on Brodie's treatments. And what if something else went wrong?

It took longer than Mallory expected for everyone to wash and spread blankets and bedrolls out in front of the fireplace in the house. Sadly, she didn't have time to soak in the tub, but they did wash their clothes and hang them over the timber rack to dry. The moment Mallory lay down, she was instantly asleep, groaning when someone tried to wake her what felt like minutes later.

"It's five thirty," Ryan said. "Half an hour before we need to have Brodie at the apothecary. Sarisa made blueberry pancakes for breakfast. Better get up and have your share before Brodie has it."

She stumbled to her feet, yawning as she staggered towards the door. "Keep me some." After using the outhouse and visiting the bathroom to put her clean, dry clothes on, she returned to the house for her share of the pancakes. She smiled when she saw the apothecary book beside her plate.

"You should have read that by now," Brodie muttered. "We all unlocked apothecary."

Having a bite of the pancakes, Mallory turned to the first page, reading over the introduction. She checked the notification the moment it appeared. *You have unlocked apothecary, a crafting ability that allows you to heal and cure injuries, illnesses and diseases.*

"Are you going to put your CAS points in it now?" Brodie put a piece of blueberry pancake in his belt pouch and his pig pulled his head back inside, snuffling excitedly.

Mallory set the book aside. She'd read the rest of it later so she could discover what she'd be able to do in the future if she continued to level up the crafting ability. "Once I have all of them. It'll help me keep track of how many I need." She glanced around. "Where's Fang?" Her gaze momentarily rested on Smudge who was sitting on Callum's lap, not having let Callum out of sight since he'd used up a revive.

"Outside." Brodie gestured in the direction of the backyard. "Eating one of those bones Ryan brought back for her."

"I hope she doesn't plan to cart it around like the last one." Finished eating, Mallory rose from the table. "We should head on over so we're there waiting for the apothecary when she opens."

Callum finished off his cup of coffee, setting the cup on the table. "We need more crafting ability books so we can learn all about the different crafting abilities." He gestured towards the book. "Apothecary has a lot of useful abilities. Who knows what other crafting abilities would also be good to level up."

Outside, Bobbi was tied to the hitching post, her panniers full and cloth bags bundled up on top of her and tied in place with a rope. They reached the apothecary minutes before she opened and Fang had to wait outside since she'd brought her bone with her.

The apothecary looked over the herbs, taking approximately two thirds of them. "I can give you eleven gold and four silver pieces. I won't need the rest of them. Maybe the trading post will be interested."

Mallory nodded. "Thank you." It wasn't as much as she'd hoped, but better than needing to pay for Brodie's next treatment. "We'd also like you to do weak rapid mend on Brodie."

Once the apothecary was finished with Brodie and paid them the balance of six gold and four silver pieces for the herbs, they headed to the trading post where they were able to sell the rest of the herbs, the bear pelt and buy oil for their lanterns, having both of them filled along with the two flasks. Mallory took the coins from the trader, slipping them into her belt pouch as she mentally calculated how much money they now had. Forty-four gold, six silver and eight copper pieces. They weren't as broke as she'd feared they'd be after their purchases. But they still hadn't regained the money they'd spent on Brodie's injury.

Outside, Mallory glanced around the group. "We should take Brodie back to Sarisa's and collect everyone else."

"I'm going with you." Brodie sat on Bug, his crutches on Bobbi. "I'm not about to sit around all day while you have fun. Besides, I can throw knives at any creatures we find."

"What if you end up setting the healing back?" Mallory asked.

Danae patted Bug on the neck. "She's a gentle horse. He should be fine. It isn't like he'll need to do anything more than a walk."

"See, Mal. I can go," Brodie said.

Mallory looked from Brodie to Danae several times before she nodded. "Just don't make your knee any worse. We do need to go home again. We're not doing too good a job at splitting our time equally between both worlds."

"We need to find out how much fountain of youth potions cost. At this rate, we might need to remain here until we earn the money to afford the potions instead of continuing to try and spend equal time between the two worlds," Ryan said.

"How can we manage that?" Mallory asked. "We still have to regularly return so our actions make a difference back home."

"We wait until the weekend," Ryan said.

"And when we've got our own place," Callum said. "That way we can return for half an hour, take a short break then return to Inadon."

"It's only Tuesday back home. That's ages away." Brodie glanced at Fang who walked beside Bug. "Can I take Fang with me?"

"Would I be able to visit your world?" Danae asked.

Mallory glanced around the group. "We have no idea how much a fountain of youth potion will cost. So let's focus on sorting out Brodie's knee and getting a place back home first."

"There was one at the apothecary," Callum said.

Mallory frowned. "One what?"

"Fountain of youth potion." Callum patted Smudge who peeked over the edge of the sling, chattering softly. "One week. Two hundred gold pieces. They only had the one."

Chapter Twenty-Six

Mallory came to a stop, staring at Callum who slowed to look over his shoulder at her. She slowly shook her head. "Two hundred gold pieces to turn back time for one week. We'd need two grand for a week."

Danae also stopped, turning to look at Mallory. "You're including me for the potions?"

"You're in our group too," Brodie said. "And we'll need potions for Fang and Smudge. Or we will eventually. When they've grown up."

Ryan returned to Mallory's side, slipping his hand in hers and tugging her forward. "I guess now we know what we're going to be spending the money, we make from the drakes, on."

"That's if we manage to make money on them." Mallory couldn't prevent herself from glancing at her brother's knee. Obviously, things could go wrong.

"You should max out your apothecary." Callum

also glanced at Brodie. "You'll be able to do things like strong rapid mend, improve potions and healing hands."

She really needed to find the time to read up on the crafting ability. "That doesn't help us now."

Ryan squeezed her hand. "Stop worrying. We've got this. Look at all we've accomplished so far." He let go of her hand and slipped his arm around her waist, drawing her close. "Simple. One thing at a time. We level you up and work on getting to Cutthroat Harbour."

Mallory took a slow, deep breath, releasing it equally as slow. "Okay. Level up, Cutthroat Harbour, then we can panic."

Ryan chuckled. "No, then we rescue everyone."

Reaching Sarisa's place, they organised themselves to head out gathering herbs and vegetables. They separated into the same groups as last night, taking yet another direction. They went further afield this time and everyone alternated, taking turns when Mallory needed a break. Even Brodie had the chance to harvest some blossoms on a tree that Danae said was used in making sweet foods. The petals were in clusters towards the ends of the drooping branches, well within reach of Brodie who remained on Bug. When he learned sugar blossoms could be eaten when freshly picked, he had to try them, picking more and sharing them around, telling everyone they needed to have some. He also shared them with Fang, Not For Bacon and Smudge. They didn't last long, everyone enjoying the sweet petals. When Danae said Bobbi and Bug could eat them, he gave them some too. Danae dropped a few petals into her belt pouch to take back for Augusta.

It was easier during the day and Mallory was able to gather a little faster. That was until they reached the point when they'd gathered most of what was in the area and started to do ever widening circles, not wanting to go too far from Wayholt and risk being slowed down by needing to fight creatures.

Mallory stopped in front of Emica and Danae who stood near some vegetables. "We've stripped the area of a lot of resources. What if the locals need some?"

"Most of it will be back in about a week," Danae said. "Things grow fast in the wild. Not so fast on farmland, unless the farmer has a high level in farming. It's part of the magic that created our world."

Mallory picked the vegetables, leaving them lying on the ground. "I also thought we'd run into a few creatures."

"We haven't gone that far from Wayholt. We've

mainly circled around it. The mercenaries keep the area fairly safe. For a price of course," Danae said.

"Are you going to keep levelling up or is it someone else's turn?" Emica asked when Mallory remained in front of them.

Mallory breathed out heavily. "Keep levelling." She smiled at Emica, whose turn it was next. "Don't worry, it'll be your turn soon enough." She was past ready for a break, but she was trying to stretch each of her turns out to twenty minutes. It was getting harder to gather for that long each time.

By the time they headed back towards Wayholt, at eleven, Mallory wasn't the only one who'd gained CAS points. But she was the only one who'd gone up a character level. Emica and Jorgen had each gained a CAS point while Ninette had gained two. Danae had gained another CAS point and had five experience points out of the one hundred and nineteen she needed for the next level. Ryan and Callum had both gained two CAS points. Ryan had twenty experience points of the hundred and twelve needed for his next CAS point and Callum had eighteen of the next hundred and twelve experience points needed for another CAS point. The experience points he'd gained also meant Smudge was close to reaching his first level. He only had another thirty-six to go, much to Brodie's annoyance who wanted Fang to level up too. But they didn't have time to do any more levelling. They had other plans for the afternoon.

Mallory was now character level three and was six CAS points into the character level with twelve of the next hundred and thirty-four experience points she needed to gain her next CAS point. She now only needed another three CAS points to reach thirty-five apothecary. She didn't care how close she was to gaining the needed levels after the hours spent gathering herbs and vegetables. She was just glad of the break that helping the frog mage would give her. She'd also drank four cups of health tea over the past four hours and was relieved they were headed back to Sarisa's place. She wanted to use the outhouse instead of having to find a shrub to go behind. She also decided to leave sorting out her next level until she was at Sarisa's place.

"What are we going to do with all these herbs?" Mallory eyed the panniers and the bags hanging from them, as well as also on Bobbi's back, that were filled with herbs and vegetables. The majority of what they'd gathered had been herbs.

"We could ask the frog mage if he'd make us health potions in exchange for herbs," Danae suggested.

"That's a brilliant idea," Brodie said. "I'm coming with you. I bet I could get us a good deal."

Mallory started to argue, Ryan speaking before she could.

"You can stay at the frog mage's place. Keep him company and out of our way while we find Cila. If you're at his place waiting for him, hopefully that'll give him a reason to return home instead of trying to come with us." Ryan looked Bug up and down. "It's not like you'll be able to hide all that easily."

Mallory smiled as she listened to Ryan continue to interrupt all of Brodie's protests. By the time they reached Sarisa's house, Brodie was silently glaring at Ryan. The glares instantly vanished when Danae suggested having their midday meal before they met up with the frog mage.

After dashing to the outhouse, Mallory helped take some of the vegetables out of the top of the panniers for Sarisa. Most of the vegetables were too difficult to reach, buried beneath the many herbs they'd gathered. Heading inside, they discovered Sarisa had prepared food for them. She'd used some of the venison Welby and Roast had caught and the vegetables and herbs they'd gathered to make venison and vegetables in a herb marinade. Some of the herbs gathered were used for both medicinal and cooking purposes. They sat around the campfire out the back while they ate the meal, Sarisa joining them.

Brodie gestured towards the meal. "I can't wait to cook like this." He looked at Sarisa. "This meal is amazing."

Sarisa smiled. "It's only a level five recipe. You have enough levels to make it. Not to the same standards, but that will come with time and putting more CAS points into cooking."

Brodie stared at her, his fork halfway to his mouth. "I can make it?"

Sarisa nodded. "If you're serious about cooking, you should buy yourself a leather-bound notebook to keep your recipes in." She glanced at Danae. "I might consider giving you some recipes. At least then I'd know Danae would have some reasonable meals while she's travelling around."

"Hell yeah. I'll cook them," Brodie said.

"I hope you're not planning on spending money on a book for your recipes," Callum said. "Aren't you the one who complained when Mallory wanted to buy a book?"

"Didn't stop her from buying it." Brodie continued to argue with Callum, Fang lying at his feet and Not For Bacon on his lap, having already been fed.

Mallory grinned when she noticed the humour

in Callum's eyes. He was doing much better than her and Ryan at managing not to smile. Although he was probably right. She doubted they'd be able to afford a leather-bound notebook for Brodie to keep his recipes in. Not after all they'd spent recently. Brand new they were worth ten gold pieces. Well out of their price range.

Chapter Twenty-Seven

As Mallory ate her dinner, she put her character point in warrior. *You have reached level two warrior. You can now wield enchanted short swords.* She tried not to sigh. It was all very good levelling up and unlocking the ability to use different things, but they couldn't exactly afford to buy the items. Trying not to think about their current problems, Mallory assigned her five attribute points. She put one point each in strength, intelligence and wisdom and two in constitution. That took her strength up to seven, constitution to eleven and both intelligence and wisdom to ten. Now her intelligence was at ten that allowed her to use level two spells, without having to level up mage.

Her health was at thirty-three, stamina at fifty-five, mana at fifty and her carrying capacity seventy kilograms. They really should have done some grinding much sooner than this. The rest of them needed to power level too. Would it be possible for everyone to gain a level before they reached Cutthroat Harbour?

She checked over her attack stats, grinning when she saw her crit attack for fireball had increased to nine due to the higher intelligence level. Hopefully that would help when they faced the hellions in Cutthroat Harbour. Finished her food, she took out the healing spell and learned it. The parchment the spell had been written on crumbled in her hands after she'd finished reading it, becoming dust then eventually nothing.

Brodie glanced at her. "About time."

Mallory opened her mouth to say she wasn't his support and not to think he could be reckless because she'd be there to heal him all the time. With a glance at Sarisa, she closed her mouth. She'd tell him later.

Ryan rose to his feet. "We better visit the frog mage and find out where he's meeting up with the kidnappers this afternoon."

Sarisa also rose to her feet, taking the plate and cutlery from Ryan. She turned to Danae, taking her plate and cutlery. "I really don't like the thought of you facing kidnappers."

Danae kissed her mother on each cheek. "I'll be

fine." She glanced at Ryan and grinned. "We've got this."

Ryan chuckled. "We have."

"What about us?" Emica asked. "Do we need to go with you to ask the frog mage about herbs?"

Mallory shook her head. "I was planning on sharing whatever potions we gain from the trade. Hopefully it'll be health potions and those without can have some."

"Who gets them first?" Jorgen asked.

"You, Emica and Ninette," Mallory said.

"Are you saying you'd give us health potions and go without if there aren't enough for everyone." Emica spoke the words slowly, as if they were hard to comprehend.

Mallory nodded. "You did help me level up."

"You helped us level up too," Ninette said.

"This is why we're always broke," Brodie muttered.

Emica met Mallory's gaze, stepping forward and taking hold of one of her hands, clasping it between both of hers. "I will repay you for all your help."

A mild sensation of static electricity crackled over Mallory's hand. "That isn't-"

Brodie interrupted Mallory before she could say the word 'necessary'. "Do you live in the castle? I'd love to see inside a castle. I didn't get the chance to go inside the lighthouse while we were at Mer Point."

Emica continued to hold Mallory's hand, glancing at Brodie. "Are you sure you're related?"

Mallory laughed. "Sadly, yes." She grinned at her brother's muttered comments.

Emica let go of Mallory's hand and stepped back. "If you don't mind, I'll remain here and have a sleep. My health points are still not full."

"Neither are mine," Jorgen said.

"Did you want me to come with you?" Ninette asked.

Mallory had no idea how dangerous rescuing Cila from kidnappers would be. "You could stay here and keep an eye on things."

Ninette nodded once. "I can do that." She glanced at Brodie. "Did you want me to have a look around at the various shops to see if I can find a reasonably priced leather-bound notebook?"

Ryan spoke before Mallory could. "How much money have we got? With the way you're levelling up, we should only have to pay for one more treatment for Brodie at the most. If we're lucky, you'll be levelled up before six tonight."

"Forty-four gold, six silver and eight copper pieces," Mallory said.

"Give Ninette twenty gold. She can take the sword to the blacksmith to get it cleaned and buy a leather-bound notebook for Brodie. I wouldn't mind eating better," Ryan said.

"Are you sure?" Mallory asked.

Ryan nodded. "We might get lucky and the sword will be worth selling."

Mallory looked at each member of her party. They all nodded. "Okay." She handed over the twenty gold pieces to Ninette. "Thanks for doing this."

Once everyone was organised, they went their separate ways. Welby and Roast remained behind to finish sorting the venison, Emica and Jorgen went to the tent and wagon to sleep, the wagoner strolled towards the tavern, Ninette strode down the road with the barnacle encrusted sword and the rest of them headed towards the frog mage's place.

Brodie rode Bug, Not For Bacon back in his belt pouch, Fang walking beside him. Callum walked in front of Brodie, Danae next to him leading Augusta as he asked her questions about Cutthroat Harbour. She was unable to tell him much, only the stories she'd heard about how dangerous it was.

Mallory linked her fingers through Ryan's, Bobbi's lead rope in his other hand. "Should the rest of you level up before we go to Cutthroat Harbour?"

"I don't think we'll have time for that." He glanced over his shoulder towards Brodie, lowering his voice before he spoke again. "I don't even know if we'll have enough time for Brodie to heal before we reach Cutthroat Harbour."

She had no idea what to say to that comment so remained silent. She wished she could as easily silence her thoughts. She might be character level three and have better health and stronger spell attacks, but she didn't feel ready. She still felt terribly under levelled. She had no idea how long it would be until she lost that feeling. Level five? Level ten?

That thought made her recall the question they'd asked Dorset. About when the dark forces might come after them on Earth. 'The earliest seems to be character level ten, but some haven't been attacked until level fifteen or twenty.' What would that mean for them? Having an enemy amongst the dark forces, would they be more likely to come after them sooner rather than later? She doubted Rass would forget about them any time soon.

Mallory was relieved to reach the frog mage's cottage so she could stop focusing on their lack of levels and all they needed to do. The frog mage came out to greet them before they'd approached the front door, a cluster of frogs following him the moment he stepped outside.

"You returned." His gaze momentarily rested on Brodie. "With your friend who was cooking."

"Do you mind if he waits here with you?" Ryan asked. "He can't exactly come with us with his busted knee. And it shouldn't take you long to give the kidnappers the potion and head home."

The frog mage nodded.

Brodie spoke before the frog mage, who'd opened his mouth, could. "Talking about potions, we've got all these herbs we were hoping to exchange for some potions. What do you say? Are you interested?"

The frog mage stared at the overflowing panniers and many bags hanging off Bobbi. "I don't know. Potion vials aren't that cheap."

"We've got eight empty vials," Ryan said.

"You have?" the frog mage asked.

Ryan nodded.

The frog mage looked from Ryan to Bobbi. "I can have all these herbs if I fill your eight potion vials? I wouldn't need to provide any vials at all."

"Depends what you fill them with," Brodie said. "Will it be useful potions?"

Mallory interrupted before the frog mage could

speak. "There are some vegetables in amongst the panniers and bags. Not many, but some."

The frog mage gestured towards Bobbi. "Mind if I have a look?"

"Go ahead," Brodie said, Danae and Callum nodding their agreement.

After he rummaged around for a bit, the frog mage faced them. "Health potions. I can fill your vials with health potions. You've got a lot of herbs here that are good for that type of potion."

Chapter Twenty-Eight

"Yes." Mallory laughed, the rest of her group having all spoken at the same time as her, each of them agreeing to the frog mage's offer. "That sounds perfect."

The frog mage gestured towards Bobbi. "Do we need to unload them now? I don't want to be late to the meeting."

"We won't be coming straight back with you," Ryan said.

"I know," the frog mage said.

Mallory nodded when Ryan looked towards her. It didn't surprise her that the frog mage wanted to leave straight away. Not with how worried he was for Cila.

Once they'd tied Bobbi up at the front of the cottage and Brodie was settled at the table inside, having brought a couple of the crafting ability books with him, Fang lying at his feet, they took the horses with them and followed the frog mage.

It was a ten minute walk to where the frog mage had to hand over the potion. They remained at the edge of the tree line, peering at a large clearing. No one seemed to be in the area, but they remained hidden in case the kidnappers were early too.

The frog mage slowly entered the clearing, glancing around as he made his way to the centre. He shifted from foot to foot as he waited, looking in every direction.

Mallory peered at the pocket watch Ryan took out. They'd been waiting for about ten minutes. "How long do you think he'll have to wait? Do you think they'll make him wait until two? Or will they also turn up early."

Ryan grinned. "Why? Are you missing gathering herbs?"

She returned his grin. "Almost."

They had to wait another half an hour before a warrior entered the clearing and took the potion from the frog mage. The two of them spoke too quietly to be heard, the frog mage's shoulders slumping as he turned and walked away, head lowered.

Mallory stared at the warrior who watched the frog mage walk away. Her gaze was fixed on the tattoo on his left cheek. A skull with dark eye sockets, the edges partially obscured by tendrils of smoke. She kept her voice low. "That is Rass." He wore a light padded gambeson this time, a dark brown that was several shades darker than his short hair. She wasn't surprised he wore armour after their last encounter.

"This can't be good," Callum said.

"Does that mean we're not going to follow him?" Danae asked.

"We have to," Mallory said. "Otherwise, we'll get Cila killed."

"He's gone up a level," Danae said. "He has a longsword and you need to be level four warrior to wield one."

Mallory momentarily closed her eyes. They were definitely under levelled.

"It looks like we all need to power level," Callum said. "I was hoping his location revive would take him home to Cape Barren."

"Some might, but you can choose which location revive to use," Danae said.

Ryan clapped his brother on the shoulder. "It's all good. It'll give you the chance to take more of his coffee."

Callum turned to Mallory. "If they've got tents like the last hellion encampment, don't burn them down.

Who knows what we missed out on in the other tent. It could have been more books."

When Rass headed back the way he'd come, they followed at a distance. A couple of times they feared they'd lost him, but Smudge set them on the right track again and they quickly caught up with Rass, staying far enough back that he didn't spot them.

Rass stopped at ruins south east of Wayholt, out past the farms. What had once been four buildings was now mostly scattered rubble, only a handful of jagged walls partially rising into the sky. Canvas had been stretched between some of the more intact walls, creating a roof over two of the buildings. He headed for the closest one.

They tied Augusta and Bug to a tree, so they'd be out of sight, before they went to the edge of the treeline to examine the area. Mallory had no idea what the buildings had once been. An extremely small village, a large farm, or something else. There wasn't enough of the buildings left. "How are we going to figure out how many are here?"

Chapter Twenty-Nine

"Maybe we should have brought Jorgen with us for his stealth ability," Callum said.

"I'll try and get closer to see what their set up is like." Ryan started to step away.

Mallory grabbed hold of his hand and drew him back to her. "That sounds like a terrible idea."

"We can't stay here all day." Ryan tugged his hand from her grip and slipped his arms around her waist. "I wasn't about to waltz in there and call out hello."

"We could cause a diversion," Danae suggested.

"What sort of diversion? Callum asked.

Danae shrugged. "I don't know. It's a pity Mallory doesn't have a levitation spell. Then she could cause rocks to fall off a wall."

"All I have is flame," Mallory said.

Callum continued to peer through the trees at the ruins. "I think there's a campfire over there." He pointed to a destroyed building left of the one Rass had entered. He shifted across half a metre. "There's firewood stacked not far from it. What if you set it on fire?"

Ryan kept an arm around Mallory, taking her with him as he moved over to where Callum stood. "Not the wood itself, the grass. You don't want it to catch fire too quickly."

"That's a good plan." Danae stared at the firewood Callum had pointed out. "It'll look natural. Sparks often start unplanned fires."

"What if they put it out before it gets going enough to cause a distraction?" Mallory asked.

Callum shifted away another half a metre. "I can't see all the area. It looks like there's a tent pitched towards the back. I can't be sure though. I might be able to see more if I can get a bit closer."

"No," Ryan said. "We remain in the cover of the trees. Draw them out."

"What about Cila?" Danae asked. "Shouldn't we check to see if she's here first?"

Before anyone could answer, a hellion came out of the far building, leading a horse. He swung into the saddle the moment he was past the buildings, heading south west.

"Should one of us follow him?" Callum asked.

"I don't know," Ryan said.

"It doesn't matter if we should," Mallory said. "None of us are going after him on our own. There aren't enough of us to split into groups."

"Are we going to create a distraction?" Callum asked.

Mallory examined the area. Nothing moved. Everything was silent. What if they attacked only to learn Cila wasn't here? That she was being kept somewhere else. "We'll create a diversion to try and learn how many are here. We won't attack until we discover where Cila is."

"What if she isn't here? How are we going to find her?" Danae asked.

"We capture one of them and interrogate them," Ryan said.

Mallory wanted to argue his words. But she couldn't think of another option. Taking a deep breath, she glanced around the group. "Are we ready?"

Ryan smiled down at her, his arm around her waist tugging her against him. "We've got this. Rass doesn't stand a chance. We've taken him out before and we'll keep doing so as long as needed."

Nodding once, she leaned in to brush her lips across his before drawing away and facing the ruins.

She scanned the area. No hellions were in sight. Picking a clump of grass against the woodpile, she cast flame, grinning when it instantly caught alight. "That is a much easier spell to use than fireball. More accurate."

"Could you imagine if it wasn't?" Callum asked. "Think of the amount of out of control fires it'd cause each time someone used it."

An archer came running into view from the back of the ruined building, trying to stomp out the flames. They were already beyond that stage. He ran in the direction he'd come from returning moments later with a dripping wet hessian bag and a rogue. She also carried a wet hessian bag. The two of them tried to put out the flames, smoke billowing into the sky as the fire spread through the grass and away from the building.

"Maybe we shouldn't have set the grass alight." Mallory stared at the flames that were rapidly getting out of control. She needed a spell that could put fires out.

The rogue pointed in the direction of the building Rass had entered earlier. The archer shook his head. The rogue shoved the archer in the direction of the building she'd indicated. The archer looked from the fire to the building Rass had entered. At another gesture from the rogue, he scurried towards it.

He didn't reach it before Rass came out, another warrior hellion with him and a woman who appeared to be carrying no weapons. "What is going on now?" Rass demanded.

Mallory winced at the anger in the words Rass shouted at the archer. "I wouldn't want to be him."

The archer pointed behind him. "The woodpile caught alight."

"Put it out," Rass said. "Can't the lot of you do anything right?"

The warrior hellion joined the archer and rogue in trying to put out the fire. The woman returned inside the ruined building, coming outside with two mages. The mages joined those fighting the fire while the woman remained beside Rass, speaking too softly for them to hear.

Mallory automatically leaned forward. "I wish there was a way to hear what they're saying."

"There's a magic spell called amplify, I'm not sure what level it is," Danae said. "There is also a potion that temporarily improves hearing and rogues have a skill called eavesdrop."

Rass gestured towards those putting out the fire. "What can you expect when I have this kind of incompetence to deal with? You tell the captain that no one could do better than I am with what he gives me."

Again the woman spoke too softly for her words to reach them.

"He was the one who came to my family with his plans. He better not go back on the deal he made. We will expect a return on our investment." Rass pointed a finger at the woman. "You can tell him that too."

The archer hurried over to Rass once the fire was out. Before he had a chance to say anything, Rass spun to face him.

"What do you want now?" Rass demanded.

The archer took a step back, gesturing towards where the fire had been. The rogue, warrior hellion and two mages remained standing around the blackened area. The archer didn't speak a word.

"Do something useful. Check on that stupid frog or something. Make sure she isn't trying to escape from the crypt again. And that no more skeletons or other creatures have spawned. I told you to check every ten minutes." Rass started to turn away, again facing the archer. "Don't mess with anything else down there. I won't be as lenient on you as your last lieutenant. And unlike him, I'm not running low on revives. You get me killed due to your incompetence, I will come after you."

The archer nodded, backing away from Rass. When he was several steps away, he turned and broke into a run, angling around the buildings to an area behind them.

"I wonder if she's in that crypt the skeletons came from the last time we were in the area," Callum said.

Mallory started to speak, stopping when the woman strode away, leaving Rass who glared after her. He spun to face the rest of the people who'd put out the fire. They scurried away before he was fully facing them. He glared at each of them until they were out of sight.

"There are too many," Callum said. "We wouldn't be able to survive facing seven enemies. Particularly ones that are probably higher levels than us."

"We need to take them out one at a time." Ryan grinned. "Like last time."

"I doubt he'll fall for that again," Mallory said.

Ryan shrugged. "He might not, but one of them has gone off on their own, giving us a chance to improve the odds."

"We're going after the one who's checking on Cila?" Danae asked.

"Might–" Ryan broke off at the sound of hooves

pounding against the ground. He spun to face the ruins.

Mallory watched as the woman galloped away, leaning low over a horse. "Looks like our odds just got better."

"We should go after the archer." Ryan glanced around the group. "We'll leave the horses here and circle around towards the back of the ruins."

It didn't take long to find the crypt which was set ten metres behind the ruins. The small building was made of rough cut stones, with an arched doorway leading into a dark interior. There were three stairs leading up to the door, demonic runes carved above it.

"I should have brought the book," Callum said.

"It'll probably be the family name of who owns it," Danae said. "The first letter is an 'N'. If you give me a few minutes, I can figure it out."

"That would be-" Callum broke off when the archer stepped outside.

"Forget translating. Take him out." Ryan readied his hunting bow.

"Attack together?" Callum drew back an arrow.

Mallory held her wand. "I'm ready."

"So am I," Danae said.

"Attack," Ryan said softly.

Mallory threw a fireball at the archer as he reached the bottom step, three arrows impaling him at the same time. He reached for his bow and she threw another fireball, her companions attacking as well. Before she could throw a third fireball, he collapsed on the ground.

Callum started forward.

Ryan grabbed his arm and dragged him back. "Careful. There might be guards inside. We'll angle around and come at the crypt from the side. You and Mallory from the right, Danni and I will approach from the left."

Once everyone had agreed, they made their way to the crypt door. When they were in position, Ryan was the one who peered inside. He motioned them forward, stepping inside first. Mallory followed him. The interior was lit by a lantern hanging from the ceiling. To her left was what looked like an altar and to the right was an opening on the floor, stone stairs leading downwards. Across from them was an extremely large frog, wrapped and tied in light blankets. Even her mouth was wrapped closed.

"Cila?" Danae took a step towards the frog.

The frog struggled against her bindings.

"I doubt there'd be another kidnapped frog." Ryan put his bow away and drew his skinning knife. "Your owner, the frog mage sent us. He and your kids are worried about you."

Cila struggled to escape again.

Ryan crouched in front of her, meeting her gaze. "You need to stay still if you want me to free you."

Mallory remained near the door, regularly glancing outside as she checked her journal notification that had appeared when they'd entered the crypt. She'd earned fifteen experience points for a location. "Should we bring in the body?"

"No, this isn't his crypt. We could drag him around the back if you want to hide him," Danae suggested.

"I'll take him around the back and check the body." Callum looked outside before stepping out, putting his bow away.

Danae remained by the door keeping her bow ready. "It'd be nice if Rass falls for the same trick."

"He seems smarter than that." Mallory remained by the door, keeping watch on Callum as he dragged the body away. She glanced over her shoulder in time to see Cila freed from the bindings.

The frog jumped towards the door and Danae stumbled back out of the way.

"Wait up." Ryan hurried after the frog. "They're still out there. The ones who caught you. Five of them. Wait here while we deal with them."

Cila turned to face him, croaking. The top of her head was level with Ryan's waist.

"I have no idea what you said." Ryan sheathed his skinning knife.

Cila croaked again, shaking her head.

"I don't think she agrees with you," Danae said.

"Do we have to take out the rest of them?" Mallory asked. "Can't we just take Cila home?"

"They might go after the frog mage," Ryan said.

Cila croaked again before jumping towards the doorway.

Mallory stumbled out of her way, Cila leaping through the doorway and landing on the ground.

Danae looked out the doorway. "She's headed for the ruins."

Chapter Thirty

Mallory joined Danae in the doorway, watching the frog jump towards the ruins. "That can't be good."

"Right, take out any who attack Cila." Ryan turned to Mallory. "And you throw at least one fireball at everything. You still have to level up."

Callum came around the building, stopping at the foot of the stairs. "What's going on?"

"We have to rescue Cila again." Mallory strode down the stairs.

Callum gave her two silver pieces. "I also got two extra arrows from him and all our arrows." He returned Danae and Ryan's arrows to them.

Ryan strode towards the tree line. "We'll try and stay out of sight. Make it harder for them to attack us." When shouts came from the ruins, he broke into a run.

Mallory ran after him, reaching the tree line and

circling around the ruins. The moment she spotted Cila, being attacked by a mage and rogue, Rass ordering the other mage and warrior hellion to check on the archer, she came to a stop.

Ryan held up a hand. "Give those two a chance to head for the crypt."

"What if waiting gets Cila killed?" Callum demanded.

Mallory smiled when the mage stumbled out of the way of Cila's darts. "She's not doing too bad on her own."

"Stop messing around," Rass ordered. "Kill her. We don't need her anymore."

"They're out of sight. Mage first and then the rogue. Mallory still attacks everyone." Ryan fired at the mage.

Mallory did as Ryan had suggested, attacking the mage first, then the rogue and lastly Rass.

"We're under attack." Rass ran towards Mallory's location.

"Relocate." Ryan grabbed Mallory's arm and tugged her to the side. "Keep attacking, but keep moving between attacks so they don't know exactly where we are."

When Ryan let her go, Mallory kept moving. She paused and threw a fireball at Rass. She hurried away when he changed directions, coming straight towards her. A glance showed the rest of her companions had moved further away. A smile slowly formed. She could lead Rass away long enough for her companions to take out the rest. He was probably the highest level and someone they didn't want to face whilst trying to fight others. She ran back in his direction, throwing a fireball at him before she headed away from the ruins and her companions.

Rass ran after her. "You can't outrun me. Not with my stamina."

Mallory checked her stamina, slowing. She'd forgotten about that. What amount was his stamina? Much higher than hers? Hearing his footsteps come closer, she glanced over her shoulder. She threw a fireball at him, hoping it hit. She didn't keep watch to find out if it did. She kept running.

"I know you."

Mallory had no idea what to do next. Her plan wasn't going the way she'd thought it would. She was going to get herself killed. It would have been nice to attack Cutthroat Harbour while having three revives. Seeing her stamina was nearly out, she spun to face Rass, coming to a stop. She threw a fireball at him, slipping behind a tree when he attacked.

"You will pay. And so will the frog mage for hiring you." Rass came around the tree, attacking again.

Mallory stumbled backwards, feeling the rush of air from his longsword. She thought of the frog mage and all his frogs. She doubted Rass would stop at killing just him. "Who?" She slipped behind another tree, angling back towards the ruins.

"The one who hired you. He owns a ridiculous amount of frogs." Rass stalked towards her. "They can die too."

"I have no idea who you're talking about. We came after you. Tracked you down." She dodged another attack, throwing a fireball at him.

"You're trying to protect him."

She considered drawing her sword, but there was no way she could beat him in close combat. She kept retreating towards the ruins. Surely they'd taken out at least half of the enemies and could cope with Rass joining the fight. "Think what you want. Doesn't change that we came after you. No one sent us. Well, not exactly. Did you know there's a big reward for your death? We're going to claim it. Once we kill you enough times to take out all your revives." She winced when her shoulder hit a tree as she dodged another attack from Rass.

"Who put a bounty out on me?" Rass stopped

attacking, but continued to stalk her as she retreated. "Give me a name and I'll let you survive this day."

Mallory shrugged, trying to sound unconcerned. "I've got revives to spare. Not that it'd matter if I didn't. I don't have a name. Only a location to collect the reward once you're permanently dead." She had no idea if it was a good idea to have warned him, but at least he was now focused on getting information instead of killing her. She was sure that would change soon enough. Nor was she about to tell him it was merfolk who wanted him dead.

"You lie."

She met his sharp, blue eyes. There was no way at all he could tell if she told the truth or not. He didn't know her. She smiled at him. "You wish."

"Is it one of my family's enemies? Or is it one of mine?"

Again she shrugged, continuing to retreat. "You're wasting your time questioning me. I've already told you everything I know."

"Then you can die since you told me nothing of any use to me."

She tried to dodge out of the way, but tripped over a branch, landing sprawled on the ground, the wand knocked from her hand. She stared up at Rass.

He grinned, not a single bit of humour in his

expression. "You shouldn't have messed with me. You're going to regret it for the rest of your very short life."

Her hand closed over her dagger. The sword swung towards her and she rolled out of the way, surging up as she drew the dagger, driving it into him before pulling it out and spinning away. Warm blood coated her hand as she ran towards her wand, trying not to think about the blood.

"Mallory!" Ryan called out to her.

Before she could reply, the sword bit into her arm, pain shooting through her. She stumbled, scooping up her wand as she faced Rass who was about to attack again. She dived to the side, again landing sprawled on the ground, quickly checking her stats as she rolled to face Rass. She'd lost twelve health points. Another two attacks like that and she'd be dead. "Ryan! Here." She launched a fireball at Rass before rolling out of the way, the sword striking the ground next to her.

"Calling for help won't do you any good. They won't reach you in time. And when they arrive, I'll kill them too."

She had a bad feeling he was right about her not surviving, but she wasn't about to let him know she agreed. "It won't stop us from coming after you." The sword came for her again and she started to roll out of the way.

An arrow struck Rass, causing him to miss Mallory. It was followed by a second arrow.

Mallory scrambled to her feet, casting a fireball at Rass and sinking her dagger into him again. Surely Rass couldn't have much health left.

"Get out of the way, Mallory," Ryan ordered.

Rass met her gaze, anger and a promise in his eyes. "I won't rest until I find you. There's nowhere you'll be able to hide from me. You and your friends." Rass struck her with his sword.

Chapter Thirty-One

Pain flared and Mallory drew her dagger from Rass' body, continuing to meet his gaze. "It won't matter. Every time we see you, you'll die." She drove the dagger into him again. He vanished and she staggered forward, her hand coated in blood, her clothes splattered with it. She spun at a sound behind her.

Ryan slipped his bow over his head and one arm as he ran forward to wrap his arms around her, holding her close. "What were you thinking?"

"That you had too many to fight already." She returned his hug, wishing she'd had the chance to put her weapons away first.

Callum joined them, Smudge still in the sling he wore. "Hope you're planning to clean that dagger before you use it to cut food again."

Drawing away from Ryan, Mallory laughed. "As if

I'd use it in the state it's in." She made a face, glancing around the area. Her smile faded. "Where's Danni?"

"Trying to convince Cila to wait for us to escort her back to the frog mage." Ryan drew Mallory back to him. "You're down to fifteen health. Have a potion."

"I was going to use my new spell," Mallory said.

"Have it in case we're attacked before you can regain a decent amount of health," Ryan said.

Mallory checked all of their health. Danae had lost none while Ryan had lost ten and Callum had lost six. "We're going to need a vat of health potion to take to Cutthroat Harbour with us." Before she drew away from him, she pressed her lips against his. She smiled up at him. "We survived. We survived a level four hellion." The feeling she normally had after facing a boss and winning, washed over her. "Maybe we can do this. Rescue everyone from Cutthroat Harbour."

Ryan grinned down at her. "Of course we can. How many times do I need to tell you? We've got this."

Chuckling, she drew away from him and had a health potion, giving him the empty vial to put in the backpack. "Do you think the frog mage will fill nine potion vials for us?" She walked beside Ryan and Callum, heading back to the ruins.

Ryan shrugged. "We can only ask. I wonder what Danni needs to make potion vials."

"We should be levelling Danni up too," Callum said. "We really need health potions. It'd be good if she has the CAS points to add to alchemy as soon as she claims her recipes from the academy. If we level both Danni and Mallory up Danni could make health potions and Mallory could improve them. We'd be set."

As they returned, Mallory worked on healing Ryan and Callum. One point each at a time, not wanting to let her mana get too low in case they were attacked. When they stepped out of the treeline, Mallory had only healed them two health points each.

Danae stood out the front of the ruined buildings, arguing with Cila who kept shaking her head. Danae threw her hands in the air. "I give up. Do what you want. Tell him we tried to escort you back, but you wouldn't listen. And let our companion know we're safe."

Cila, who had started to turn away, faced Danae again. She croaked.

"You do know I can't understand you," Danae said.

Cila croaked, moving closer to Danae.

"While you finish talking to the frog, we'll search

the ruins." Callum strode towards the nearest ruined building.

Mallory started to follow him, pausing when the journal icon appeared in the corner of her vision. It was another notification about location experience. "Twenty XP for finding ruins. They're as good as a dungeon."

"Brodie's going to want to come here. I bet he's sitting at the frog mage's place watching every little bit of XP we gain." Ryan headed towards one of the other ruined buildings.

Cila jumped in front of Ryan, croaking several times.

Ryan gestured towards the building he'd been heading towards. "Are you trying to stop us from searching?"

Cila shook her head.

Mallory moved closer to Ryan, staring at the extremely large frog. She was a lot bigger than her children. "I think it's the mention of Brodie."

Cila looked towards her, nodding.

Danae joined them. "Finally. What about Brodie?"

Cila croaked.

Danae sighed. "Sorry. I forgot. Yes or no questions only. But it's not easy when I have no idea what question to ask."

"She obviously wants to know something about Brodie," Mallory said.

"I'll leave you both to figure it out while I search the place with Callum." Ryan stepped around Cila.

Mallory stared at the frog. "I really don't think we're going to figure it out. Unless she suddenly learns how to speak English. Or how to write in the dirt. I guess we can ask the frog mage what she was going on about when we collect Brodie."

Callum came running out of the ruined building.

Mallory reached for her wand.

He waved an object above his head. "Look what I found."

Ryan came out of the building he was searching. "Try holding it still so we can actually see what you're waving around."

Callum stopped waving the object and held it with both hands. One at each end. "A brass spyglass. We finally have a brass spyglass."

Mallory took several steps towards him. She stared disbelievingly at the object. "It works? It's not broken or anything?"

Callum peered at her through the spyglass. "I can see your health. It works."

Ryan took the spyglass from Callum and looked at Mallory through it. "Yep, it works."

Callum took the spyglass back. "You've got the pocket watch. And the compass. You can't have all the good gear." He took a holster out of his satchel. "And look what it came with."

Mallory laughed. "Brodie is going to be so annoyed he had to stay back with the frog mage."

Cila croaked, making them all laugh. The frog looked at each of them, croaking again.

Callum finished putting the brass spyglass on his belt. "This is going to change everything. We'll know how much health they have and can sort out our plan of attack much better."

"It'd be even better if we could use it while fighting." Mallory couldn't help thinking about her fight with Rass. She looked at the blood that coated her hand and was splattered across her clothes. "I need to get cleaned up."

Ryan gestured towards the ruined building he'd been checking. "They've set up a wash area back there. A bowl and jug of water and a barrel nearby that's three quarters filled with water."

Mallory was halfway towards the building when she realised there were only three bodies scattered across the area. "Where's the second mage?"

Ryan shrugged. "Must have had a revive."

"Great," Mallory said dryly. "I hope that doesn't

mean we're going to have two enemies hunting us down."

"I don't think so," Danae said. "He didn't seem like the sort of person interested in tracking down those who'd killed him and risking his life again. At the end, he was trying to run."

Mallory nodded. Danae was probably right. But they still had Rass after them. An image of his sharp, blue eyes filled her mind. His eyes as they'd been when filled with anger and a promise to come after her. And she didn't doubt he would. Heading for the wash area, she tried to convince herself it was better that he came after them rather than the frog mage. Right this minute, she didn't find that thought comforting.

Chapter Thirty-Two

Once she'd cleaned the blood off her hands and dagger, Mallory helped search the ruins and bodies. Besides the brass spyglass, they also got a tent, two bedrolls, enough coffee for six cups, four iron throwing knives, a brown dress that looked like it would fit Mallory, a dagger, a short sword, a three metre square piece of canvas, a wooden bucket they tipped the water from, a leather belt, two pairs of dark brown trousers, a four metre length of rope, a book titled Legend Of The Ancestral King and a small corked jar with a fine white powder in it. They also gained three gold, nine silver and fifteen copper pieces and a letter addressed to Rass telling him to see that the extended invisibility potion was in Cutthroat Harbour by the fifteenth of the month. In four days time.

Not finding the potion Rass had taken from the

frog mage, Mallory held up the book. "Do you think the potion they wanted the frog mage to make has something to do with the dark forces going after the ancestral king?"

Ryan took the book, flicking through the pages. "It could be."

"Do you think it'll be a problem for the frog mage that the potion won't work?" Mallory asked.

Ryan closed the book, meeting Mallory's gaze. "Shouldn't be a problem if we stop Hisoki."

"I hope so." Mallory couldn't help thinking about Rass threatening to go after the frog mage when he'd thought that was the reason they'd come after him.

Callum glanced skywards. "That took longer than I expected. Who wants to help me load the gear onto the horses?"

While Ryan and Callum loaded everything onto the horses, the two of them brought back to the ruins, Mallory showed the jar she'd found in the wash area, to Danae. "Do you know what it is?"

Danae uncorked the jar. "Tooth powder. I was going to need to buy some of this soon. My jar is getting low."

Mallory frowned, Danae's comments not having made sense. "Tooth powder?"

Danae nodded. "Yes, to clean your teeth."

Mallory stared at the powder. "How does that work?"

"You rub it over your teeth and leave it for a few seconds before rinsing it off." Danae pushed the cork back into place. "How do you clean your teeth in your world?"

Callum looked up from where he strapped the bedrolls onto Bug. "Toothbrushes and toothpaste."

"You use a brush on your teeth. Like you use for your hair?" Danae asked.

Ryan chuckled. "Nowhere near that large." He gestured towards the jar Danae continued to hold. "It works? It keeps your teeth from getting cavities."

Danae held the jar out to Mallory. "It keeps your teeth clean and healthy."

Mallory took the jar and slipped it inside her satchel. "Perfect. It might be a bit lame, but I was starting to miss brushing my teeth every day."

Ryan put the rolled up tent on Augusta. "You weren't the only one."

As soon as they'd finished putting all the gear on the horses, wrapping most of it up in the canvas, they headed back towards the frog mage's place, leading the horses. Cila jumped along beside them. Mallory continued to heal everyone. The half hour walk back gave her enough time to not only heal Ryan, Callum and herself, but also repair her shirt with mend I. During the walk, Callum talked about the fact that Smudge had levelled up and had gained the ability to wear leather armour. The only stat that had changed was that Smudge's crit attack had gone up by one, which had disappointed Callum who'd hoped his health would go up.

As they neared the frog mage's place, Callum turned to Ryan. "What's the time?"

Ryan took out the pocket watch. "Almost four. Why? You got plans?"

"Yep. I was invited to check out some musical instruments," Callum said.

"I don't think that was all he was interested in sharing with you," Ryan said.

Callum smiled. "Good."

Brodie came out of the frog mage's cottage to greet them, using his crutches, Fang at his side. "About time you got back. Although it wasn't too bad waiting here for you. Did you know the frog mage likes to cook too? He gave me several recipes. They're on the table because I don't have a belt pouch for them. I don't suppose you found one on any of the kidnappers. My pig really needs his own belt pouch."

"We found something better." Callum held up the brass spyglass.

"Hell yeah. Who gets it?" Brodie asked.

"Callum found it," Mallory said.

"That's not fair. I wasn't there to find it. And what about all the XP for locations you got. I saw your XP jump up," Brodie said.

Ryan tied Bug up beside Bobbi. "We'll take you there once we're finished here." He turned to the frog mage who was making a fuss of Cila. "She was trying to tell us something, but we couldn't figure it out."

The frog mage rose to his feet, frequently glancing at Cila. "She was worried about me being here on my own. She's glad to hear you left Brodie behind to keep me company."

"Lucky she hadn't met him then," Callum said softly.

Mallory tried not to laugh. She cleared her throat. "I don't want to rush you, but we have other things to do this afternoon."

Ryan grinned at his brother. "Callum has somewhere to be before sunset."

Callum smiled, remaining silent.

Brodie nodded towards the frog mage. "He said he'd fill any potion vials you emptied. I told him Mal had to use a health potion while rescuing Cila."

"What did you do? Spend the entire time watching our stats?" Mallory asked.

Brodie shrugged. "It wasn't like I could go with you. And what were you doing letting your health get so low?"

Mallory glanced at the frog mage before returning her attention to her brother. "I'll tell you all about it later. On our way to the locations so you can gain some XP."

Ryan handed over the nine empty potion vials to the frog mage. "I'll put the gear the horses are carrying in the panniers you emptied while you sort the potions."

The frog mage nodded. "I put all the bags in the panniers." He headed inside with one last look at Cila.

"Someone needs to get my recipes off the table for me." Brodie glanced at his belt pouch, Not For Bacon poking his head out of it. "I can't exactly carry them while using crutches."

Mallory followed Brodie inside. On the table were several pieces of paper and a small frog. She eyed the frog, wondering if it was safe to pick up the paper.

"Isn't he cool?" Brodie gestured towards the frog.

Mallory kept watch on the frog as she took the paper from the table. "Ahh… yeah. Sure."

"The frog mage said I can have him if I want. Think he'd get along with my pig and Fang?" Brodie asked.

Mallory folded the paper and tucked it into her satchel. She faced the door where Cila blocked their exit. "He might be little now, but you do realise how big he'll grow, don't you?"

Brodie faced the doorway. "How long do you think it takes to reach that size?"

Mallory shrugged.

Brodie looked from Cila to the frog on the table. "He probably wouldn't like some of the places we're planning to go."

"Probably not." Mallory headed for the door, waiting for Cila to get out of the way before she stepped outside.

Ryan looked up from his conversation with Callum. "We ready to go yet?"

Before Mallory could answer, the frog mage joined them, carrying a basket that contained potion vials and two parchments. "There were too many for me to carry." He pointed to the health potions. "The nine you wanted filled, plus two extra."

Mallory took the potions and put them in her satchel. "Thank you."

"These four are invisibility potions." The frog mage pointed to the vials that contained a milky coloured liquid. "They last for thirty seconds."

The frog mage pointed to the last two potions

in the basket. They were a shimmery blue colour. "Water breathing potions. Ten minutes each." When Mallory took the two potions, he picked up the parchment. "A level one and a level two spell. I hope you find them useful."

Mallory slipped them into her satchel as well. She would look at them later. It seemed kind of rude to check them now. "Thank you."

"No, thank you for helping me get Cila back." The frog mage looked down at Cila who was at his side. "I'd be devastated if anything happened to her." He glanced around the group. "Good luck with whatever other plans you have this afternoon."

Ryan chuckled, glancing at his brother. "I'm sure some of us will appreciate that luck."

Chapter Thirty-Three

Mallory thanked the frog mage, her words echoed by the rest of her companions. Once Ryan had helped Brodie onto Bug, they headed towards the ruins. As they walked, Mallory checked her journal, assuming that the icon in the corner of her vision was from the completed quest. *Kidnapped Frog: You escorted Cila home to the frog mage. You were rewarded with a variety of potions and two spells for your party. You also earned twenty experience points each.* Mallory smiled. It didn't matter what the spells were. The potions had been worth the effort of going after Cila.

"We can go after the stick now we have water breathing potions," Brodie said.

"It's a staff," Mallory said. "And have you forgotten about Cutthroat Harbour?"

"Not yet. After. My knee still needs to heal too," Brodie said.

"What about the undines?" Callum asked.

Danae glanced around the group. "You're going after the missing mage staff people have been talking about in Wayholt?"

Mallory spoke before Brodie could. "We haven't decided. There are other things we need to do first. Someone else might find it before we have the chance to look for it."

"We're taking too long to do everything," Brodie muttered. "All the good quests will be gone if we don't get things done quicker."

Mallory glanced at her brother's knee. "We aren't the ones slowing things down." She smiled when he muttered under his breath, his words too quiet for her to hear. When he remained silent, she scanned the area. Other than a couple of rabbits, the area was quiet.

Fang started after the rabbits. Brodie called her back. He had to call her to him several times when she spotted one of the small creatures. Each time she reluctantly returned to his side.

Reaching the ruins, Brodie didn't need to dismount to gain his experience points. He rode to the crypt the moment he'd gained them, needing to dismount and enter the building to gain experience points from visiting that location.

Brodie crossed the room, his crutches loud against the stone floor, to stare at the stairs leading downwards. "I bet this is the crypt the skeletons came from that attacked us the last time we were in Wayholt. We should do the quest for here."

"Mallory needs to finish levelling up. Preferably before six," Ryan said.

"I thought we were heading back to Wayholt." Callum glanced in the direction of the village.

"She only has another fifty XP to gain her next CAS point," Ryan said. "There are a lot of herbs in this area."

"Probably because we haven't been here harvesting any." Mallory dreaded the thought of gathering herbs again.

"Gain your next CAS point then we'll head to Wayholt and take a break," Ryan said.

"Can we come back here and do the crypt quest after a break?" Brodie headed outside.

Ryan nodded towards Brodie's crutches. "How are you meant to do a fighting quest hobbling around on them?"

"You can all do the fighting and I'll be here to get the XP at the end of the quest." Brodie handed the crutches to Ryan and let Callum help him onto Bug.

Mallory gathered the herbs she saw nearby while

Brodie argued with Ryan. She smiled at Danae when she pointed out another lot of herbs. It was a slower process without the extra help. They worked their way through the area, heading towards Wayholt. It took Mallory twenty minutes to gain a CAS point, not bothering to earn any experience points towards the next CAS point before continuing directly to Wayholt. She only had another two CAS points to gain to reach level thirty-five apothecary. She didn't like her chances of getting them done today.

Ryan checked the pocket watch as he entered Wayholt. "Five thirty. There's no way Mallory is going to gain another two CAS points before six."

Mallory smiled at hearing him confirm what she'd been thinking.

"You don't need me to go to the apothecary with you, do you?" Callum glanced at the tavern ahead of them.

Ryan chuckled, clapping his brother on the back. "We'll meet you at Sarisa's."

With a nod and a smile, Callum strode towards the tavern.

Mallory watched him enter the building. "Do you think he'll be okay? I mean, how safe is it to walk around Wayholt on your own?"

"It's safe," Danae said. "He'll be fine."

They headed to Sarisa's place so they could leave Augusta and Bobbi behind and let Sarisa know Danae was safe. They learned Ninette and the wagoner were still out and Emica and Jorgen had gone for a walk.

Mallory stared at Welby when he told them the information. "Together?"

Welby nodded, Roast also nodding.

Mallory slowly shook her head. It was the last thing she'd expected to hear.

Brodie remained on Bug. "Are we going to the apothecary shop? I don't want to be late and miss out."

They reached the shop early and had to wait ten minutes before Brodie could have his treatment. The apothecary also reminded Mallory to use the salve on him. She paid the apothecary the five gold pieces for the treatment before she used the salve on Brodie.

He stared at his knee as it was splinted again. "It feels heaps better."

"That'll be because you're forty-five percent through the healing process," Ryan said.

"Stay off it," the apothecary warned. "Do not ruin all the work I've done."

"Or waste the money we've spent on you," Mallory said.

"I didn't say I was going to walk on it. Just that it

feels a lot better." Brodie got to his feet with the help of the crutches.

When they returned to Sarisa's place, they found Ninette waiting for them. "I was hoping to be here when you returned earlier, but the blacksmith took longer than I thought he would to clean the sword."

"Where is it?" Brodie asked.

Ninette gestured to the back of the wagon. "It's a longsword so it was a bit awkward for me to carry." She took off her cane backpack and rummaged about in it. "I also bought a leather-bound notebook. There was an accident during transport and the cover's been scratched up. I managed to talk them down to six gold pieces. There are a hundred pages. That should give you plenty of space for your recipes." She held out the leather-bound notebook to Brodie. "Uhm." She lowered her hand with a look at the crutches. "Sorry."

"How much did the sword cost to clean?" Ryan asked.

"Seven gold pieces." Ninette gave the remaining seven gold pieces to Mallory, along with the notebook. "He said it cost more because it was a longsword."

Ryan picked the sword up off the back of the wagon. "Nice." He frowned. "You weren't wrong about it being awkward to hold. Not as awkward as a dagger or something that isn't suited to my class."

"What's it made of?" Brodie came closer.

"Steel. The blacksmith said it's been enchanted. He doesn't know how many enchantments are on it, but considering it's superior quality and that it contains a gem, the sword could have two enchantments and the gem might have one on it to magnify the sword's enchantments." Ninette glanced at the sword. "It could be a pretty powerful weapon."

Ryan returned the sword to the back of the wagon. "It might be worth keeping. I doubt we'd be able to afford a powerful weapon any time too soon."

Mallory sighed. "Why do we always need to level up?"

"We're going to have to spend more time on levelling up," Ryan said. "Instead of getting caught up in questing and exploring."

Mallory met his gaze. "Are you saying we shouldn't be doing all these quests?"

"Time sensitive quests are different," Ryan said.

"We need to level me up as soon as my knee is better," Brodie said.

Mallory laughed, catching sight of the humour in Ryan's eyes before she turned to Brodie. "Yeah, we know. It's not fair."

Chapter Thirty-Four

While they waited for the sun to set, they sorted out their new gear. Mallory gave the four throwing knives to Brodie and Ryan helped her wash the new clothes. Danae also set a batch of health tea to steep since they'd run out. This new batch would restore two health points a cup.

When Emica and Jorgen returned, Mallory gave each of them a health potion and Ninette two since she'd be staying behind to guard the wagoner. The other six she kept in her satchel to share amongst her and her companions for when they needed them.

When the sun set, they lit one of the lanterns and headed to the tavern to collect Callum, rather than wait for him to return. As they left, Sarisa let them know dinner would be ready in half an hour. On the way they talked about Kruth's offer and Deneg's request, deciding to accept both.

Entering the tavern, Mallory spotted Callum at a table not far from where Deneg sat on a stool playing his gittern. Kruth sat with him, but neither seemed to be talking. Both listened to the music. She led the way to the table. Her gaze was drawn to the two marks at Callum's neck as she sat across from him.

"Looks like you had an interesting afternoon." Ryan's gaze momentarily rested on Callum's neck.

"What were you doing making out with-" Brodie began.

Mallory elbowed her brother who was sitting beside her before he could finish his sentence. Had he forgotten how good Deneg's hearing was? She turned to Kruth. "If you're still interested-"

"I am," Kruth said.

"Think you can be ready to leave by morning?" Ryan asked.

"I can be ready to leave tonight," Kruth offered.

"What about Deneg?" Callum asked.

"We can help him get to Velkden." Mallory looked towards the vampire who nodded at her. She smiled, returning his nod before she faced her companions. "What if I don't get enough XP tonight?"

Ryan rose to his feet. "You will. We better head back to Sarisa's so we're not late for dinner."

"I wonder what it is." Brodie used the crutches to

get to his feet and crossed the room, leading the way once he'd said goodbye to Kruth.

Along with the rest of them, Mallory echoed Brodie's goodbye and hurried after him through the crowded tavern. The walk back to Sarisa's was quiet. Mallory had no idea why everyone else was silent, but she was tired after her late night and early morning. As well as all the gathering she'd done. She dreaded the thought of the last two CAS points she needed to earn. All she wanted to do was have dinner, soak in the tub then go to sleep. Maybe even read the book they'd found at the ruins while she soaked in the tub. She doubted that was going to happen.

Once again they sat around the campfire to eat, Sarisa joining them. She'd made a creamy vegetable bake seasoned with herbs which Fang also ate, Smudge happily having the raw fish Sarisa gave him. While Sarisa and Brodie talked recipes, Mallory tried not to nod off over her meal. She considered checking the recipes and spells from the frog mage, but it seemed like too much effort.

Ryan, who sat beside her, nudged her. "Do I take it your vote for doing the crypt tonight will be no?"

"I'm so tired I don't know how I'll stay awake long enough to get those last two CAS points." Mallory had another mouthful of her food.

Danae leaned close after glancing at her mother. "Rass and his people might have been all that was keeping the skeletons from escaping the crypt."

"What if we told the mercenaries?" Mallory asked.

"I doubt they'd go. The reward you gain is random," Danae said.

"What reward?" Ryan asked.

"At the end, after you've dealt with whatever is preventing the dead from resting in peace. You place your hand on the altar and tell them 'rest in peace' and a gift will appear on the altar in front of your hand. Certain gifts and coins are stored in a special vault that the magic accesses when things go wrong and someone fixes the problem. Sometimes though, there's nothing left for the magic to access," Danae said.

"But the crypt isn't that far from the village. Surely the mercenaries wouldn't let something happen to their own village." Mallory had the last mouthful of food.

"They'll expect to be paid." Danae took Mallory's empty plate, putting it on top of hers. "A random reward that might or might not appear will not be good enough for them."

Ryan turned to Mallory. "If something happens, it could be our fault."

Mallory sighed heavily. "What if we get up early in the morning and deal with it? I really can't do it tonight. I'd probably get myself killed. And what are we going to do about going home? We can't exactly leave while Brodie's knee hasn't healed. And that won't be until the morning of the fourteenth. Three days away."

Ryan shrugged. "I guess we wait until he's better before we return home."

"What if it's somewhere dangerous? How can we leave everyone to deal with that on their own?" Mallory asked.

Ryan captured her hand, cradling it in his. "We wouldn't do that to them. We'll figure something out. When we know where we are then. Anything could happen in three days. Look how much we've done in eleven days."

"I suppose." She paused a moment. "I'm just worried about not spending equal time between the two worlds while we can't afford those potions."

Ryan momentarily tightened his hold on her hand. "We'll figure it out. Now, are you ready to keep gathering? You should gain three CAS points so you have a point spare. It won't take much longer to gain a third point. It also makes sense to gain enough CAS points to reach character level four when you're so close."

"I suppose I should get it over and done with, but I'm not gaining three." She rose to her feet, holding onto his hand.

They argued it out, needing to head twenty minutes from Wayholt before Mallory was able to start gathering resources. In an effort to be done as quickly as possible, she didn't take turns with anyone to gather resources, eventually convinced to gain three CAS points. She doubted she'd manage to stay awake long enough if she took any breaks. Instead, she had some of the health tea half an hour after beginning to gather and was able to continue for another half an hour and gain the four hundred and eight experience points she needed for the three CAS points. It brought her up to character level four.

This time, instead of waiting until she arrived at Sarisa's place, she sorted out her stats on the way back. She started with adding points into apothecary, bringing it up to level thirty-five. She checked her journal, wondering why she'd waited to do it all at once when she saw the long list of notifications. She glanced past the ones that didn't mention any new abilities, reading over the rest of them.

You have reached level one apothecary. You now have

the ability to use diagnostic and surgical instruments. You have reached level five apothecary. You now have the ability to recognise common ailments. You have reached level six apothecary. You now have the ability to use enchanted tools and instruments. You have reached level eight apothecary. You now have the ability to treat common ailments. You have reached level ten apothecary. You now have the ability to recognise common diseases. You have reached level thirteen apothecary. You now have the ability to treat common diseases. You have reached level fifteen apothecary. You now have the ability to set broken bones. You have reached level seventeen apothecary. You now have the ability to do basic surgery. You have reached level twenty apothecary. You now have the ability to recognise uncommon ailments. You have reached level twenty-three apothecary. You now have the ability to treat uncommon ailments. You have reached level twenty-five apothecary. You now have the ability to recognise uncommon diseases. You have reached level twenty-eight apothecary. You now have the ability to treat uncommon diseases. You have reached level thirty apothecary. You now have the ability to recognise rare ailments. You have reached level thirty-three apothecary. You now have the ability to treat rare ailments. You have reached level thirty-four apothecary. You now have the ability to recognise *rare diseases. You have reached level thirty-five apothecary. You now have the ability to use weak rapid mend on broken bones.*

She couldn't help wondering if any of those new abilities would make a difference for her back home. And if they did, what kind of difference. She smiled at Ryan when he slipped his arm around her waist when she stumbled. He looked as exhausted as she felt. She had no idea how they'd manage if anything attacked.

Chapter Thirty-Five

Returning to sorting out her stats, it took Mallory a few minutes to decide what to put her attribute points in. Her character point went in mage, but she was worried about her health levels and mana since they were heading to Cutthroat Harbour and wasn't sure how many points to put into them. In the end, she decided to put one point in each of strength, intelligence and wisdom and two in constitution.

She frowned as she looked over her new stats. Did she need to start putting some points in dexterity, charisma and luck? They were only at five. Her strength was now eight, constitution thirteen and both intelligence and wisdom were eleven. Which made the other three attributes look really low. She had no idea what she should do, just like when it came to a lot of things in this world. But at least now she had thirty-nine health, sixty-five stamina and fifty-five mana. That should help when they faced the dark forces in Cutthroat Harbour.

Arriving back at Sarisa's they took turns using the bathroom, sitting around the campfire talking while they each waited for their turn. Brodie had a cup of his ale, also giving a cupful to Danae, while Callum had a cup of his wine. He sat close to the fire so he could use the light to read Legend Of The Ancestral King. Mallory used the bathroom first, joining everyone once she'd had a quick wash, having longingly eyed the fireplace while washing her clothes and hanging them over the wooden rack to dry overnight.

She sat by the fire, taking out her notebook. "I thought you'd have had some of your ale long before now." She grinned at her brother.

He glared at her. "You won't buy any so I have to make it last."

She laughed at his comment, writing in her notebook, only half listening to her brother when he began to complain about how far behind he was in levels and that they needed armour. She grinned at Ryan's reply.

"Just for your knees or full body armour?"

"Very funny," Brodie muttered when everyone laughed.

Callum came out of the bathroom. "What is funny?"

"Armour for Brodie's knees," Ryan said as Emica strode to the bathroom.

Finished writing in her notebook, Mallory slipped it inside her satchel and took out Brodie's recipes, thinking she should probably distract him from the insults he was trading with Callum. Before things went from friendly to nasty with how tired everyone was. "Did you want me to tuck your recipes inside your book?"

Brodie held out his hand. "I can't believe he gave me so many. He also kept thanking me for everyone going after Cila."

Mallory leaned forward to give him the recipes, glancing at Callum who'd returned to reading the book.

"What recipes did you get?" Danae asked.

"Coastal crab salad, spaghetti and bear bolognese, butterscotch shortbread, creamy vegetable soup and also spicy pancakes," Brodie said.

"Creamy vegetable soup sounds like something that could be made in a pot over a campfire." Callum looked up from the book, turning to Mallory. "What spells did he give you?"

She took them out and angled them so she could

read the details by the light of the campfire. "Poison dart which is a level one spell and lightning trap which is level two."

"Why haven't you learned them yet?" Brodie asked. "Lightning trap sounds cool."

Mallory looked at Danae. "Is there a maximum amount of spells you can have?"

Danae shook her head. "You can learn hundreds if you want."

Yawning, Mallory put the spells in her satchel. "I'll learn them in the morning. I'm so tired I'd probably read them out incorrectly."

"It wouldn't matter. You just keep reading the words until you get them correct," Danae said.

"Then I'm definitely reading them in the morning. It'd probably take me an hour to get them right and I'd rather be sleeping." Mallory started to rise to her feet, remaining where she was when Callum spoke.

"We can't let them set the ancestral king free." He closed the book, glancing around the group. "If this book is the story of what happened, like it says it is, then it'd be a really bad idea to let the crown be removed."

Danae glanced at the book Callum held. "It's the truth."

Mallory started to ask what was in the book,

shaking her head instead. "I don't want to know. Not tonight." She rose to her feet. "I'll read it tomorrow." Stumbling inside, she removed her boots, weapons and belt before stretching out beside the fire, tugging a blanket over herself. Closing her eyes, she fell instantly asleep.

Mallory woke, heart racing, sitting up to glance around the room. It was filled with shadows, only the glow of the coals in the fireplace casting any light. She tried to forget the dream that had woken her, but the final images remained. Rass as he'd looked in those few moments before she'd killed him.

"Mallory?" Ryan, who'd been lying beside her, sat up. "What's wrong?" He spoke softly, leaning close to her.

"We're going to have to spend more time levelling up." She leaned against him when he wrapped his arms around her. "We need to out level Rass."

Ryan's arms tightened around her. "We'll figure something out."

Brodie sat up. "Is it morning already?"

Ryan let go of Mallory and rummaged around in his belt pouch, which was lying on the floor beside where he slept. He took out the pocket watch, leaning close to the glow of the coals. "It's only five. It won't be daylight until six."

Callum groaned. "Why is everyone talking? Go back to sleep."

Smudge made several soft sounds, snuggling in closer to Callum.

"I'm too awake to go back to sleep." Brodie grabbed his crutches. "We should get up and have breakfast then get started on the crypt." He awkwardly rose to his feet.

Mallory doubted she'd be able to sleep now either. Not after her dream about Rass. Instead of her being the one to stab him, he'd been the one to stab her. "The sooner we get finished with the crypt the sooner we can head to Cutthroat Harbour."

Brodie stared at her for a moment. "We can start getting ready?"

Before Mallory could speak, Callum did. "No. Go back to sleep."

"I can make spicy pancakes. Sarisa said I can help myself to any ingredients I want since the vegetables we brought back for her will save her a lot of money." When Callum made no comment, Brodie continued speaking. "I'll make a cup of coffee for you too."

Callum rolled over onto his back, Smudge protesting about being disturbed. "I hung my satchel on the back of one of the kitchen chairs."

Brodie started towards the table, stopping and

turning to face Mallory. "What about Danni? We can't wake her without disturbing her mum." Brodie glanced at the closed door of the bedroom.

"Don't worry, we're not about to leave her behind," Mallory said. "We'll get organised as much as possible and then wake her. Maybe by then it will almost be daylight."

Chapter Thirty-Six

Ryan built up the fire while Brodie prepared the food and Mallory got ready for the morning. By the time Brodie was serving breakfast, Danae and Sarisa were awake. So too was Ninette and all three joined them. The meal was fairly quiet, none of them talking much until it was almost over. Mallory read Legend Of The Ancestral King while she ate, having started it while she waited for breakfast to be cooked. Reaching the end, she wondered if she should have waited until after they'd been to Cutthroat Harbour to read the book. It would be very bad if they failed their quest and Hisoki removed the crown of the ancestral King.

Ryan turned to Ninette. "Can you see what you can do about crutches for Brodie? Find out if there's a pair we can purchase. I don't know when, or if, we'll be back here."

"Remind everyone we're leaving for Cutthroat

Harbour when we get back from the crypt," Callum said.

Ryan shook his head. "Velkden will be far enough for the day. We don't know what we might face at Cutthroat Harbour. So it'd be best not to arrive exhausted."

"Let Kruth know too," Mallory said. "How much money do you think you'll need to buy crutches?"

"I'll arrange for you to buy them when you return. It won't take long. You could buy them on the way out of the village or I could go back and pay for them while you finish getting ready to leave," Ninette said.

"That'll work." Ryan rose to his feet. "We should probably get started. It'll take us five hours to reach Velkden so we need to be done with the crypt by midday at the latest." Ryan checked the pocket watch. "That's just over six hours away."

"It shouldn't take that long." Danae helped her mother clear the table.

"What about those spells you're going to learn?" Brodie asked Mallory.

She'd forgotten about them. "We haven't left yet." She took out the spells. She probably would have remembered them when it was time to leave. Once she'd finished learning poison dart, the parchment became smoke and dissipated. Upon learning lightning trap, it crackled and flared, vanishing in a streak of lightning. She stared at her hands. "Do they ever harm you when they vanish?"

"Not that I've heard of," Danae said.

"They shouldn't do." After a glance at Mallory and her companions, Sarisa turned to Danae. "Don't go rushing into danger."

Danae hugged her mother. "I'll be fine."

Mallory noticed Danae hadn't promised her mother anything.

Brodie held up his belt and belt pouch, not having put them back on when he'd woken. "Where is my pig?"

It took them ten minutes to find him. Sarisa was the one who found him under her bench, munching on an apple. "He can stay here with me while you're at the crypt. It might be safer for him."

"You sure?" Brodie asked.

Sarisa nodded, patting Not For Bacon on the head. "I'll look after him and keep him out of mischief."

"Now he's been found, time to heal your knee a bit more." Mallory gestured towards the chair, her gaze on Brodie.

Once seated, he looked up at her. "You do know what you're doing, don't you?"

She grinned as she knelt in front of him and rested

her hands on his knee. "Guess we'll soon find out." Ignoring Brodie's protests, she activated weak rapid mend. It used ten mana. She rose to her feet. "Well?"

Brodie stared at his knee for a moment. "It feels a lot better."

"Don't go using it yet," Mallory warned.

"As if." Brodie used his crutches to help himself to his feet. "I can't wait for it to be better. Broken bones are the worst."

After saying goodbye to Sarisa, Mallory headed outside to help Ryan saddle the horses and put the panniers on Bobbi. It didn't take them long and they told the wagoner, Welby, Roast, Emica and Jorgen of their plans for the day since they were in the process of getting up.

Emica looked at each of them. "Make sure you are back by midday. I need to get to Cutthroat Harbour."

"We all do," Welby said.

Mallory couldn't stop thinking about what a disaster it would be if the crown was removed from the ancestral King. "We'll be back on time."

They were on the road and heading towards the crypt only a little after six. The journey was uneventful and Mallory couldn't help scanning the ruins for danger as they passed by. Everything was quiet within the jagged buildings.

Danae gestured to the crypt ahead of them. "I've worked out what the name is above the door of the crypt. I'm not very fluent in demonic runes, so it took me a bit of time. The name is Nesdin. The family owns South Peak Mine. They lived in this area for generations, moving to Sendale a decade or two ago."

"One family owns South Peak Mine," Brodie said.

Danae started to answer, breaking off when a bow wielding skeleton appeared in the doorway as they approached the crypt, firing at them.

Mallory threw herself to the side as she drew out her wand, casting a fireball at the skeleton while she was still moving. She missed. She tried again. This time the fireball hit the skeleton, which had already been struck by several arrows and a throwing knife. The skeleton collapsed on the floor. Before Mallory could start forward, another skeleton appeared in the doorway.

Brodie, who remained on Bug, threw a throwing knife at the skeleton. "How are we meant to get in there?"

Mallory didn't answer, attacking along with the rest of her companions. She had no idea what to tell him. What if they were stuck outside, a steady stream of skeletons keeping them from finding out what had happened in the crypt? Before she could throw a third fireball at the skeleton, it collapsed on the floor, sprawled across the other skeleton in the doorway.

Ryan ran forward, jumping over the skeletons and disappearing inside.

Mallory hurried after him. "Don't run off alone." She stepped inside the dimly lit interior to see that he peered down the stairs. The lantern hanging from the ceiling was still alight.

Ryan held his hunting bow, an arrow drawn back. "Organise lanterns. I can't see anything down there."

Brodie entered the crypt on his crutches, Fang at his side. "Can someone get my throwing knives? It's a little hard to do it while I'm on crutches."

Callum entered, Smudge still in his makeshift sling, peering over the edge. "I'll get them." He crouched by the skeletons.

Ryan, who remained by the stairs, glanced over his shoulder. "Is anyone getting the lanterns?"

Callum looked up from the skeleton he searched. "Danni is."

"I think there's something moving around down there. But I don't have enough light to see what it is," Ryan said.

Mallory started for the doorway, stopping when Danae entered, stepping over the skeletons. She took one of the lit lanterns from Danae. "I wonder how much it costs for a magelight spell. It'd be good not to have to carry a lantern while fighting." She'd prefer to have her sword drawn in case of close combat rather than cart around a lantern.

Callum rose to his feet, returning arrows and throwing knives and giving Mallory five copper pieces and five knucklebones. "I have no idea what they're for."

"Alchemy," Danae said. "Knucklebones of the undead are a rare drop."

Mallory slipped them inside her satchel. "We could do with a few rare drops. That's if they're worth selling."

"Knucklebones of the undead is one of the ingredients that can be used in a fountain of youth potion," Danae said.

Chapter Thirty-Seven

Mallory looked from the satchel to Danae. "We could collect all the ingredients needed for the potion?"

Ryan stepped back from the steps. "Forget about potions for now. Bring a light over so I can see what's down here. Other than the archer that shot at me."

Mallory came forward, holding the lantern above the opening in the floor. She stumbled back when a skeleton fired an arrow at her, having caught a glimpse of four warrior skeletons with him. "I don't know if this is such a good idea."

"What's down there?" Callum came forward.

Mallory waved him back, hearing the sound of footsteps coming up the stairs. "Five skeletons." They came out of the depths of the crypt as she spoke.

Callum backed away, checking the skeletons with the brass spyglass. "The archer has twenty-five health and the warriors have thirty."

"That is going to be extremely useful." Mallory threw a fireball at the skeleton archer, placing the lantern on the floor.

Callum slipped the spyglass back in its holster. "We should have brought Ninette with us to use the spyglass and tell us which one is getting low on health."

They focused on the skeleton archer, taking him out before they faced the warriors.

When Fang barked, Mallory spun to see her brother sprawled on the floor, a warrior skeleton standing above him. She ran towards him, throwing a fireball at the skeleton. He spun to face her, Fang attacking his leg. She drew her sword, casting poison dart as she swung it.

The skeleton blocked her sword, attacking immediately. Before he could make contact, Ryan got between Mallory and the skeleton, blocking with one sword and attacking with the other.

Mallory took several steps back, throwing another fireball at the skeleton. About to throw a third fireball at him, she stopped when he was pierced by an arrow and collapsed on the floor in front of Ryan. She started to turn so she could face the rest of the room. A skeleton slashed at her arm. Pain radiated through her, making her turn in the other direction.

"Mallory!" Ryan attacked the skeleton. "You okay?"

She nodded, helping Ryan attack the skeleton after checking she'd only lost four health. She was tempted to use her healing spell, but didn't want to risk running out of mana during a battle. And it wasn't like she was low on health these days. Well, at least not when she was being attacked by skeletons. They didn't do anywhere near as much damage as Rass. "I only lost four health." The pain from the wound was starting to ebb.

Brodie struggled to his feet. "At least you've got the health to spare now." He nearly dropped one of his crutches as he took out a throwing knife and threw it awkwardly at one of the skeletons. "Yes! I'll get some XP for that one when you kill it." He threw a knife at another skeleton, this time dropping one of his crutches.

Mallory attacked the skeleton with a combination of sword swings and casting fireball. "Are you trying to get yourself killed, Brodie?" If anything, trying to keep an eye on her brother when she should be focusing more on the skeleton attacking her, was likely to get her killed.

Brodie managed to pick up the crutch he'd dropped. "I'm not the one who lost health."

Finished helping Ryan take out the skeleton she looked around for the next one. There were none. Only fallen skeletons scattered across the floor. She checked everyone's health. Brodie was the only one who hadn't lost any. Callum and Danae had both lost two health each while Ryan had lost nine. Mallory checked her mana. As she watched, another point regened. She joined Ryan, Callum and Danae in searching the skeletons. As she did, she healed Ryan for two health since he'd lost the most.

Ryan looked up from the skeleton he was searching. "Thanks." He smiled at her.

Mallory returned the smile he gave her. "Should we remain in here while I heal everyone and let my mana regen?"

Danae straightened, having finished searching one of the skeletons. "We don't want to take too long. Skeletons, and whatever else might be guarding this place, will continue to spawn until we solve the problem that's preventing those laid to rest here from resting in peace."

"How do we figure that out?" Callum asked.

"Sometimes it can be impossible," Danae said. "Then stonemasons are called in to seal off the crypt and no more members of the family can be laid to rest in it."

"I'll be okay," Ryan said. "It's not like my health dropped that much. I still have twenty left. You should heal everyone at least once, including yourself, to take away the pain."

Mallory did as Ryan suggested before checking over what they'd gained from searching the skeletons. An extra arrow, twenty-seven copper pieces and bone dust of the undead. Before she could suggest going down the stairs, Brodie spoke.

"Aww, come on. Ryan and Callum both got a CAS point. They're halfway to their next character level. I'm so far behind all of you. And why are you hoarding all of your CAS points, Callum? Put them into something. There has to be something you'd find useful."

"Keep moving and you might have the chance to gain a CAS point today. You've only got twenty-seven points left before you gain one." Ryan led the way to the stairs.

Mallory sheathed her sword and picked up the lantern, following Ryan. She paused on the stairs, looking over her shoulder at Brodie. "Can you manage the stairs with them?" She nodded to his crutches.

"I'm not about to wait behind." Brodie followed at

a slower pace, Fang at his heels, Danae and Callum behind him.

Mallory continued down the stairs, stopping at the foot of them to stare at the stone coffin at the end of the long, narrow room. A door led off to the left. "What direction are we heading in?"

Ryan took out the compass, moving closer to her so she could see the directions too. He glanced at the door on the left. "It looks like our only option is to go east."

Brodie joined them at the foot of the stairs. "Do we get to see what's in the coffin?" He turned to his sister. "Like you do in that RPG you play."

Danae stepped around Brodie so she could face him. "You want to loot graves? That's one of the reasons why the dead become restless and the creatures set to guard them spawn."

"How was I supposed to know?" Brodie asked.

"Some of the tabletop and computer games in our world are based on Inadon. But there are a lot of inaccuracies," Mallory said.

Danae looked from Brodie to Mallory and back again. "You must come from a very strange world."

Ryan chuckled. "You'd probably think so. But not for that reason." He took a step towards the door. "Everyone ready to continue?"

Mallory looked from the coffin to the stairs that led outside into the sunshine. If they only had until midday to finish up, they needed to keep moving. "Yeah." She remained close to Ryan, holding the lantern up so they could see what was ahead of them. The room they entered was two metres wide and three metres long. At the far end of the room was another door. "How big are crypts?"

"That depends on how wealthy the family is," Danae said. "They can also grow larger over the years as more rooms are added to them."

"I'll get the next door." Ryan strode towards it, flinging it open and jumping back out of the way. An arrow flew through the room, missing everyone. "Three archer skeletons and two ghostly looking creatures."

Callum had the brass spyglass at his eye as the five creatures entered the room. "The archers have the same amount of health as the previous ones and the other two are called shades and have thirty health." He returned the spyglass to the holster and readied his bow.

"Why aren't they coming further into the room?" Mallory attacked the same archer that Danae and Callum shot.

"Shades usually have magic attacks," Danae said. "They don't need to come any closer."

Mallory threw a fireball at each of the creatures, noticing everyone else attacked each creature, including Brodie. One of the shades dropped to the floor in a puddle of robes.

"We should do that every-" Callum broke off, staggering back as the remaining shade attacked him.

Chapter Thirty-Eight

Before Mallory could attack the shade, he was taken out by attacks from Ryan, Danae and Brodie. She checked Callum's health as she attacked one of the other archers. He'd lost seven health. After finishing off the archer, she used the health spell on Callum. "I think I need a stronger healing spell."

Danae joined Ryan and Callum who were already searching the creatures. "Putting CAS points into it will make it a better spell. You'll eventually be able to heal people from a greater distance, have it cost less mana and heal them for more health points."

"Why does everything take so long to level up?" Brodie muttered. "Even after these five, I still need another five XP to gain a CAS point. Danni got to earn a CAS point this time."

Mallory helped search the creatures. "Are you sure

we can't stay in this room long enough I can finish healing Callum? He's down to fourteen health."

Finished searching one of the creatures, Danae rose to her feet, shaking her head. "The longer it takes us, the more creatures we'll end up needing to fight."

Sighing, Mallory got to her feet. "If we let our health get too low, we won't be able to finish this quest."

"We've got health potions." Brodie came further into the room. "Can someone get my throwing knives?"

The throwing knives were handed over to Brodie and the rest of the items they found were put away. Two silver and thirteen copper pieces were given to Mallory along with one bone dust which she put in her satchel. The rest was given to Ryan to put in the backpack. A wand, a dagger and a satchel, which Brodie planned to use once he was no longer on crutches.

They entered the next room. There was a door leading to the north, two to the east and one to the south. In the north east corner were two stone coffins and the room was about five metres wide from north to south and four metres east to west. Mallory stepped further into the room. "How are we going to choose which direction to take? Did you want to take turns like last time?"

"What if we rolled one of the dice?" Ryan pointed first to the door heading north. "That can be one, then two, three, four. If we roll a five or six, we roll again."

Brodie tried to get one of the dice out of his belt pouch. In the end, Callum needed to help him. Callum looked up from the floor where he'd rolled it. "One."

"Who's to say it was your turn to roll?" Brodie demanded.

Callum picked it up and put it back in Brodie's belt pouch. "You can't even get it out to have a turn." He glanced around the group. "Anyone object to opening the northern door?"

They'd been standing around long enough that Mallory had healed Callum twice more. "I don't care which door we take. If it takes us too long to decide, we won't get to finish this quest before we leave for Velkden."

Ryan headed for the door. "Time to get moving then." He glanced at Brodie. "At least completing this quest will make sure you level up."

Brodie glared at Ryan, muttering under his breath.

Mallory was too far from him to hear the words,

but she doubted they were complimentary. She followed Ryan. The door led into a narrow corridor, one metre wide and three metres long. It ended in another door. She remained close to Ryan, holding up the lantern so he could see when he opened the next door. It was a room two metres square with a stone coffin along the northern wall and another door. This door headed east. "So far the crypt hasn't been too bad."

"Rass' people probably attacked anything that came out of the crypt. It will have helped," Danae said. "Especially for the creatures with a longer respawn time."

Nodding, Mallory healed Ryan and Callum, one health point each. She smiled. Being able to heal with mana, rather than potions was going to save them a lot of money.

Ryan moved over to the door. "Everyone ready? I doubt it's going to stay quiet in here for too much longer."

Mallory tightened her grip on her wand, nodding. She continued to remain close to Ryan. He swung the door open and she peered past him. It was another corridor. This one was longer than the previous one. "It's empty." She followed Ryan along the corridor which was eight metres long, turning sharply to the south where it travelled another four metres before reaching a corridor that ran east to west. "Do you think Rass' people came in here?"

Danae looked in both directions of the next corridor. "I don't know. I can't see why they'd bother."

Mallory looked in each direction of the corridor as well. To the left was a door about three metres away. In the other direction, the door was about seven metres away. "Which way?" Again she healed Ryan and Callum.

Ryan grinned. "Maybe we should let Brodie pick. Then he might stop muttering under his breath about how unfair everything is."

"I bet you wouldn't have liked it if someone laughed at you for getting shot in the knee," Brodie said.

"Which direction?" Callum asked. "I want to get this over and done with as quickly as possible so we don't have to worry about being attacked by too many creatures. I'd prefer not to have low health any more than I need to. Especially since I've only got one revive left."

Brodie nodded towards the east. "We take the short end."

Ryan headed towards the next door, flinging it

open. He scrambled back. "Two skeletons. Retreat to the intersection." An arrow struck him in the arm. He slowed as he looked over his shoulder towards the oncoming skeletons.

Reaching the intersection, Mallory slipped around the corner and threw fireballs at each of the skeletons. One was an archer and the other was a warrior.

"Nice." Callum peered through the spyglass, crouching at Danae's feet while she fired at the two skeletons. "You got a crit on both of those skeletons, Mallory. Danni didn't."

"Someone get out of the way so I can attack too," Brodie said. "How can I level up if I can't attack?"

"And risk my brother's revives? You can't do anywhere near the damage with your throwing knives." Callum continued to peer through the brass spyglass. "That's it. One more attack on each and they should be done."

Mallory launched a fireball at the one that had remained by the doorway while Danae took out the one that had chased Ryan. She checked Ryan's stats. He was down to twenty-one health points. She healed one, not wanting her mana to get too low.

Callum put the spyglass away and joined Ryan in the corridor. He stopped beside his brother who searched the warrior skeleton. "Are you sure there were no more in the room?"

Ryan got to his feet, having found a sheathed short sword. "It was a small one and has a stone coffin like the last room we were in. It's the same size too. The only difference is that the doors are in different locations." He strode towards the archer skeleton.

Mallory hurried after Ryan and Callum, Danae and Brodie following her. "How are we meant to figure out why all the skeletons are wandering about the crypt? I mean, will it be obvious? Or do we have to search for the answer?"

"It could go either way," Danae said.

Ryan turned to them with a grin, holding out a folded piece of paper. "A drop for you, Brodie."

Reaching them, Brodie eyed the piece of paper suspiciously. "What is it?"

Ryan's grin broadened. "A recipe."

When her brother didn't take the recipe, Mallory took it. She opened it, laughing when she read what it was. "Beef bone broth."

"Very funny," Brodie muttered.

Ryan gave Mallory three copper pieces and bone dust of the undead. "We might not do too bad out of this place if we keep getting bone dust."

Mallory put the bone dust and recipe in her satchel

and the coins in her belt pouch. "How are we doing for time?" She completely healed Danae's health so that at least two of the party had full health.

Ryan took out the pocket watch. "It's seven forty. If this place isn't too big, we might get it dealt with before midday."

Chapter Thirty-Nine

They entered the room the skeletons had come from. Mallory looked around the crowded space. It was exactly as Ryan had described it. Fairly identical to the previous room. There was a coffin along the northern wall and a door heading south. She readied her wand, watching as Ryan opened the next door. It was a short corridor, two metres long and taking a sharp turn to the west with another door two metres away from them. Before Ryan opened the door, Mallory healed him for one point. She really needed more mana. A pity they only gained five attribute points each time they gained a character level.

Ryan opened the door, closing it even quicker. He backed away. "There are too many for us to face."

What was in there?" Danae asked.

"A lot of warrior skeletons and two or three shades," Ryan said.

Danae pushed past them to fling open the door. "Shades can go through solid objects. We don't want to be trapped in the corridor when we fight them."

Mallory entered the large room to see three shades heading towards them, skeletons following. They were completely outnumbered. She set the lantern on top of a nearby coffin, this one made of marble. There were another three coffins in the room, set in two rows running east to west.

Callum put the spyglass away, that he'd just finished using. "They all have thirty health." He readied his bow.

Deciding it was more important they have full health, and that she could use a sword, Mallory completely healed Callum as she ran towards the closest warrior. She was also able to heal two of her health points and one of Ryan's before she was out of mana. "Stay back in the corridor, Brodie. You can't do anything in here."

The sound of swords clashing filled the room. It echoed around them, bouncing off the stone walls. The room was five metres square and other than the four coffins and various enemies, was empty.

Mallory continued to attack the skeleton, forced to block more than actually attack. Each time she regained six mana, approximately every half a minute, she worked on healing Ryan. It seemed like she'd no sooner nearly completely healed him than he lost seven health, taking him down to eighteen. She quickly checked everyone else's health. They'd all lost some. Although Ryan's was the worst. Before she could heal anyone else a second warrior attacked her, quickly followed by a third. Two of the warriors managed to get in an attack and pain flared through her. Using the healing spell caused the pain to vanish as quickly as it had arrived.

She was down to thirty-one health. Which wasn't much when she was surrounded and outnumbered. Especially since she could do little more than block the attacks.

Brodie hobbled forward, hitting at one of the warriors with a crutch. "Leave my sister alone. Go on, back off." Fang joined him, attacking and barking at the warrior, ignoring Brodie when he ordered her to retreat.

Mallory attacked the same warrior Brodie focused on, barely managing to avoid the sword of one of the other warriors. She wished there was a way to see their health without using the spyglass. This time when her mana came back enough to use the health spell, she used poison dart instead. Three seconds later the skeleton she attacked was down.

"We took one out," Brodie called out.

"I took one down too," Callum said.

Mallory didn't have time to glance around the room to see how many were left. She was too focused on the skeletons wanting to kill her. And trying to prevent either of them from getting any attacks in on Brodie. "You shouldn't be in here. You're going to make your knee worse." Had she done the right thing attacking rather than healing? Although if she hadn't she doubted they could have lasted much longer being attacked by three skeletons.

"As if. I'm not putting any weight on it." Brodie continued to brandish one of his crutches, leaning heavily on the other one. All he seemed to be doing was blocking the attacks and ensuring that the skeletons had more than just Mallory to focus on.

"One of the shades is down," Ryan called out.

Mallory checked Ryan's health. "You need a healing potion. You've only got four health left." Her mana came back enough for her to heal him for a single point.

"I can't," Ryan said. "There's no way I can stop long enough to drink a potion while they're attacking me."

Mallory glanced at Brodie. "Help Ryan. I can manage these two." She healed Ryan again the moment she had enough mana. She looked between Brodie and the skeleton that tried to attack him. "Go on. Hurry up."

"I've taken one out," Danae called.

"I killed the warrior skeleton, I just have the shade left," Ryan said. "Brodie can continue to help you, Mallory."

She healed Ryan again before she spoke. "My health isn't as low as yours." She drew in a sharp breath as a sword cut into her flesh. She didn't have the mana to take away the pain this time. But even if she did, she would have used it to heal Ryan. He needed it a lot more than she did. Again she healed him the moment she had enough mana. She'd barely done so, when his health went down to one point. "Ryan!" She knew he'd be able to revive, but still she wanted to run to his side and fight with him against the shade. Pain shot through her again as one of the warriors managed to get past her defences. Surely once they'd finish this fight, they could wait long enough to heal before going on. They couldn't face more creatures on next to no health. That would be crazy.

"We've taken out one of the shades," Callum said. "Danni can help you, Mallory, and I'll help Ryan."

Mallory was able to heal Ryan as Danae joined her.

"You should retreat, Ryan. Leave the shade to Callum so you can have a potion." With Danae's help, she finished off one of the warriors.

"We got him," Brodie called out.

As she watched, Ryan's health went up by ten points and she was able to heal him once more. He now had thirteen health. The moment the last warrior was down, Mallory sheathed her sword and flung herself at Ryan. "Are you okay?"

He wrapped his arms around her. "Heal yourself next. You must still be in a lot of pain."

She was in some pain, but it was nothing compared to the fear she'd felt as she'd watched his health drop low. "I know we have revives, but they aren't infinite."

Ryan's lips met hers and his arms tightened around her momentarily. He drew back to meet her gaze. "Once we've finished with Cutthroat Harbour and Ruby Isle is safe again, we'll work on getting better gear."

"Are you pair going to kiss all morning, or are you going to help search the bodies so we can keep moving?" Brodie leaned against one of the coffins.

Mallory looked over at Brodie, grinning back at him. She checked his stats. "You levelled up." No wonder he was so happy. She noticed he'd also lost seven health. "We need to heal before we move to the next room."

"Won't we have too many creatures spawn?" Callum asked.

"With how much health we lost, we'll end up dying if we continue. If we heal before we go on, we should have a better chance of surviving," Mallory said.

Callum shrugged. "We can try it your way if you want." He turned to Brodie. "What did you do? Attack every single creature in the room at least once?"

"Not quite. I tried though." Brodie looked at Fang who sat at his feet. "What did you think you were doing, girl? You don't have enough health to join in the fights yet. Wait until you're older."

Chapter Forty

In the ten minutes it took to search all the creatures, Mallory alternated between healing each of them. She also gave Ryan one of the health potions from her satchel since he'd needed to use his. They were still a long way from being healed and Mallory was half tempted to have a potion herself and get Ryan to have another one. But they didn't have an endless supply. She needed another twelve health, Ryan ten, Brodie and Danae four and Callum none.

They put all the items they'd gathered on top of one of the coffins. The one in the south west corner. "Look at everything we got," Brodie said. "I wonder how much money we can get for all of it."

Mallory surveyed the items. "I don't know that it was worth nearly losing a revive. And the cost of the potion."

Danae nudged the mage robe. "This should cover

the cost of the health potion. Unless you want to keep it."

Mallory shook her head. "It's the same as the last one. I'd probably trip over the hem." Her attention was caught by something poking out from underneath the edge of the robe. "What's that?" She pulled out the rolled up piece of parchment. Unrolling it, she stared at the writing. "It's a spell. I have another spell."

Ryan chuckled. "I wondered when you were going to notice it."

She turned to him. "You couldn't have told me it was there?"

He drew her to him, keeping his arm around her waist. "You seemed determined to worry about everyone's health. I thought it'd be a nice surprise."

"You should just give in and accept you're the healer," Brodie said.

Mallory glared at him. "I am not your healer."

Ryan turned slightly so he could briefly kiss her. He met her gaze. "Being a healer doesn't mean you can't also be a warrior, or a mage. Or anything else you want to be."

She relaxed against him. "I just don't want to be the support class."

"You're not," Ryan assured her.

Seeing she had enough mana to cast the healing spell ten more times, she healed Danae's health, two of hers and three of Ryan's.

"Aww, come on. That's not fair," Brodie protested.

"What isn't?" Ryan asked.

Brodie gestured towards Mallory. "She healed everyone except me."

Ryan chuckled. "Do you blame her?"

"I told you I'm not your healer," Mallory said.

Brodie glared at everyone when they laughed at him.

Mallory returned to checking over what they'd gained from the fight. The spell was level three and was called weak reanimate. It would allow her to reanimate the dead that were level three and below for the cost of twenty mana. Sadly, whatever she raised from the dead would only last for a minute. It would take longer than that to regenerate the mana used. It might be a spell worth putting CAS points in to reduce the mana cost and extend the amount of time the spell lasted. Even with the drawbacks of the spell, she was glad to have it and glad she'd be able to use it since her current intelligence points allowed her to cast spells one level above her mage level.

As well as the spell and mage robe, they got an iron pick, ten knucklebones of the undead, two bone dust of the undead, another satchel, four silver and nine copper pieces and a sheathed short sword.

They put everything away, most of it going in Ryan's backpack, or tied to it in the case of the pick. The handles of the two short swords they'd gained stuck up out of the edge of the backpack opening. They remained in the room as Mallory continued to heal them. Brodie gestured towards the bodies scattered around the room on the floor. "Why do they give us such good drops when we beat the creatures?"

"What we gain from killing these creatures has nothing to do with those who are buried here. It's to do with the magic used to spawn creatures to protect the crypt in times of danger. And it has absolutely nothing to do with the reward we might gain at the end," Danae said.

Mallory finally finished healing all of them. She was out of mana though. She checked Brodie's knee, relieved it was still splinted.

Brodie tried to push her away. "I'm okay. Stop fussing over me."

She brushed his hands aside, examining his knee more closely. "You haven't damaged it at all." She frowned. "I have no idea how I know that, but I do."

"You're a level thirty-five apothecary," Danae reminded her.

Mallory stepped away from Brodie. "It's going to take awhile to become accustomed to that."

"Can we go now?" Brodie asked.

Mallory turned to Ryan. "What's the time?"

He took out the pocket watch, glancing at it before returning it to his belt pouch. "Nearly eight thirty. Or it will be in five."

"Can we wait five minutes for my mana to regen?" She gestured towards the closed door in the middle of the western wall. "We don't know what could be waiting for us in there. And five minutes isn't that long."

Ryan chuckled. "Were you hoping if you talked about it long enough you wouldn't need us to agree because five minutes would already be up?"

"No, but now you mention it…" She let her voice trail off, smiling at him.

Ryan nodded. "It makes sense to wait until your mana is back, especially since it won't take too long. We wouldn't have survived the last battle without your help." He moved closer to her. "I wouldn't have survived."

She met his gaze, her smile fading at the look in his eyes. "I didn't want you to die. I know you can revive, but still…" She finished her comment with a shrug.

He slid his arms around her waist. "I didn't want to die either."

"You're not going to kiss again, are you?" Brodie demanded.

Ryan chuckled. "Don't look if it bothers you."

Mallory wrapped her arms around Ryan before she looked at Brodie, grinning at him. "Jealous?" She glanced at Danae to make sure he knew exactly what she was talking about.

Brodie muttered under his breath, looking away.

Ryan chuckled, his arms tightening around Mallory before he kissed her. He drew back slightly. "He must be. But if you don't speak up…" He chuckled again.

Brodie headed towards the door, after glancing at Danae several times. "We should keep moving before we have a tonne of creatures spawn and we all die."

Mallory drew away from Ryan, her gaze resting on Danae who stared at Brodie. After collecting the lantern, she moved closer to the half-elf as they headed towards the door. "As I said the other day, you'll be the one that'll have to make the moves." She kept her voice low so the rest of their party wouldn't hear.

"What if I don't know how to do that?" Danae asked softly.

Mallory shrugged. She had no idea what to suggest.

Ryan opened the door to the next room. It was empty. The room was two metres wide and four metres long, two coffins along the northern wall. There was another door directly across from them in the western wall. Ryan opened the next door and they stepped into a larger room.

Mallory looked around the room, holding up the lantern. "We're almost back to where we started." It was the room where they'd let a random roll decide which direction they went. "There are only two doors we haven't opened." She looked at the door in the north east corner. "That one probably leads to the long corridor where we fought the archer and warrior skeleton."

Ryan stepped ahead of her and opened the door before she could. After looking along the corridor, which was empty other than two dead skeletons, he smiled at Mallory. "Just because you have the highest health out of all of us, that doesn't make you the tank."

She grinned. "Aren't you the one who said I could be whatever I want?"

Ryan chuckled. "Fair enough." He turned to face

the door that was across the room in the southern wall. "This is the only direction we haven't taken yet. Everyone ready to continue?"

Fang ran over to the door and growled softly.

Chapter Forty-One

Mallory stared at Fang for a moment before her attention was caught by Smudge who quietly made his warning cry. "There goes my hope that it's another empty room."

Ryan waited until everyone was near the door before he opened it. He ran inside and attacked the nearest warrior skeleton before the four warrior skeletons, two archer skeletons and two shades had the chance to move towards him or attack.

Mallory hurried after him, glancing around the room. It was four metres wide from east to west and six metres long. There were three pillars down each side of the room, each row of pillars approximately a metre in from the eastern and western walls. There were no coffins in this room. Instead, there were large niches in the walls with cloth wrapped bodies placed in them. The niches were four high with three tiers of them on each wall, except for the eastern one where there was only two, part of the space being taken up by a door that hadn't been placed in a position to allow a third row of niches. Unlike the door they'd entered the room through, which was located in a corner of the room.

Not wanting to use up all her mana, Mallory cast a single fireball at each of the eight creatures. She was forced to dodge two of the warriors and a shade during the process. She assumed Brodie did the same as a couple of times throwing knives struck the same creature she attacked. Many of them were also impaled with arrows. She left the lantern near a pillar she'd retreated to, hoping that would prevent it from being knocked over. Drawing her sword, she attacked a nearby warrior who was going after Ryan.

He was surrounded. Attacking and blocking the three warriors, archer and shade that seemed determined to kill him. He began to focus more on the warrior Mallory attacked and it wasn't long before they'd finished him off.

Mallory checked Ryan's health, seeing he'd lost eight. Before she had the chance to heal him, an arrow pierced the side of her arm, pain shooting through her. She moved to put the nearby creatures between her and the one attacking from across the room. There was no way she could turn her back on the nearby ones. Seeing she'd only lost three health, she healed one of hers and one of Ryan's then decided to test the new spell on the fallen warrior.

The warrior skeleton rose to his feet and turned on the nearby archer, attacking with his sword.

Mallory joined him, grinning. "This is going to be so handy at Cutthroat Harbour."

Ryan joined the two of them in their attacks on the archer. "A healer necromancer. Interesting combination."

Callum joined them as the archer skeleton was taken out. "Is this what you plan to do with the patients that die on you?"

Ryan chuckled. "If we can't heal you, we'll reanimate you. Sounds like it could be a good motto."

Mallory started to reply, frowning when her reanimated skeleton crumpled to the floor. "That doesn't last anywhere near long enough." The warrior they attacked dropped to the floor and she focused on the shade.

Danae joined them, helping attack the last of the creatures. "There are stronger versions of that spell when you go up in levels."

"There are so many things I want to level up and put CAS points in, but what about when I get better versions of them? Won't that be a waste of CAS points in the early levels?" Mallory asked.

Danae fired an arrow into the shade and he sprawled across the stone floor, unmoving. "Powerful demons have the ability to reassign CAS points."

Mallory surveyed the room then checked everyone's health. Her and Ryan weren't the only ones who'd lost some. Brodie had lost six and Callum had lost four. She started healing everyone. "Lucky we waited until my mana came back before moving on."

Ryan chuckled. "Is that your way of telling us we're waiting again this time?"

Mallory sheathed her sword and tucked the wand in the canvas loop. She looked at the canvas for a moment. One day, she'd replace it with something better. "I don't have enough mana to heal everyone completely. And then I'll need approximately five minutes to regen again after that. We're probably looking at between ten to fifteen minutes all up. It'll give us time to search the bodies."

Ryan looked up from the body he was searching. "We won't need that much time." He smiled at her. "But we can wait for your mana to regen."

"Look what I found in the corner." Brodie stood in the north east corner, behind a pillar.

Mallory hurried over to see what he was up to. There were two bodies that they hadn't killed, a full backpack lying on the floor beside them. "Do you think they were some of Rass' people?"

"Check in the backpack for me." Brodie glanced at his knee. "Isn't there a quicker way to fix bones?"

"Mallory would need to be a higher level apothecary." Danae joined them. "They might have been the ones who caused the problem to start with." Danae crouched by the backpack, opening it to rummage around inside.

Brodie stared at the contents of the backpack. "Do we get to keep all the weapons, jewellery and stuff?"

Danae closed the backpack and hoisted it onto her shoulders, picking up her bow with her left hand. "This is probably what made the dead restless. They want the items, they were buried with, returned to them."

Mallory glanced around the room. "How do we know where to put all their items?"

Danae returned to the middle of the room, standing between two of the pillars. "It isn't any of these ones. Or the ones in the other rooms. We'll know which ones when we see them."

Brodie followed her, Fang beside him. "How will we know?"

"They'll have been disturbed." Danae gestured to the door in the southern wall. "Are we ready to continue?"

"I've healed everyone and my mana is back," Mallory said.

"I've just got to put away the things we found and then I'm ready." Ryan handed three silver and seven copper pieces to Mallory along with bone dust of the undead. There was another mage robe he put in the backpack along with a wand. He held studded, leather vambraces out to Danae. "See if these fit you."

Danae leaned her bow against her legs as she tried them on. "They're perfect. And just what I needed." She grabbed hold of her bow. "I'm ready to continue."

Ryan glanced around the group and when they all nodded, he strode to the door and swung it open.

Mallory peered past him. It was another long corridor. Five metres long. "I'm beginning to think we'll never find the end to this place. How big can crypts be? Surely they can't be much bigger than this."

Danae laughed softly. "I've heard of ones that are four or five times this size. But there are also ones that are smaller."

Ryan checked the time on the pocket watch as he

strode along the corridor. "It'll be nine thirty soon. With how long this has taken us, there's no way we could manage one five times this size." He returned the pocket watch to his belt pouch. "Not and be done before midday."

Mallory walked beside him. The corridor took a sharp turn to the right and was about two metres long before it ended in a door.

Ryan opened the door and stepped inside, moving to the left. "What are these?"

Mallory followed Ryan into the room, heading to the left with him while the other three went to the right. She glanced around the room. It was six metres long from east to west and four metres wide. On the eastern and western walls, there were three columns of niches that were four rows high. Cloth wrapped bodies were in each of them. Directly across from the door was an altar, the family name carved on the wall above it in demonic runes. A metre in from both the eastern and western walls, centrally located, were two marble coffins, the lids on the floor beside them. On the floor between the coffins was a scattering of bones and a single skull. None of these details held Mallory's attention for long.

What her gaze remained focused on, were the two creatures in long robes that hovered a good ten centimetres off the floor, towering over them, a stiletto in each hand. "That doesn't look good. They must be at least six and a half feet tall."

Callum lowered the brass spyglass. "They're wraiths and they each have forty-five health."

"What are they waiting for?" Brodie demanded.

"Maybe some of the other creatures are close to respawning and they're waiting for reinforcements," Danae suggested.

"That sounds like a really bad idea." Callum put the spyglass away and readied his bow.

"Sounds like a bad idea to me too," Ryan said. "I'll keep the one on the left distracted while the rest of you take out the one on the right." He waited until everyone nodded or murmured an agreement before running towards the wraith on the left.

Chapter Forty-Two

Mallory cast two fireballs at the creature on the right, moving forward in preparation for attacking with her sword. The creature vanished, reappearing in front of her and attacking with its daggers. She threw herself to the side, colliding with one of the coffins. She hadn't moved quickly enough. One of the stilettos slashed across her cheek and she felt the warmth of blood coat the side of her face, gritting her teeth against the pain. She spun to face the wraith as she healed herself for a single health point out of the eight she'd lost.

Callum fired another arrow at the wraith. "I wish I could see what his health is currently at."

This time, Mallory attacked with poison dart. It was a pity she had no creature to reanimate. She thought of the ones in the previous room. The corridor between her and them was too long and the spell didn't last long enough. "I wish we could see what his health is at too." She checked Ryan's health, shocked to see he'd lost fourteen health. That left him with only thirteen health to face the wraith.

"Diplomats wear special glasses that have some similarities to a spyglass." Danae shot the wraith again. "I wouldn't mind a pair of them right now. The only problem is, they're easily broken."

When Brodie and Callum attacked again, Mallory started to throw another fireball at the wraith. He disappeared before she had the chance. She scanned the room, trying to find a clue as to where he was. He reappeared beside her a moment later and she blocked one of his stilettos. The second one managed to get her. This time she lost six health. She healed herself and Ryan one point each as she attacked the wraith. He dropped to the floor in front of her and she spun to face the other one, heart racing as she prepared to attack him.

The second wraith vanished, reappearing a moment later in front of Brodie. He raised a crutch to block. It wasn't enough. The stiletto caught him in the side for eight health points.

Mallory cast poison dart at the wraith before healing Brodie for one health point. She checked

Ryan's health. It hadn't changed. She needed more mana. Or less costly spells.

Brodie recovered his balance then hit the wraith with his crutch after having thrown a knife at him. Callum and Danae also attacked at the same time as Brodie. Again the wraith vanished, this time appearing in front of Callum. He blocked the attack with his bow. The wraith was close enough to Ryan that he was able to attack, taking the wraith out with his swords.

Mallory scanned the room, half expecting another creature to appear. "Lucky there was only two of them. I don't know if we'd have been able to manage three."

Danae ran towards the coffin on the left and sat the backpack down beside it. "Hurry. We have to sort out these bones and figure out which coffin each of them and these items belong in."

"But we've killed them and there's no other door." Brodie nodded to the wall ahead of them. "There's only an altar. Unless it hides a secret door." Brodie started forward. "Not that I can search for hidden doors on my own. I can't wait until my knee is healed. It's impossible to do anything with this splint on."

Danae peered in both of the coffins. "They'll keep

on spawning until we fix the problem. And they'll respawn with extra creatures each time."

Mallory hurried forward, nearly colliding with Callum who did the same. She picked up the skull that had been lying on the floor. A glance around showed there was no other skull. She peered in both of the coffins. The coffin on the left contained a skull. Mallory put the skull in the coffin on the right. "How are we meant to sort out the rest of the bones?"

Callum studied two bones that were fairly similar looking. "The smaller skeleton is a female. There are some differences between male and female skeletons. Not just that the pelvic bones of the female are more rounded. When you compare the bones together, you can see the one belonging to the male is longer and thicker." He held up the bones. "We can figure it out. It'll just take time."

Danae continued to sort through the contents of the backpack. "We don't have time." She took out a ring with a square, low setting and two daggers. "Which coffin belongs to the male?"

Callum put several bones in the coffin on the left. "This one."

The five of them sorted the bones, at one stage needing to chase Fang away from them when she sniffed at a longer bone.

"How do you know about which ones are female and which are male?" Brodie sat amongst the bones, sorting them into two piles.

"I watched a documentary on the differences. It was fascinating." Callum placed two bones in the coffin on the left.

"I should have known," Brodie muttered.

Danae compared two bones with each other. "This is taking too long." She put one bone in each coffin. "Wraiths will respawn before we're done."

Mallory took some of the bones her brother had sorted. "Can't we just take out the next lot then continue to sort the bones and items?" She placed the bones in one of the coffins. The garments the skeletons had once worn were torn, left behind in the coffins and the bones were randomly dropped into the coffin on top of them.

"We barely managed to defeat those two. The next time we'll have to face more creatures. Possibly more wraiths. If we're lucky it'll be more skeletons with the two wraiths." Danae again rummaged in the backpack. She took out two golden candleholders. After examining the altar, she placed them one at each end, putting a candle in each.

"We need to come up with a plan before the next lot of creatures spawn," Ryan said.

"Someone should continue to sort bones," Callum suggested.

"Wouldn't it be better to take out all the creatures as quickly as possible so we can all return to sorting bones?" Danae placed a ring in the female's coffin.

Mallory continued to alternate between healing everyone as she sorted bones, trying not to let her mana get too low. "How often do they respawn?"

"The wraiths can respawn every five to ten minutes, which can trigger other creatures to respawn with them. Ones that would normally take longer to respawn. The more they respawn, the shorter the time becomes between each spawning," Danae said.

"There must be a quicker way to do this." Brodie looked around himself. Bones surrounded him.

"Yeah, it includes not stopping," Ryan said.

Mallory finished healing Brodie to full health. She now only had seven health left to heal for Ryan and six for herself. "This is worse than doing a jigsaw puzzle without a picture."

"It's not that hard." Callum shifted one of the bones Brodie had sorted, into the other pile. "Okay, maybe it is for some."

"Not everyone thinks documentaries are fun to watch," Brodie muttered. "There are other-" He broke off when two wraiths and two warrior skeletons appeared in the room. He reached for his crutches.

Ryan drew his swords. "Keep sorting, Brodie. Everyone else focus on the skeletons. I'll try and keep the wraiths busy."

Chapter Forty-Three

Mallory ran towards the closest skeleton, drawing her sword. She was torn between wanting to use her magic to attack in the hope the fight would be over quicker and continuing to use it to heal her and Ryan. The decision was quickly made for her when Ryan's health went down dramatically. He'd either been hit for twelve or there'd been two close hits together. Whichever it was, he was now down to eight health. She healed him as much as possible as she continued to fight the skeleton. It wasn't enough. She was only able to bring him up to thirteen health.

"Ryan, do you need-"

Ryan interrupted his brother. "Stick with the plan. Once the skeletons are down, you can focus on one of the wraiths."

One of the skeletons collapsed to the floor, two arrows having impaled him at the same time.

"Mallory and Danni can take care of this last skeleton. The way you're going, you'll get yourself killed, Ryan," Callum said.

"That isn't necessary," Ryan said.

Mallory continued to attack the skeleton, dodging the sword that swung towards her. "Help him, Callum. He's going to get himself killed and then he won't have enough revives for when we get to Cutthroat Harbour."

Callum remained where he was, spinning to face Ryan and the two wraiths. "You're not a tank either, so stop acting like you are." He released an arrow that struck one of the wraiths who were focused on Ryan.

The wraith spun to face Callum, vanishing.

"I hate it when they do that." Callum stepped to the side just in time. The wraith appeared to the side of him, failing in his surprise attack.

"We should have seen if the others wanted to join us this morning." Brodie continued to sort bones. "Are you sure you don't want me to help?"

"You are helping." Ryan stepped back and to the side when the wraith he fought vanished. When it still didn't reappear, he shifted his location. The wraith appeared to the side of him and he spun out of the way.

Finished with the second warrior skeleton, Mallory

faced the wraith Callum fought, unable to do much more than block with his bow, his hunting knife also in hand. She came in swinging her sword, healing Ryan as well. It was a good thing the room wasn't overly large so that everyone remained in range of her healing spell.

Brodie threw a knife at each of the wraiths. "I should have done that to the skeletons. I'll never level up at this rate."

"Forget about levelling up. Focus on the bones. You can level up later." When the wraith vanished from in front of her, Mallory looked around trying to figure out where it would appear. "How long can they remain invisible?"

Before anyone could reply, the wraith appeared in front of Brodie aiming his stilettos at him. Fang launched herself at the wraith, throwing off his aim and giving Brodie enough time to roll out of the way, scattering some of the bones he'd sorted.

Mallory checked her brother's health, relieved to find he'd lost none. She ran at the wraith and attempted to heal Ryan at the same time. She'd obviously put too much distance between them because her target was now out of range. She looked from Brodie to Ryan. "Move, Brodie. Get out of the way."

Brodie stumbled to his feet, one of the crutches out of reach. He hobbled away from the fight. Which meant he also put more distance between himself and the other crutch. "Stay back, Fang."

Mallory wanted to retreat so she'd be closer to Ryan and able to heal him. Then she remembered her new spell. Dodging an attack, she reanimated a warrior skeleton. In the process, the sword was knocked from her hand. There wasn't time to draw her dagger. Curling her hand into a fist, she struck out at the wraith. The creature knocked her from her feet in retaliation. It came towards her.

"Get up, Mal," Brodie ordered.

Mallory had no idea what the journal notification in the corner of her vision was for and didn't have time to check. She drew her dagger as she got to her feet, blocking the wraith's attack. The skeleton she'd raised from the dead, joined her in attacking the creature, taking the wraith's attention from her. Before she could attack the wraith again, he was dead. She moved towards Ryan, shocked to see his health was down to five and they still had one more wraith to take out. She healed Ryan, bringing him up to eight health. She needed more mana. Remembering the three mana potions in her satchel, she fumbled in it and took one out. Ten mana points weren't much, but it would help. She downed the contents. It gave her enough to heal Ryan two more times.

"Return to sorting bones, Brodie," Ryan ordered as he continued to swing his swords.

Brodie threw a dagger at the wraith before he collected his second crutch and lowered himself to the floor amongst the bones.

Mallory picked up her sword, shaking her head. "Didn't you learn anything last time you did that, Brodie?"

"Obviously he didn't," Callum said.

"He's not about to come after me." Brodie gestured towards the wraith that was surrounded. "You lot are keeping him busy."

The wraith vanished and the four of them backed away. Callum glanced at Brodie. "You better hope he didn't take that as a challenge."

The wraith appeared in front of Danae who stumbled backwards as he started to attack her with his stilettos.

Mallory cast a fireball at him at the same time as Callum released an arrow. The wraith dropped onto the floor at Danae's feet, not having had the chance to finish his attack. Mallory scanned the room, her breath coming fast as she searched for danger.

Nothing attacked. Around the room Ryan, Callum and Danae also remain poised and ready to fight.

Brodie looked up from the bones he continued to sort. "Isn't anyone going to help me?"

Slowly letting out her breath, Mallory put her weapons away. "Yeah. Let's get these bones sorted before any more spawn. I don't want to know how many extras they bring with them next time." She took a health potion from her satchel and held it out to Ryan. "Have this. If they respawn quicker than last time, there's no way I can heal you enough for another fight."

Ryan downed the contents of the potion and put the empty vial in his backpack. "I think we need to spend a week levelling up once we're done with Cutthroat Harbour."

Mallory checked her notification as she sorted bones. Her hand stilled as she read it over. "You have learned unarmed combat, a skill that allows you to fight without the need to use weapons."

"I forgot about that skill," Callum said.

"I mustn't have punched you hard enough then," Brodie said.

Callum checked over the bones Brodie had sorted, rearranging the piles slightly. "Okay, these can go in each of the coffins and then we only have to finish sorting the backpack of items."

Mallory helped Ryan and Callum put the bones in the coffins. "Do we have to put them in order? They're all jumbled up."

Danae placed a dusty bottle of wine on the altar, sections of the bottle having been roughly wiped clean. "Depends on the dead. They might be happy with their bones being back in their coffins or they might want to be laid out properly."

Mallory checked inside the backpack. There were three rings and a dagger left. All were made of gold. "How do I know which coffin these belong in?"

Danae took two of the rings. "I think the last ring and the dagger belong to the male skeleton." She placed the two rings in the female's coffin.

Mallory healed Ryan for two health as she took the items to the male skeleton's coffin. Before she had the chance to place the objects inside, three wraiths and four warrior skeletons appeared. "We can't face that many."

"Drop the items in the coffin and if everything is back to normal, they'll vanish," Danae said.

Mallory placed the items in the coffin as her companions attacked the creatures. She looked from the coffin to the creatures. "It didn't work."

"Then try something else," Ryan ordered.

"Like what?" Mallory demanded. Fear rushed through her. What happened if every single one of them died at the same time? Would they revive again after the battle was ended? Or not, since technically they would be on the losing side.

"I don't know, but you better figure it out quickly." Ryan blocked an attack from one of the wraiths, dodging out of the way of a skeleton. "We can't face this many for long."

Chapter Forty-Four

Mallory tried to rearrange the bones, hoping that would be enough, but she had no idea where everything went. At least not exactly. It didn't help that she kept glancing over her shoulder, wanting to join in the fight and help her companions. She considered using her reanimate spell in the hope that the bones would put themselves in a better order. She might even be able to tell the dead to lie in place, but would that upset them more? They didn't need any more creatures sent to kill them. There were already too many to fight.

Callum joined her, dropping Smudge into the coffin. "See what you can do to sort the bones, Smudge." Callum rejoined the fight.

Smudge held up a bone to Mallory. It had been snapped in two.

"You think that's the problem?" Mallory took the pieces from him.

Smudge chattered at her, shifting a couple of bones around.

Mallory slowly shook her head. "You look like you're shifting them around as randomly as I was." At least she'd managed to put the skull in the correct place. That had been easy. Taking a deep breath, she placed the two halves of the bone together and used rapid mend on it. She was down to three mana.

"Hurry up." Brodie blocked a warrior skeleton with one of his crutches. "Are you trying to get us killed, Mal?"

"Nothing is working." Gathering Smudge, she took him to the second coffin so he could help her sort the bones. "I'm doing the best I can." None of the bones in this coffin were broken. Not that it had helped repairing the other bone. A glance over her shoulder showed her companions were still outnumbered and checking her journal let her know they were rapidly losing health.

"Are we sure all the bones are in the correct coffins?" Ryan asked.

Mallory shifted the jewellery and items to places they should logically go. Rings near the hands, a dagger near the hip and a necklace below the skull.

The sounds of fighting didn't change. Her fingers brushed across a torn garment. She tugged it over the rib bones. "Come on, Smudge. I need some ideas here." She ran a finger along the tear. It was different from the other tears. Torn apart rather than worn through.

Smudge patted her arm, chattering softly.

She smiled at him. "Thanks for the confidence. But I don't know what to do."

"Do something. Anything," Brodie yelled. "They're killing us."

"I don't know how much longer we can keep them from going after you," Danae said.

Mallory checked her mana, her gaze again drawn to the tear. She didn't have enough. Did she wait a few more seconds for enough to regen or drink a mana potion? She drank a potion, repairing a small section of the aged cloth. Not only was the tear repaired. The cloth returned to new.

"Whatever you did, do it again," Ryan said. "One of the wraiths and half the skeletons vanished."

Mallory spun to face the room. Excitement raced through her. She'd figured it out. Or at least figured it out for one of the skeletons. Gathering Smudge, who held his paws out to her, she returned to the other coffin.

Smudge tugged the aged fabric over the rib bones, chattering excitedly.

Mallory helped him, her hands shaking as she tried not to rush and tear the material further. It didn't help putting it back into place. She guessed she'd have to repair the material like last time. Checking her mana, she found she was eleven short. A potion vial wouldn't be enough. But it'd help. Downing the contents of a mana potion, she returned the empty vial to her satchel.

"Mal! Look out," Brodie called.

Mallory spun to see a warrior skeleton coming towards her. At the same time, she noticed her mana had regened enough she could use mend I on the material. If it didn't work, the skeleton would attack her before she could defend herself. Taking a deep breath, she faced the coffin, using mend I on the material, bracing herself for the attack. It didn't come. Silence filled the room and she slowly turned to see what was happening.

Ryan sheathed his swords, grinning. "We did it." He strode across the room.

Returning his grin, Mallory met him partway, throwing her arms around him. "I can't believe that worked." Her lips met his and she clung to him, trying not to think about how low everyone's health was. It had been too close.

"I'm surprised none of us died in that last fight." Callum scooped up Smudge and returned him to the makeshift sling. "That was close."

Mallory remained in Ryan's arms. "We should search the bodies." She didn't let him go.

He continued to hold her. "It can wait a few minutes." He smiled down at her. "I'm not in any hurry to move."

"What did you do to make them happy?" Brodie asked.

"Mended the material that had been torn," Mallory said.

"How could we have made them happy without the mending spell?" Callum asked.

"Repaired the clothes by sewing them," Danae said.

Mallory checked her mana. There was enough to cast her healing spell a few times. She could begin healing everyone again. She started with Ryan. "We are not leaving the crypt until everyone has full health."

Ryan ran his fingers across her cheek. "Sarisa is going to freak when she sees the amount of blood on all of us."

"We could sneak into the bathroom and clean ourselves before we see her," Brodie suggested.

"We'd be better off cleaning ourselves at the well." Danae dropped onto the stone floor by the coffins, leaning against one of them. "I'm exhausted. It's a good thing we can ride in the wagon and not have to walk or ride all the way to Velkden."

Mallory momentarily closed her eyes. Five hours in a wagon was going to make it a really long day. "Don't remind me."

Ryan chuckled. "Give it time. Once we're all healed and have had a rest, the trip to Velkden will be easy."

"What if we're attacked along the way?" Mallory asked.

"We'll have enough with us that any fight should be quickly won," Ryan said.

"I hope so." Mallory slowly drew away from him, surveying the room. Her gaze was drawn to the candles that were alight. "When did they light themselves?"

"When the creatures vanished." Danae struggled to her feet, taking the hand Callum held out to her. She smiled at him in thanks. "We need to put the lids back on the coffins. If we take too long to do it, wraiths will respawn."

"Why didn't we need to do it straight away?" Mallory made her way to one of the lids.

"They can be left open for short periods of time for those who prefer to open them to pay their respects." Danae grabbed the edge of the lid.

When everyone was in place, other than Brodie, they lifted the lid back onto the coffin, doing the same for the second one. Mallory slowly shook her head, staring at the lids. "I can't believe how easy they were to lift up. I was expecting us to struggle."

"Look at how much each of us can carry." Ryan crouched beside a wraith and began to search it.

"I'd forgotten about that." Mallory searched one of the warrior skeletons. "There are so many differences between our two worlds."

"I'd love to see some of them," Danae said.

"We're trying to get our own place," Brodie said. "You could visit then."

"I'd love that. When do you think you'll have your own place?" Danae asked.

Brodie shrugged, turning to Ryan. "How long do you think it'll take?"

"I don't know. All I know is Dorset said the guardians would vouch for me when it came to getting a place. Or at least they'd vouch for me once during the testing phase and to make sure I wanted to waste that on a rental property." Ryan moved onto another creature, having finished searching the wraith.

"What happens if you don't get the first place you apply for?" Callum asked.

"I asked him about that. He said that as long as I was realistic about the places I applied for they'd keep vouching for me until I was accepted for one." Ryan grinned. "I have no idea how long it'll take, but I'll keep applying until we have our own place."

Brodie turned to Danae again. "I could take you to see my favourite places. Show you around Brisbane. If you wore your hair down, it should cover your ears."

Danae smiled at him. "You'd do that? Show me your favourite places."

Brodie's cheeks flushed. "Ahh, yeah."

Danae moved closer to him. "I could show you around Simria if you ever visit there."

"Cool." Brodie looked over to Mallory. "We should do that, Mal. Take Danni to Simria instead of leaving her to catch a ship."

Ryan spoke before Mallory could. "What about all the quests you want to complete?"

Brodie shrugged, the movement awkward while using crutches. "I'm beginning to think that isn't possible. The longer we stay in an area, the more we seem to get."

"Finally," Callum said.

Danae laughed softly. "You'll get accustomed to not being able to complete every quest you come across. Although as an adventurer, you have a better chance of being able to complete them. It used to frustrate me when I came across a quest I'd like to complete, but didn't have the skills to complete it."

"Do you have some you need a hand with?" Brodie asked. "After Cutthroat Harbour." He glanced down. "And my knee is better."

Danae shook her head. "Not around here."

Ryan put some items on top of one of the coffins. "How about we finish searching?"

Mallory nodded, doing the same. "Another mage robe. At least we should do all right by selling them."

Callum put five knucklebones and a handful of coins on top of the coffin. "And we gained some potion ingredients that we'll eventually need."

Chapter Forty-Five

Mallory went through all the items they'd found. As well as the mage robe and five knuckles, there was also two gold, six silver and eleven copper pieces, two stilettos, a silver armband that Danae said might be enchanted, two essence Danae told them were an alchemy ingredient but didn't know what potion they were used in, full leather leg armour that Callum teased Brodie he'd needed days ago and also a spell.

Mallory unrolled the parchment. "Vanish I. Twenty-five mana and it lasts for one minute on target."

"On target means you could use it on anyone or thing, including yourself," Danae said.

"Use it on me," Brodie said.

Mallory slowly shook her head at her brother's enthusiasm, putting the parchment in her satchel.

"I'm still healing everybody. I don't have the mana to waste."

"Once you finish healing everyone," Brodie said.

Ryan spoke before Mallory could tell her brother no. "We still have to get back to Wayholt and just because there's been no creatures every other time, that doesn't mean it will remain that way."

"We should take the two grave robbers outside and clear out the upstairs area," Danae said. "If we leave the grave robbers we might not get a reward. Same if we leave a mess in the entrance room."

Ryan gathered up the gear that was to go in his backpack. He gestured to the backpack the grave robbers had brought with them. "You can grab that, Callum. We'll take the grave robbers upstairs and search them while we wait for Mallory to finish healing us."

"Will it be safe to wait upstairs when our health isn't full?" Mallory put the knuckles and coins away.

Ryan shrugged. "I guess we'll soon find out."

They returned to the room with all the pillars and the bodies of the grave robbers, collecting them and taking them upstairs to the entrance room. Before taking them outside, they checked over the bodies and found two hand drawn maps, a letter, six silver pieces, a sheathed long sword, a sheathed stiletto, a pair of leather boots and a tin that contained four small, cloth balls that were about two centimetres in diameter and a tiny corked vial.

Brodie peered into the tin, cautiously touching the contents. "What are they for?"

"Sleeping mist." Danae took the tin from him and closed it. "You put a couple of drops of the liquid, from the vial, on the ball and set it where you want everyone in the area to fall asleep. It takes about five minutes before it activates and the cloud that rises from it puts everyone to sleep in about a four metre radius. Or more if it's a higher strength potion."

"Why do you need the balls? Can't you put the potion from the vial on something else?" Callum asked.

Danae shook her head. "There are special herbs in the balls that the potion reacts with. They cut the herbs up finely and put them inside the cloth balls and stitch them closed."

"That sounds like a rogue thing." Brodie held out his hand. "I should have them."

Ryan took the tin before Danae could give it to Brodie. "That sounds like a disaster waiting to happen in your hands." He handed them to Mallory. "They can go in your satchel."

Ignoring her brother's protests, Mallory put the tin

inside her satchel. "How far do we need to take the bodies?"

Danae gestured towards the doorway. "Not far. Just as long as they're not left on the steps."

Ryan checked outside. "We'll do that while we're waiting."

Once the bodies were taken outside, Mallory did the last of the healing. Relief washed over her. Somehow, they'd survived.

Ryan tugged her towards him. "What are you looking so pleased about?"

She smiled up at him. "We didn't die."

He chuckled. "So we didn't." He kissed her before drawing back and checking the time. "It's ten thirty. We better collect the reward and head back to Sarisa's place."

Mallory made her way to the altar. "How does this work?"

Danae joined her. "Once everyone has placed their hands on the altar, we say 'rest in peace' together. A gift for each of us should appear in front of our hand." She placed her hand on the altar, palm against it.

Callum stood on the other side of Danae, placing his hand on the altar. He smiled when Smudge chattered and reached out a paw towards the altar. "I don't think it'll work for you."

Smudge scolded him, placing his paw on the altar anyway.

After Mallory had placed her hand on the altar, she checked that everyone else had done the same. "Are we ready?" When everyone nodded, she asked, "On the count of three?" Again they nodded. "Okay. One. Two. Three. Rest in peace." The altar warmed beneath her hand. A single pearl on a gold necklace appeared on the altar close enough to touch her fingertips. She looked across the altar to see what everyone else had received, the journal icon appearing in the corner of her vision. Guessing it was the quest completion notification she didn't bother checking.

There were ten gold pieces in front of Ryan, a ring for Callum, a sheathed knife for Brodie and a belt pouch for Danae. Smudge made disappointed sounds as he lifted his paw and examined it then looked at the altar. He spotted Mallory's necklace and reached for it, chattering excitedly.

Smiling, she handed it over to Smudge. "Here you go. It seems fair that you should get to play with it since you let me have yours." She ran her hand across Smudge's head. "Those pearl earrings we got in Mer Point would have gone well with the necklace. A pity we sold them."

Brodie picked up the knife, taking it out of the sheath. "You shouldn't give that to Smudge, it's probably worth a lot of money. Look how much that single pearl was worth and it wasn't on a necklace." Brodie slipped the knife back into the sheath. "Why did I end up with such a lame gift?" He looked at the belt pouch Danae had picked up. "Not that yours is much better, but it would have been more useful for me. I need one for my pig."

"I don't mind swapping if you want," Danae said. "Utility knives always come in handy and can be used by anyone. And judging by the quality of the ring Callum received and the necklace Mallory was given, it wouldn't surprise me if all of these items were enchanted."

"If we got enchanted stuff, then why did Ryan only get coins?" Brodie asked. "And not many."

"You tend to get something related to your class or your crafting ability. Ryan is a warrior and they often get paid," Danae said. "Back when those bodies that were disturbed were buried, ten gold pieces was probably worth a lot more than they're worth today."

Brodie eyed the coins Ryan handed to Mallory. "I would have rather been paid. What sort of enchantment can you put on a utility knife?"

"Quite a few different ones. Cutting straight, stay

sharp, never miss which means you'll never accidentally cut yourself, unbreakable or never lost which means it reappears in the sheath if it's left lying around for too long," Danae said.

Ryan chuckled. "Maybe that is the correct gift for Brodie after all. Particularly if it's a never miss enchantment."

Brodie glared at Ryan. "Very funny."

Chapter Forty-Six

Once she'd finished laughing, Mallory nodded towards the necklace Smudge was playing with, putting the chain around his neck only to have it slip down. "What sort of enchantment would be put on necklaces?"

"Too many to list. Jewellery is a popular item to use for enchantments," Danae said. "Especially since you can wear approximately twenty separate pieces for enchantments between rings, earrings, a necklace, piercings, bracelets, armbands and anklets."

"How do we find out what, if any, enchantments were put on the items we were given?" Mallory asked.

"Someone with a high enough level barter would be able to tell you. My father could, but there's no one in Wayholt that can," Danae said.

"Callum has a heap of CAS points he hasn't used," Brodie said.

Danae smiled. "They wouldn't be anywhere near enough."

"Is that the only way we can tell what the enchantment is?" Ryan asked.

"You could put them on and if you're lucky they might be an enchantment that's easy to figure out. Such as adding an attribute point or giving you a buff that would be listed in your journal," Danae said.

Callum slipped the ring on. Before he could speak, Brodie did.

"How unfair. Plus two for bow attacks. I want one for stiletto attacks. And throwing knives." Brodie turned to Mallory. "Put your necklace on."

Mallory looked down at Smudge who remained in the sling, trying to get the necklace to stay around his neck. "Could I have it back for a minute please, Smudge? I'll return it to you afterwards. I just want to find out what it does."

"What if it's a good buff?" Brodie demanded. "You're not going to give it back to him if it is, are you?"

Mallory took the necklace Smudge held out to her. "Of course I am." She slipped it over her head. "I said he could play with it for now."

"Huh! Told you you're a healer," Brodie said. "Even the dead people think you are. Double your healing."

"That's probably because of how much healing she did while we were in the crypt," Danae said. "Their magic isn't omnipotent. It could only judge by our actions while we were here."

Mallory slipped the necklace over her head and returned it to Smudge. "We could have done with this earlier."

"What are you doing?" Brodie demanded. "Put it back on."

Mallory smiled as she watched Smudge try and put the necklace on again. It continued to slip down and he kept trying to put it back in place. "I'm finished healing everyone for now. I can get it back off him if I need to do more healing later."

"What if he loses it?" Brodie asked.

"He won't lose it." Callum lifted up the necklace and twisted the chain to make a double loop before slipping it over Smudge's head. "He's smarter than that."

"He better not lose it," Brodie muttered.

"Do you think it will increase the healing I do with my apothecary abilities?" Mallory asked.

"It might help you fix my knee quicker?" Brodie asked.

Danae shrugged. "I don't know. Wear it next time you heal Brodie and find out."

"If it works with rapid mend, you could level your apothecary up another ten levels to do average rapid mend and then you'd be able to reduce healing time by twenty percent instead of ten. I wonder if it works with the salves you apply," Callum said. "It'd be pretty overpowered if it did. Between those two you'd heal by fifty percent in one go if it worked with both."

"You better try it tonight," Brodie said. "And level up another nine CAS points."

"Then you'll be complaining even more about how far ahead of you I am," Mallory said.

"I'm sick of not being able to do anything. It's not like I wanted to be shot in the knee," Brodie muttered.

Grinning, Ryan glanced at Brodie's knee before he headed for the exit. "It's time to get back to Wayholt. Especially if we plan to be on the road by midday."

Outside, Callum helped Brodie onto Bug and they headed towards Wayholt. Mallory checked her journal, seeing she was right and it was a notification about completing the quest. *Ancient Crypt: You discovered the reason why the dead were restless and ensured they could rest in peace again. You were rewarded with gifts, from those you laid to rest, for the members of your party. You also earned fifteen experience points each.* They'd also gained two reputation for Wayholt. She smiled when she realised both her and Callum had gained a CAS point. She guessed Brodie hadn't realised yet since he hadn't said anything. And with all the money they'd gained she didn't feel as broke as she'd felt after paying for Brodie's visits to the apothecary. They now had forty-one gold, thirty-eight silver and ninety-eight copper pieces.

The journey was quiet and they arrived just after eleven. They stopped at the well and cleaned up a bit before they continued to Sarisa's place. Brodie stepped away from the well. "You have to be kidding. Mal and Callum got a CAS point. I'm never going to catch up." He glared at them when they laughed.

"I would have thought you'd have noticed that ages ago," Ryan said.

"I was checking other things. Like how Fang only needs another hundred experience points to reach level one and trying to decide what to put my CAS point in. There are so many things I want to unlock and improve."

Mallory looked them over as they strode along the road. Cleaning the blood off their arms and face hadn't made a great deal of difference. Their clothes were streaked and splattered with their blood. The potions and healing spell might have fixed their wounds, but they hadn't got rid of the evidence. "Maybe Danni should sneak out the back of her mother's cottage and have a wash while I get some clothes for her to change into."

Ryan chuckled. "I don't think it'll help. Not with the state the rest of us are in."

Danae smiled at Mallory. "Thank you for the offer. She'll have to become accustomed to how this is part of my life now." Danae's smile widened into a grin as she looked around the group. "And I couldn't be happier." Her gaze rested a moment on Brodie before she turned to Mallory again. "Meeting all of you was one of the best things to ever happen to me. I never thought I'd find another friend like Sidree. I was devastated when he moved away from Simria."

"Who is Sidree?" Brodie asked.

"He's my best friend. We grew up in Simria together. Or at least we did once I moved there." Danae laughed softly. "We stumbled into so much trouble together that I think my father was relieved the day he left."

"Why did he leave?" Mallory asked.

Before Danae had the chance to speak, Sarisa came

out of the house, hurrying to meet them. "You're unharmed?" She stopped in front of Danae. "You suffered no serious injury?"

Danae smiled. "My health is at full again." She held out the belt pouch she'd received. "I was given this for laying the dead to rest. We think it might have an enchantment on it."

Sarisa took the belt pouch, looking it over. "The easiest one to test for is reduced carrying weight." She glanced around the group. "If you wish to clean up, I've cooked chicken and vegetable pasties for you to eat before leaving. As well as some to take with you so you don't have to worry about your meal when you stop for the night. I made enough for everyone."

"Hell yeah!" Brodie urged Bug forward. "I'm first in the bathroom."

Ninette came to meet them as they went around to the back of the cottage. She held out a letter. "Deneg left instructions for you. His coffin and chest are in the wagon. Kruth helped me collect them."

Chapter Forty-Seven

Mallory took the letter and looked past Ninette to Kruth, nodding at him in thanks.

Kruth grinned at her, his lower canines becoming more noticeable. "I'm ready to go whenever you are."

Mallory glanced around the area. Nearly everything was packed. Welby, Roast, the wagoner, Emica and Jorgen all sat around the fire talking softly. Welby and the wagoner were playing a game that involved dice. "Sarisa said she made lunch for us to have before we leave."

Kruth nodded. "She brought out food for us to pack for dinner."

Mallory glanced at the letter. "I better read this."

With a nod, Kruth returned to the group around the fire.

Ninette gestured in the direction Brodie had taken. "The apothecary said for an extra two gold pieces you could keep the crutches. Did you want me to take the money to her?"

Mallory nodded, handing over the coins. She opened the letter as soon as Ninette raced off. She looked up at Ryan when he joined her, smiling at him. She held the letter at an angle so he could read it too. Finished it before him, she said, "It looks like Deneg doesn't need to go all the way into Velkden. The person he wants to visit is on a farm before you reach Velkden. Just over the river. About twenty minutes away from Velkden."

Ryan looked up from the letter. "That might work out better. We can ask them some questions about the village. None of us have been there before. It'd be nice to have some details about it before we arrive."

Mallory folded the letter and put it in her belt pouch. "I sent Ninette to pay for the crutches from the apothecary. Maybe we can sell them once Brodie's knee is healed."

Ryan grinned. "Or keep them in case he needs them again."

"I hope not." Mallory slowly shook her head. "This has been a lot of trouble. And what are we going to do about going home? We're meant to regularly return so our actions can have an impact on our world. Not to mention we're meant to split our time between the two worlds until we can afford the potions we need to turn back the ageing process."

"They didn't say it was a requirement. Or tell us how often we need to return," Ryan said.

"Should we return for a few minutes before we leave here? Just long enough for the quests we completed to have an effect," Mallory asked.

Ryan shook his head. "We can't risk it. What if something happened to slow us down? It'd make you late to school."

"I suppose." Mallory sighed. "Danni is so lucky her mother knows and she doesn't have to hide any of this from her."

Ryan chuckled. "I doubt your mum would be so tolerant."

"I know she wouldn't be." She leaned against Ryan when he slipped his arm around her waist. "It'd just be nice if it wasn't such an effort to travel between the worlds."

Ryan held her gaze for a moment. "You won't be in school and living at home forever."

Mallory's lips slowly curved into a smile. "No, I won't."

Danae and Callum joined them, Brodie also coming over. "What are you talking about?" Brodie looked from one to the other.

Mallory briefly explained, including Ryan's final comment.

"Hell yeah," Brodie said. "I can't wait."

Callum took a step towards the bathroom, looking over his shoulder. "We'll be finished school before you." Grinning, he hurried away.

Brodie glared after Callum. "That doesn't mean you can come here without me."

Mallory chuckled. "You know he wouldn't want to come here without you." She glanced at those standing with her. "We're a team." Her gaze momentarily rested on Danae. "All of us."

Danae smiled back at her.

It didn't take long to wash themselves and their clothes and change into clean ones. As she sat by the fire eating her lunch, Mallory looked down at the brown dress she wore. It was surprisingly comfortable and not as long as she'd feared it would be, only reaching midcalf. Although she wouldn't want to fight in it. Her attention was caught by Brodie and Sarisa who were talking.

"You want to keep him?" Brodie asked.

Sarisa patted Not For Bacon who was lying on her lap. "No, look after him while you're in Cutthroat Harbour. He's such a tiny, little thing that he might end up getting hurt."

"His name is Not For Bacon," Ryan said.

Brodie glared at Ryan. "It is not. He hasn't got a name."

"You should have named him sooner if you didn't want us to name him," Callum said.

"We don't even know if we're coming back this way," Mallory said.

Danae laughed. "Which is probably why my mother wants to look after him. To make sure we do come back so she can see for herself that I survived Cutthroat Harbour."

"It'd be nice to see you once you're done in Cutthroat Harbour," Sarisa said. "But my concerns are real. Look what happened this morning. What if he escaped and was lost when you were somewhere on the road? You might never find him."

Brodie's gaze remained on Not For Bacon. "She's right." He looked at Mallory. "We can't take him with us, Mal. We'll have to come back and get him."

"What happened to finding a home for him?" Callum asked.

Brodie gestured towards Not For Bacon. "Look at him. He's so cute. How can I give him away?"

Callum patted Smudge on the head. The river otter still wore the pearl necklace. "What was it you said to me when I wanted Smudge because he's cute?"

"That was different," Brodie argued. "Besides, how would I know if someone else would look after him properly."

Ryan grinned. "Yeah, Callum. It was different. Smudge wasn't for Brodie."

Chapter Forty-Eight

Mallory interrupted her brother's protests. "We vote on it. And it doesn't necessarily mean we'll get to come back to Wayholt straight after Cutthroat Harbour. There might be other things we need to do first."

Callum shrugged. "I don't mind."

Danae glanced at her mother before returning her attention to Mallory. "I'd like to see my mother again before I travel to Merrow."

Brodie interrupted Mallory. "Majority rules. We're coming back here."

"If you'd given me the chance to speak, I was about to say the same thing." Mallory smiled at Danae. "I decided yes the moment Danni said she wanted to say goodbye to her mother before heading to Merrow."

Sarisa met Mallory's gaze. "Thank you. It's good

to know Danae now has friends who can handle the trouble they get into."

"Sidree isn't that bad," Danae protested.

Sarisa smiled at her daughter's comment. "I think it is more a case that you are both as bad as each other." She turned to Brodie. "I'll take good care of him." She glanced down at Not For Bacon.

"Thanks," Brodie said.

Sarisa took four pieces of folded paper out of her belt pouch and handed them to Brodie. "And I know you'll all take good care of my daughter."

Brodie unfolded the paper, looking at each one. "Cool. Recipes. Bacon, egg and herb bake. Blueberry pancakes. Herb muffins. Ginger crepes. I can't wait to make some of these." He tucked them into his belt pouch. "Thanks."

Sarisa inclined her head and held out the belt pouch to Danae. "I figured out what the enchantment is. It reduces the weight of things by fifty percent. That's not to say there isn't another enchantment on it as well. It seems to be a fairly well made item."

Danae took the belt pouch and held it out to Mallory. "You should have this since you're carrying the group money. I'm sure it gets heavy at times."

Mallory took the belt pouch, glancing at Brodie. "Not lately." She changed belt pouches, putting the contents of hers in the new one before putting it on, leaving out the two maps and the letter they'd found on the grave robbers. "What do I do with this belt pouch?"

"Brodie could have it for Not For Bacon," Danae said.

Brodie groaned. "Not you too. He doesn't have a name."

Danae glanced at Not For Bacon. "Everyone needs a name. Even little pigs."

Brodie sighed. "Fine. Not For Bacon." He glared at Callum and Ryan when they laughed. "But I'm shortening it to NFB." He turned to Danae. "Did you want the utility knife?" He wore it on his belt.

Danae shook her head, smiling. "You keep it."

Mallory handed the spare belt pouch to Sarisa before she held up the maps. "I don't suppose anyone knows the location of these maps."

Emica leaned forward. "I don't recognise the locations, but I do recognise the names written in demonic runes at the top of each map." She pointed to the first map. "That is a family that owns Dead Hope Mine. Brower. They live in a mansion in Shadhurst." She pointed to the second map. "That one says Frostwell. They live in Rolling Meadows and own the Eastern Mine."

Mallory looked from one map to the other. "That makes a terrible kind of sense. Especially with the letter from someone called Tivon in Morlee who is interested in the gems and jewellery they talked about selling. They were grave robbers." Noticing the journal icon was in the corner of her vision, she checked and found a new quest. She laughed when Brodie began to complain.

"What is wrong? Sarisa asked.

"A quest," Ryan said. "Grave Robbers: Notify the authorities or take the matter into your own hands and see if the dead are still at peace."

"If you don't want to do it, I can complete it when I return to Shadhurst," Emica said.

"You can do the quest too?" Brodie asked.

"If you don't want to share a quest with people who aren't in your party, you shouldn't read it aloud." Emica gestured around the fire. "Everyone here now has that quest."

"So we won't be able to do it?" Mallory asked.

"I won't notify them if you don't want me to, but even if I do, that doesn't mean the quest will be finalised for you. They might take awhile to deal with the situation allowing you to complete the quest too," Emica said.

Jorgen rose to his feet. "It's nearly midday. We should make a start."

"How do you know it's nearly midday?" Brodie asked. "You don't have a pocket watch, do you?"

Jorgen shook his head. "I don't need one." He indicated the sun that was overhead. "As long as you know the rising and setting times you can estimate what the time is." He smiled. "And midday is the simplest time of all to figure out."

Mallory put the maps in her belt pouch, which was far lighter than she was accustomed to. "Everyone should use the outhouse before we leave. Next stop isn't for five hours."

It didn't take them long to finish getting ready and after saying goodbye to Sarisa everyone clambered into the wagon except for Danae who was still saying goodbye to her mother. Mallory smiled at all the wet clothes hanging from every available space of the wagon and the canvas stretched over the top of it. They would make an odd sight travelling down the road, but at least their clothes would dry. She turned to Emica and Jorgen who were sitting on the coffin that was taking up a fair amount of space. "Do either of you dual wield?"

Both nodded, only Jorgen speaking. "I prefer to use two stilettos."

"We have spares now. If you want to borrow them." Mallory rummaged in the gear, taking out a sheathed stiletto and short sword. "You're probably going to need them when we get to Cutthroat Harbour." She gave the stiletto to Jorgen and the short sword to Emica.

Danae climbed into the wagon, waving to her mother as they drove off. The horses and donkey were tied to the back of the wagon and Sarisa stood there waving to them until they were out of sight, cradling Not For Bacon.

Mallory moved closer to Danae. "Are you okay?"

Danae nodded. "I always feel bad when I leave her behind. This is where she wishes to stay. It's her home." Danae paused a moment. "I'm not sure where mine is yet."

Mallory looked at those around her and out at the village they were leaving behind. "Who says home has to be a place?"

"Certainly not the travellers," Jorgen said. "To us, home is our clan. Those who remain at our side, fight alongside us, celebrate with us, die with us."

Mallory slowly nodded. "I like that idea of home." She reached for Ryan, linking her fingers through his.

"I like that idea of home too," Danae said.

Mallory leaned against Ryan as he moved closer to

her. She looked out the back of the wagon, Wayholt no longer in sight. Five hours was a long time to spend in the wagon. She could get a start on writing in her notebook or gain some experience points. That might help the time pass more quickly.

Ryan let go of her hand and slipped his arm around her shoulders, smiling down at her when she looked up at him.

She returned his smile. Experience points and updating her notebook could wait. She was too contented to move. Jorgen was right. She was home. It wasn't just the people she was with. It was the adventures and being able to make a difference in both worlds. She couldn't wait to see where the next adventure would take them.

Final Stats

Character weight does not include any backpacks, satchels, their contents or items carried by livestock.

Mallory

Character Level: 4	CAS XP: 5/139
Health: 39	Available CAS Points: 2
Stamina: 65	Available Class Points: 0
Mana: 55	Level Progress: 4:1/10
Weight: 5kg 865g/80kg	

Attributes

Strength: 8	Dexterity: 5
Constitution: 13	Charisma: 5
Intelligence: 11	Luck: 5
Wisdom: 11	

Class

Mage: 2
Warrior: 2

Class Skills
None

Spells

Fireball: 0
Mend I: 0
Health I: 0

(Expand For More Details)

Weapon and Armour Affinity

Dagger: 1 (+1% damage)
Wand: 1 (+1% damage)
Cloth Armour: 0
Short Sword: 0

(Expand For More Details)

Crafting

Alchemy: 1
Apothecary: 35
Wheelwright: 1

(Expand For More Details)

Reputation

Global: 0
Local Areas:
Ruby Isle
(Expand For More Details)

Buffs and Negative Stats

Necklace: doubles healing done

Available Revives 4

Mallory

Spells Expanded

*All attack spells have +34% damage to base attacks.

Level 0

Fireball: 0
Mana cost: 3
Cooldown: 2 seconds
Damage: low 3, normal 5, critical 7
Duration: Instant

Mend I: 0
Mana Cost: 17
Cooldown: 5 seconds
Area Of Effect: 1cm2
Duration: Instant

Flame: 0
Mana cost: 5
Cooldown: 3 seconds
Damage: low 4, normal 6, critical 8
Damage Over Time: 4 every 2 seconds
Duration: Non-flammable materials 6 secs,
flammable materials until runs out of fuel

Level 1

Health I: 0
Restores health to target
Mana Cost: 6
Cooldown: 3 seconds
Area Of Effect: +1HP to target within 2m
Duration: Instant

Poison Dart I: 0
Mana Cost: 6
Cooldown: 3 seconds
Damage: low 4, normal 6, crit 8
Damage Over Time: 5 every 3 seconds
Duration: 3 secs

Level 2

Lightning Trap: 0
Mana Cost: 10
Cooldown: 5 seconds
Damage: 10
Duration: damage on contact

Level 3

Weak Reanimate: 0
Mana Cost: 20
Cooldown: 5 seconds
Area Of Effect: reanimate one of the dead
level 3
Range: 2m
Duration: 1 min

Mallory

Weapon and Armour Affinity Expanded

Dagger (and enchanted): 1 (+1% damage)
Wand: 1 (+1% damage)
Cloth Armour: 0
Unarmed: 0

Chain Mail Armour: 0
Short Sword (and enchanted): 0
Shield (and enchanted): 0
Dual Swords: 0

Crafting Expanded

Alchemy: 1
Apothecary: 35
Bard: 0
Bartering: 0

Cooking: 0
Diplomacy: 0
Fishing: 0
Hunting: 0

Husbandry: 0
Languages: 0
Sailing: 0
Scribe: 0

Shipwright: 0
Wheelwright: 1
Woodcutter: 0

Reputation Expanded

Ruby Isle:
Buckneth 22

Mer Point 10
South Peak Mine 5

Surith 5
Wayholt 10

Wildebay 10

Ryan

Character Level: 1
Health: 27
Stamina: 45
Mana: 20
Weight: 10kg 387g/90kg

CAS XP: 108/113
Available CAS Points: 7
Available Class Points: 0
Level Progress: 1:5/10

Attributes

Strength: 9
Constitution: 9
Intelligence: 5
Wisdom: 4

Dexterity: 5
Charisma: 5
Luck: 6

Class

Warrior: 1

Class Skills
None

Spells

None

Weapon and Armour Affinity

Chain Mail Armour: 0
Short Sword: 1 (+1% damage)
Shield: 1 (+1% damage)
(-1% damage taken)
Dual Swords: 0

Crafting

Hunting: 5
Wheelwright: 1

(Expand For More Details)

Reputation

Global: 0
Local Areas:
Ruby Isle
(Expand For More Details)

Buffs and Negative Stats

None

Available Revives 2

Ryan

Crafting Expanded

Alchemy: 0

Apothecary: 0

Bard: 0

Bartering: 0

Cooking: 0

Diplomacy: 0

Fishing: 0

Hunting: 5

Husbandry: 0

Languages: 0

Sailing: 0

Scribe: 0

Shipwright: 0

Wheelwright: 1

Woodcutter: 0

Reputation Expanded

Ruby Isle:

Buckneth 22

Mer Point 10

South Peak Mine 5

Surith 5

Wayholt 10

Wildebay 10

Bradie

Character Level: 1
Health: 27
Stamina: 45
Mana: 25
Weight: 6kg 458g/50kg

CAS XP: 98/111
Available CAS Points: 1
Available Class Points: 0
Level Progress: 1:3/10

Attributes

Strength: 5
Constitution: 9
Intelligence: 4
Wisdom: 5

Dexterity: 8
Charisma: 7
Luck: 5

Class

Rogue: 1

Class Skills
Stealth: 0 (30 seconds,
1 hour cooldown)

Spells

None

Weapon and Armour Affinity

Stiletto: 1 (+1% damage)
Throwing Knives: 2
(+2% damage)
Leather Armour: 0

Crafting

Bartering: 1
Cooking: 7
Wheelwright: 1

(Expand For More Details)

Reputation

Global: 0
Local Areas:
Ruby Isle
(Expand For More Details)

Buffs and Negative Stats

None

Available Revives 1

Bradie

Crafting Expanded

Alchemy: 0
Apothecary: 0
Bard: 0
Bartering: 1

Cooking: 7
Diplomacy: 0
Fishing: 0
Hunting: 0

Husbandry: 0
Languages: 0
Sailing: 0
Scribe: 0

Shipwright: 0
Wheelwright: 1
Woodcutter: 0

Reputation Expanded

Ruby Isle:
Buckneth 22

Mer Point 10
South Peak Mine 5

Surith 5
Wayholt 10

Wildebay 10

Callum

Character Level: 1
Health: 21
Stamina: 35
Mana: 25
Weight: 6kg 283g/60kg

CAS XP: 9/114
Available CAS Points: 13
Available Class Points: 0
Level Progress: 1:6/10

Attributes

Strength: 6
Constitution: 7
Intelligence: 5
Wisdom: 5

Dexterity: 9
Charisma: 4
Luck: 7

Class

Archer: 1

Class Skills
None

Spells

None

Weapon and Armour Affinity

Short Bow (and enchanted): 1 (+1% damage)
Hunting Knife: 1 (+1% damage)
Studded Leather Armour: 0
Sling: 0
Slingshot

Crafting

Wheelwright: 1

(Expand For More Details)

Reputation

Global: 0
Local Areas:
Ruby Isle
(Expand For More Details)

Buffs and Negative Stats

Silver Ring: +2 damage to bow attacks

Available Revives 1

Callum

Crafting Expanded

Alchemy: 0
Apothecary: 0
Bard: 0
Bartering: 0

Cooking: 0
Diplomacy: 0
Fishing: 0
Hunting: 0

Husbandry: 0
Languages: 0
Sailing: 0
Scribe: 0

Shipwright: 0
Wheelwright: 1
Woodcutter: 0

Reputation Expanded

Ruby Isle:
Buckneth 22

Mer Point 10
South Peak Mine 5

Surith 5
Wayholt 10

Wildebay 10

Danae

Character Level: 2
Health: 27
Stamina: 45
Mana: 25
Weight: 5kg 889g/60kg

CAS XP: 113/120
Available CAS Points: 2
Available Class Points: 0
Level Progress: 2:2/10

Attributes

Strength: 6
Constitution: 9
Intelligence: 5
Wisdom: 5

Dexterity: 11
Charisma: 4
Luck: 8

Class

Archer: 2

Class Skills
None

Spells

None

Weapon and Armour Affinity

Short Bow (and enchanted): 1
(+1% damage)
Hunting Knife: 1 (+1% damage)
Studded Leather Armour: 0

(Expand For More Details)

Crafting

Alchemy: 9
Bartering: 1
Cooking: 1
Glassblowing: 5

(Expand For More Details)

Reputation

Global: 0
Local Areas:
Ruby Isle
(Expand For More Details)

Buffs and Negative Stats

None

Racial Bonus

Archer +10% damage
Mage capable of using spells
one level above class level

Available Revives 2

Danae

Weapon and Armour Affinity Expanded

Short Bow (and enchanted): 1 (+1% damage)
Hunting Knife: 1 (+1% damage)
Studded Leather Armour: 0

Sling: 0
Slingshot
Enchanted Arrows
Unarmed: 1 (+1% damage)

Crafting Expanded

Alchemy: 9
Apothecary: 0
Bartering: 1
Clothier: 0

Cooking: 1
Diplomacy: 0
Fishing: 0
Glassblowing: 5

Husbandry: 0
Languages: 0
Sailing: 0
Scribe: 0

Shipwright: 0
Wheelwright: 1
Woodcutter: 0

Reputation Expanded

Ruby Isle:
Buckneth 4
Mer Point 10

Simria 22
South Peak Mine 5

Surith 5
Ursen 0

Wayholt 18
Wildebay 10

COMPANION ANIMALS' FINAL STATS

Smudge 8HP (Callum)

1168XP/2000XP

Fang 6HP (Brodie)

900XP/1000XP

Free Ebook

Subscribe to Avril's newsletter and receive a free ebook. This ebook is exclusive to those on her mailing list. To find out more about this offer visit:

www.avrilsabine.com/free-ebook

*

We value your privacy and will not sell, rent, exchange or loan your email address to third parties. Your information is confidential and you are under no obligation to remain on the mailing list and can unsubscribe at any time.

Acknowledgements

Thanks to the usual crew. We appreciate your help and are grateful for the time you spend working with us to improve this series. Each and every one of you are invaluable.

To The Reader

If you enjoyed this book, why not consider leaving a review to help other readers discover it too? Reader engagement is one of the few ways that lets an author know readers want more books in a particular series or genre. So leave a review and tell friends, not only about this book but also about other ones you've enjoyed, so you can continue to enjoy books by your favourite authors for years to come.

Dreams are meant to be lived,

Avril, Storm and Rhys.

About The Authors

Avril is an Australian author who lives with her family on acreage in South East Queensland. She writes mostly young adult and children's speculative fiction, but has been known to dabble in other genres. You can find more information about her at www.avrilsabine.com where you can also subscribe to her newsletter to be kept informed about new releases, current projects, blog posts and exclusive news.

Storm has a wide range of interests from gaming and blacksmithing to cooking and sewing. It's not unusual to find him cooking at any hour of the day or night, particularly after a long gaming session.

Rhys loves books and gaming and has thoroughly enjoyed combining two of his favourite things. He has been running tabletop gaming sessions for the past few years and enjoys creating characters and doing in depth worldbuilding.

Titles By Avril Sabine

Stories about strong characters and characters who discover their strengths.

SERIES

Assassins Of The Dead- Young Adult Fantasy/ Paranormal

Book 1: Dark Blade

Book 2: Dragon Touched

Book 3: Society Against Vampires

Book 4: King's Request

Dragon Blood- Young Adult Urban Fantasy (with elements of romance)

(5 book series)

Book 1: Pliethin

Book 2: Wyvern

Book 3: Surety

Book 4: Knight

Book 5: Mage

Dragon Mage- Young Adult Urban Fantasy (with elements of romance)

(Series two of Dragon Blood series)

Book 1: Promise

Dragon Blood Chronicles- Young Adult Urban Fantasy (with elements of romance)

(Companion stand alone series to Dragon Blood)

Book 1: Oath

Book 2: Betrayed

Guardians Of The Round Table- Young Adult Fantasy LitRPG

(Co-written with Storm and Rhys Petersen)

Book 1: Dexterity Fail

Book 2: Goblin Boots

Book 3: Singed Feathers

Book 4: Frog Mage

Book 5: Crystal Mine

Book 6: Cursed Harp

Rosie's Rangers- Young Adult Western Steampunk

(6 book series)

Book 1: Justice

Book 2: Vengeance

Book 3: Treachery

Book 4: Accused

Book 5: Wanted

Book 6: Corruption

Mark Of Kings- Children's Fantasy

(Upper middle grade/preteen)

(4 book series)

Book 1: The Arena

Book 2: The Island

Book 3: The Assassin

Book 4: The King

STAND ALONE SERIES

***Demon Hunters- Young Adult Urban Fantasy/
Horror (with elements of romance)***

Book 1: Blood Sacrifice

Book 2: Retribution

Book 3: Tainted

Book 4: Premonition

Book 5: Cursed

Book 6: Feud

Book 7: Extrication

Plea Of The Damned- Young Adult Urban Fantasy/Paranormal

(6 book series)

Book 1: Forgive Me Lucy

Book 2: Forgive Me Aiden

Book 3: Forgive Me Jena

Book 4: Forgive Me Kobe

Book 5: Forgive Me Marti

Book 6: Forgive Me Dawson

Realms Of The Fae- Young Adult Urban Fantasy
(with elements of romance)

The Sword (short story in Like A Girl Anthology)

Heart Of Stone

Book 1: A Debt Owed

Book 2: Marked By The Hunt

Book 3: The Magic Collector

Book 4: An Unexpected Betrayal

Book 5: Imprisoned By Iron

Fairytales Retold (Short Stories)

Snow-White And Rose-Red

The Twelve Brothers

The Light Princess

Beauty And The Beast

Sleeping Beauty

Aschenputtel

The Golden Bird

The Frog Prince

The Death Of Koshchei The Deathless

Myths And Legends Retold (Short Stories)

Ion, Son Of Apollo

Sir Gawain And The Maid With The Narrow Sleeves

Princess Ilse, The Giant's Daughter

YOUNG ADULT NOVELS

Young Adult Fantasy (with elements of romance)

Elf Sight

Earth Bound

Young Adult Urban Fantasy

Stone Warrior (with elements of romance)

The Jungle Inside

Young Adult Contemporary (with elements of romance)

Through Your Eyes

The Ugly Stepsister

Perfect Little Princess

Young Adult Contemporary/Paranormal

Whispers In The Dark (with elements of romance and same sex relationships)

Over Too Soon (with elements of romance)

Young Adult Sci-Fi

Experiment X-One-Six (Urban Sci-Fi/Superheroes)

An Endless Dawn (Post Apocalyptic Sci-Fi)

CHILDREN'S BOOKS

Dragon Lord (Preteen/early teens) (Fantasy)

The Irish Wizard (Upper middle grade) (Urban Fantasy)

SHORT STORIES

Urban Fantasy

Eternally Late

Dealings With Joe

Glimpses (short story in That Moment When Anthology)

Contemporary

The Brat Next Door

Fantasy LitRPG

(Set in the same world as Guardians Of The Round Table Series)

Tales Of Inadon 1: The Disc (Co-written with Storm and Rhys Petersen) (short story in Game On! Anthology)

Post Apocalyptic Sci-Fi

Compulsive Directive

NONFICTION

A Year Of Weekly Writing Exercises (Creative Writing)

Cooking For Families With Allergies (Cooking) (Co-written with Storm Petersen)

Tell Me A Story, Grandma (Memoir)

For the most up to date details on available titles visit:

www.avrilsabine.com/books/bibliography

Guardians Of The Round Table Series

To learn more about this series visit:

www.avrilsabine.com/series/gotrt

Find maps, more stats and details about the next book.

BOOKS AVAILABLE IN THE GUARDIANS OF THE ROUND TABLE SERIES

Book 1: Dexterity Fail

Book 2: Goblin Boots

Book 3: Singed Feathers

Book 4: Frog Mage

Book 5: Crystal Mine

Book 6: Cursed Harp

Book 7: Treasure Seeker

BOOKS SET IN THE SAME WORLD AS THE GUARDIANS OF THE ROUND TABLE SERIES

Adventurers Guild Handbook (Lore Book)

Legend Of The Ancestral King (Lore Book)

Lost And Powerful: Myths Of Misplaced Staves (Lore Book)

Disclaimer

This is a work of fiction. Names, characters, businesses, places, events and incidents are either the products of the author's imagination or used in a fictitious manner. Any resemblance to actual persons, living or dead, or actual events is purely coincidental. The opinions expressed or beliefs held are those of the characters and should not be assumed to be the opinions or beliefs of the author.